EMMA NEALE, a poet and prose writer, was born in Dunedin and raised in Christchurch, San Diego, CA, and Wellington. After gaining her first literature degree from Victoria University, she went on to complete her MA and PhD at University College London. She has written five novels — *Night Swimming, Little Moon, Relative Strangers, Double Take* and *Fosterling* — and a number of poetry collections, and has edited anthologies of both short stories and poetry. Neale won the Todd New Writer's Bursary in 2000, was the inaugural recipient of the NZSA Janet Frame Memorial Award for Literature (2008), and was the 2012 Robert Burns Fellow at the University of Otago. Her poetry collection *The Truth Garden* won the Kathleen Grattan Award for poetry in 2011, and *Fosterling* was shortlisted for the Sir Julius Vogel Award in 2012. Her collection *Tender Machines* was longlisted in the inaugural Ockham New Zealand Book Awards. She teaches, works in publishing and looks after her two young sons.

BILLY
BIRD

EMMA NEALE

VINTAGE

VINTAGE

UK | USA | Canada | Ireland | Australia
India | New Zealand | South Africa | China

Vintage is an imprint of the Penguin Random House
group of companies, whose addresses can be found at
global.penguinrandomhouse.com.

Penguin
Random House
New Zealand

First published by Penguin Random House New Zealand, 2016

10 9 8 7 6 5 4 3 2 1

Text © Emma Neale, 2016

Design by Carla Sy © Penguin Random House New Zealand
Cover illustration/art by Abe Baillie
Front cover photograph by Graham Warman
Printed and bound in Australia by Griffin Press,
an Accredited ISO AS/NZS 14001 Environmental Management
Systems Printer

A catalogue record for this book is available from the National
Library of New Zealand.

ISBN 978-0-14-377005-3
eISBN 978-0-14-377007-7

The assistance of Creative New Zealand towards the
production of this book is gratefully acknowledged by
the publisher.

ARTS COUNCIL OF NEW ZEALAND *TOI AOTEAROA*

penguin.co.nz

Birds in human shape.
The apple trees in blossom.
The great enigma.

— Tomas Tranströmer

PART
ONE

THE HOW DO WE BEGIN?

WE'LL BEGIN THIS STORY with a true Once Upon a Time.

There was once a young man called Liam and a young woman called Iris. They were Just Very Good Friends. They were Just Very Good Friends for years and years. About four. That's an aeon for the young, especially when the small blue pilot-light of unspoken attraction burns steadily.

Various complex circumstances kept on prevailing — like a difficult headwind — until one particular night. It was after a mutual friend's wedding, where the optimism and openness in the bespoke wedding vows, the free champagne glowing in the warm summer air, the sweet idealism and the lusty basslines in the DJ's playlist meant that Liam and Iris finally fell over the line between friendship and more-than-that into bed.

If this were a film, now would be a good time for a musical interlude.

Liam took off his watch
(metal-linked silver strap heavy as a weapon)

because he wanted nothing between him
and the astonishing Iris
as he stretched himself the length of her,
lay himself he hoped gently as muslin
over her skin, which was printed
with a gleaming beaded trail of moon
as light slipped through the thread-holes
of the Roman blinds.

He placed his watch on the bedside table, said,
'Is this all right, are you okay, what kind of talk do
                                            you like?'
She answered, 'Nothing,' let her knees fall open
like lupin pods unhusked in the sun,
remembered the way
her grandfather used to clean his knife
between spreads of butter and honey
by neatly sliding it lengthwise into thick bread
                                            crust.

Which made her think, 'How strange to recall that
                                            now.
Can it be Freudian when it's in the middle of sex,
or isn't that the opposite of Freudian?
Does it maybe even mean it's bad sex
if for years and months we've hedged round this
                                            question,
yes, years, with that intoxicating, agonizing
does he want me, does he not,
if he calls for coffee every fortnight
is it just platonic,
is there something I'm doing wrong,

can't he *tell* I think he's
the All New Gorgeousness Guaranteed?
Yet here after all that thrilling
high-wire waiting now I'm thinking
of cushions, sequins, cider bottles,
starlight, supermarket aisles,
amber-coloured filigree beetles,
motorbikes, neon EAT signs,
seaside rocks old-bridal with spray,
phosphorescence, open roads, orange dirt,
the way in the night club the lint on his shoulders
shone like an alien radioactive dust;
that time when I said I didn't smoke,
he flicked the lid of the mint tin open
like a Zippo, little joke,
ohhhhhh, something has burst inside me
as if he has painted a Georgia O'Keefe poppy
with a hot welding iron plunged in ice water,
over-ripe strawberries,
molten toffee-apples stretched and lost—'
and then Iris felt his sudden, shudderous heave
as he rowed like a shipwrecked boatswain
desperate for rescue, last stroke to reach the shore,
as the prow of the bed slammed into the coast of
                                          the wall,
the watch hurtled off, hit the wooden floor,
and stopped.
11:08 p.m.
And the sign hung in the tiny date window
                                          declared

December 28.
For weeks Liam forgot to get it fixed.

Iris would ask the time, the date, and Liam would
say,

'Eleven-oh-damn' or 'December twenty-shit.'

NOW WE'VE REALLY STARTED SOMETHING

WEEKS AND WEEKS LATER, Iris was sick-gilled and green as lake-weed.

She spilled herself in all unlikely places: flowerpots, saucepans, gumboots, rubbish bins. (Oh, but that one *is* quite likely, actually: it's always a relief when pregnant to find a rubbish bin is close at hand.) Popcorn buckets, handbags, desk drawers, plastic bags, wheelbarrows. Her eye was always on what could quickly be grabbed and made *receptacle*, so she made less of a spectacle of herself, and the floor. She counted back, and would always believe that 28 December, 11:08 p.m., was the precise date and time of the baby-on-the-way's conception.

Once upon a time, she thought. *And so we started you upon all your once upon a times.*

She just didn't quite know how to tell Liam. She mulled. She whispered it to herself. She reconsidered and rehearsed in front of the mirror, shook her head, rephrased, took another run at it, and then when she met him, defaulted to blurt.

'I'm going to have a baby.'

Then came the eponymous, quintessential, most pregnant of pauses. A woman waits on a fulcrum, feeling her life tip towards the maelstrom.

Liam looked blank.

This was almost worse than a look of shock. There was nothing to go on! Nothing to work with! Not even to fight!

Days of held-back tears rushed to the surface. Yet before the tears could hit air, Liam's expression careened into wonder. 'We're officially a couple?'

She swallowed. 'I'm sorry. It's too soon. Should've been more careful, I—'

'What have you got to be sorry for?' He gave her a tender, somehow teasing hug. 'A quick game's a good game.'

'Of Monopoly, maybe, Liam. Or cricket. This—'

He started nuzzling her, laughing. 'Tiddlywinks! Pick-up-sticks! Poker! I'll have someone who'll learn my card tricks!'

'You have card tricks?' Iris had a tissue at the ready. 'I didn't know that. You see? Four years and still I hardly know you. How can I raise a child with you?'

'There's still time to teach you my card tricks before the baby's here. Promise. In eight months, you'll know me and my card tricks upside down or your money back.'

She was crying now, and laughing, yet not sure she wanted laughter to shoo away the tears: crying was such a relief. 'Seven months. I think it might be only seven months left.'

'Nyeh.' He pinched thumbs to index fingers, lifting them in a mock-Italian shrug. 'So, fewer card tricks. Still a bargain.' He noticed her expression then. He put his arms around her shoulders, kissed her forehead. 'It's going to be okay. It was bound to happen some time, right? All that pent-up, incredible sex. The life force has been *using* us!' He was using a false, appalled lisp: a cross between Sylvester the Cat and a drag queen. 'That's just what biology wants. And secretly I've known for a while now that you're the one. *You're The One!*'

Oh, God. Could she have a child with someone this hyper? 'Liam, there might be someone for everyone, but that's *some*one, not The One.'

He managed to goggle his eyes and glower at the same time. 'I just said something very committed. You're meant to swoon.'

'I'm trying to be realistic. This is huge, Liam. Most people have more time to just be a couple. To really get to know each other first.'

'Iris.' He pressed his forehead to hers. 'We've been friends for years *and* I'm a very shallow guy. It won't take you long to know every tiny thing there is left to know about me.'

And he did this thing — this thing — with the tip of his tongue, and his thumb, and then this patch of skin on her waist, of all places; she'd had no idea there were such sensitive nerve-endings there . . . Rather soon, she forgot to be the serious, sensible one. It seemed now quite logical: who better to have a child with than someone with such boyish high spirits? She moaned, and he mumbled with his mouth against hers, 'Wait till you see my card tricks.'

Fun and games; heedless sex; briefly insouciant youth: December 28, 2003, 11:08 p.m. The unconscious start of we're-going-to-be-a-family.

It was also, she swore, the moment when the sharp-toothed silver cogs of love were finally set running. All that sugar-swim-comet-works, soaring-surge canyon-glide . . . (You can see the appeal in not sharing what's behind the bedroom door. Isn't one point of sex that it's a separate language? Yet how typical of Iris to set off a cascade of *words* for any significant episode . . .) Anyway, until then, her relationship with Liam had been so wrapped up in self-denial (*We're just friends!*) that she hadn't known herself what was going on.

Yet from that moment, in her view, they hadn't just had sex. Something existed that hadn't before. Invisible weft. Not-quite-sculpture-of-air, not-quite-bower-of-heat. A presence, yet not as solidly *there* as cake, potter's bowl, dance, melody . . .

Which is why she went quiet whenever her older, garrulous, pharmacist sister laughed at the phrase *making love*. 'Why do people say that? Love-shmuv. Screwing will do me.' Cue trademark smutty bark.

'Carrie!'

'What? Don't be a prude. You've heard it plenty of times, haven't you?'

'Yeah, but I don't like "screwing", it sounds so — what, light bulbs and metal and mechanical and I don't know, crumple it up and throw it away. Like sex is throwaway. It's not for me, okay?'

'No kidding. It's taken you long enough to even *find* a screw. Why would you want to chuck it so soon?'

'Carrie, cut it out.'

'Sorry, princess, can I say *have sex*?'

'Well, if you're going to split idioms . . .'

'Booooooring!' sang Carrie. 'You brainy-ise everything. Wanna catch a movie?'

Later Iris repeated this (post-coital, of course) to Liam.

'So I said, screw sounds so *throwaway*. What we do is—'

'Infinitely renewable,' he said, giving her the glad-eye, feeling the nap of her like velvet and silk and sometimes bumpy cotton because this is real, not Photoshopped, not Hollywooden. His hands were earth parched for the rain of her, because sometimes, actually, reality feels like poetry, and these are the time-fragments we want to remember, the moments that impel momentous decisions.

How could she say to Liam, well, in a way, I *didn't* really love you until we had sex? It seemed dangerous for a feminist to admit. There was excitement, attraction, giddiness and urgent hope, yes, but not deep love. That grew gradually: perhaps when it felt safer, because there, she had him.

And really, if sex can accidentally make something as wild, complex, erratic, dogged, miraculous, sensitive, vulnerable, solid, unaware, bizarre, intractable, awful and joyful as a human child, why, in a specific instance, couldn't it be said to help make love?

SIDESWIPE

ALL THIS POST-COITAL OVER-THINKING was the prelude to Billy. And as they slowly began to recover from the paradigm shift of the first child, of course they began to wonder. Pushing Billy on the swing, dressing him in the new astronaut-style jumpsuit with hood and visor that Iris designed, or watching him toil away at the job of growing (how to aim a twisty stream of milk *into* a cup; how to react when a bigger kid, of whom you are in awe, bursts into tears) they thought: there. That fleeting minute, can we pause it, replay it? Can we have another toddler puddling about like a penguin, leaving surrealist art installations all over the house — a tiny cow in a teapot in a hat on the doorstep, of course! A stuffed crocodile in a silk camisole perched beside a woollen chick in a beanie on the bread-bin, why not!

Billy shadowed them everywhere — following so closely that sometimes, if they turned around mid-thought, they'd step right on him. They started to say: 'I think Billy's lonely. I think he needs an ally.'

So they tried for another child, feeling the chill cast by

the friend who said, 'Most animals have more than one offspring, of course. It's Nature's insurance policy.'

Did the effort begin in greed for love? In fear, or even in over-confidence? (Look what we can do!)

Was the mistake not to be happy with Billy for his own sake?

Why think in terms of mistakes?

Well, why *think* at all? Life sideswipes you anyway. For there they were, wondering if they were unable to conceive again (was it the stress of Liam's work at TVNZ, was it Iris's irregular cycle), when wham, they had to take in Liam's nephew, Jason.

'Another bairn,' Iris's mother said. 'Any bairn's a blessing. This could be an answer to your prayers.'

'Who's been praying?' asked Liam.

'*Lee*-am,' warned Iris.

Billy was two; Jason was six. Liam's sister-in-law, Steffie, had died of breast cancer. Almost a year on, his brother, Pete, couldn't cope. Liam and Pete's parents had died several years ago; Jase had no maternal grandparents alive either. There was one aunt on Steffie's side, but she lived overseas. Besides, Pete had once said, 'Wouldn't trust her with a dog, let alone a kid. She's high half the time, pissed the rest. Changes boyfriends fast as pants. You'd never know whether the bloke she was with would be any good for a child.'

Looking after Jase was meant to be until Pete could get back on his feet down in Wellington; get himself well again. But the thing was, he couldn't. The poor guy couldn't, and his body was found in the Akatawara Forest one weekend by a couple of polytech students with trail-bike permits. Pete didn't have a permit. That was a detail the police officer emphasised when he knocked on their door. Iris felt something in her throat fold over and over, which was just as well, because it meant she couldn't spit out

This man's brother, this child's father, and you —

This man's brother, this child's father, and you —

Liam managed better. Expressionless, he said, 'Not many people in that frame of mind would be thinking legal particulars.'

'I am sorry for your loss, sir.' Something tutored and robotic in the officer's manner, Iris thought. Not that he didn't feel it. She saw how he watched Jason valiantly trying to play swing-ball with his little cousin out there, in raincoats, on the lawn, though Billy couldn't follow the rules. The man didn't know how to convey it, yet still stay within the guidelines of his brief.

Unfair of Iris, unfair. Because when they both sat down to tell Jason that they loved him, they would always look after him, but they had very tough, very sad news, the small, cruel words peeled off, dry and unrelated to the facts.

The facts were more than facts. They were a great tumbling mist: confusion that warped and cracked open into flash-fissure caverns of *Oh, no. Oh, no.*

But you had to hold on. You had to take deep breaths and play 'We can manage this', and face it, for the children.

When they told Jason, he bit the ulcerated patch on his lip that had been there since he'd come to them, and asked, 'So — am I a norphan?'

A gnaw-fin. A small fish eating at itself. Iris quickly tipped her head back as if tears could roll clean away.

Liam's hands worked to pull words from the air. 'Technically, I guess. But you don't have to think of it that way. You've got us, eh, Jase?'

Iris and Liam sat there with Jase sandwiched between

them. Even terrible-two Billy, nose raw with winter sniffles, fell quiet and clambered up on Iris's knee. Liam took his nephew's hand. As they sat there, Iris with not-knowing-what-to-say battering like a giant moth in her throat, Jason, drawn and pale, began not to cry, but to yawn. Great aching, stretching yawns. The sheer fact of taking in the massive change in his circumstances meant they had to say, *Jase, you need a rest. Have a lie-down, as long as you need. You're safe here. We'll keep you warm and safe.*

He was a lovely kid. A lovely, poor, sad, unfortunate, ordinary, annoying, delightful nuisance of a ratbag of a hoot of a kid. Taking him in was the best of things, the worst of things. It meant Liam had no time to wallow in regret for what he should have done for his brother. On the other hand, there were days he felt he'd had no time to really let it all sink in — but — on the fourth hand, was it? — what Jase had lost mattered more.

After a while, Jase and Billy acted like siblings, almost. That was a comfort. By the time Billy, too, had started school, the pair of them wanted another word for what they were. 'Cousin' wasn't close enough, they said. They'd heard of cuzzy-bros, but everybody said it like a joke, so that was no good. They tried bruzzins, bruth-cuzzes, cuzz-bruths, but everything sucked, apart from pretty-much-brothers, or basically-brothers.

Iris and Liam were glad the boys so easily found their equilibrium. Of course there were fights, whinges, jealous jabs and selfish pouts. There were, yes, even flashpoint rages of don't-you-dare-pull-that-one-on-us, when Jase tried, 'I *hate* you. You're not my mother!' Or 'I don't have to listen to you, *you're* not my father!' And even, 'Get out of my room, Billy, y' yabber-mouth. You talk diarrhoea.' There were raised voices, ultimatums, punishments. There were also long, sometimes sullen, sometimes tearful talks on the couch; misspelled sorry notes pinned to the fridge; and hugs, lots: even the embarrassing at-the-schoolgate kind.

Over the next few years, they had the normal ups and downs of any other family.

'For when we're up, we're up; and when we're down, we're down; and when we're only halfway up, we're neither up nor down,' sang Iris, regularly, to her grand little dukes of orcs.

'Orcs they are,' sighed Liam, whenever the boys dropped undies, socks, fruit peel, cotton buds, milk-soaked oats, athlete's foot cream or tissue clumps, or left piddle dots on the loo seat — name a yuck, they'd trail it behind them.

In other ways, Billy and Jase were opposites: Billy already diligent, sprinting away with literacy and numeracy at only five; Jason an average student, more interested in people than paperwork. They were chalk and cheese who met in the cheerful in-between. Rousting around in the altogether: the Nuddy Butt Club, the boys called it; or, when they were *supposed* to be heading off to bed, the Naked Wakers. They hid out in huts made of picnic rugs and chairs, driftwood and sand, or lavalava and the hole in the backyard hedge. They sketched side by side, everywhere from the living-room to summer campsite tables; they pottered over Lego, co-building a universe called Doctor Topper's Scrinching Vortex; shared an intense and often sweaty obsession with *Star Wars*. They both begged regularly for some fresh costume accessory from Iris, as if the point of her sewing/ design workroom were to cater for their games; they frequently commandeered her dressmaker's dummy, Coco, as a character (usually a corpse) in make-believe; they developed private amusements like Twitch. Twitch was a birdwatching game that grew out of a family debate on a car trip to the Bay of Islands: whose first word was bird?

'It was Billy's: he pronounced it "bid".'

'No, but my mum, she said it was mine.'

'Really? How strange. Sure you're not mixing up your memories with stories we've told you?'

'No, it was definitely bird. Or actually, *bir-duh*. I know because whenever we saw a magpie, she'd blow a kiss and say that rhyme. One for sorrow, two for joy, and she'd remind me. *Bir-duh. Bir-duh.*'

'You might have even been saying two words,' said Liam, glancing at Jase in the rear-view mirror, checking for wistfulness, traces of the losses the boy had borne. 'A bird, a bird, a bird.'

The boys now imitated themselves as babies, whenever they saw a magpie on farmland, or the fingered wingtips of a harrier ('No, say *kāhu*, Mum') scissoring across the sky, or, once, a gangly white-faced heron (*matuku moana*), landing on a concrete water-tank. Whoever said the babble-word first won points.

'Can words run in families?' asked Billy.

'You *learn* words, Dillbrain,' said Jase. 'It's not like a nose or something.'

'Don't say Dillbrain, Dorkmoron.' Billy landed a soft punch to Jase's arm.

'Hey. Stow it,' warned Liam.

'Peace, love and happiness, please,' Iris sighed, scanning the scenery sliding past for a flash of kingfisher, or any other bright relief from car-cabin fever.

'I do love him,' said Jase. 'He's my most favourite dill-brain in the world.'

'That's nice. You're the best dorkmoron I know.'

'*Boys.*'

'Point to Aunty Iris! We're boys!'

'Better give you two points, Mum, because you never see the birds first.'

Twitch was mainly for holidays or the dull torpor of car travel, when they'd also swap bird facts to fill the gaps between sightings. *Did you know that herons stab frogs? Kāhu are bigger than falcons, eh? What's Māori for falcon? Kārearea.* But even during term time, now and then, at the end of a yelling match over who got the blue and who the red light sabre, or who'd messed up Iris's thread spools (for the love of all the gods of little brats!), a truce could be signalled by:

'Bid.'

'Bir-duh.'

Or possibly:

'Bir-duh.'

'Bid.'

How Iris wanted to suspend them in this phase; where Jase seemed happy to play at Billy's level, as if he needed to regress, just a little, into a safer era of his own boyhood, after the floodwrack of his orphaning. Sure, there were already days Jase said to Billy — 'Fifty cents if you just zip it for *five minutes*.' But what would it be like in a few years? When Jase had moved on to desire, to late-night dances, to drink, and—

'Don't speed things up, Iris,' Liam said. 'We'll worry about that when we get there.'

True, some days, the teenage years did seem distant. She'd feel the serpent of worry start, and then — just as she was sure some issue would destabilise the entire family dynamic — there'd be a reprieve. Like when Jase started guitar lessons, in his final year of primary school. He wanted a leather jacket for his birthday, refused Iris's offer to sew him a denim version, then put up a large poster of Luna Lovegood from the *Harry Potter* movies on his wall. Iris thought, *Holy Hendrix, not puberty so soon?* How do we talk about this? How do we talk about telling the difference between love and a crush? How do we talk about safety? How do we talk about respect? How do we — no, he can't have the jacket. It costs far too much. She and Liam bought him a digital tuner for his birthday instead.

Not long afterwards, Iris thought both boys had fallen unnaturally quiet in Jase's bedroom — increasingly, a place out of bounds for Billy, when Jase wanted to escape the constant broadcasts of what he was *not* allowed to call *The Billy Bulletin*. (It was the *tone* he used.) The unlikely silence drew her up to the door. Her suspicions of monkey business were reinforced by a thin, scaling sound, like a strong zip being undone, perhaps, and then a duet of disbelieving, delighted sniggers. She tapped on the door and walked straight in — to discover the boys getting the new guitar tuner to register their farts. The tuner's screen raced wildly through wavering chromatic arpeggios — up for Billy, down for Jason. The more they laughed at Iris's facial expression, the more they accidentally farted, and the wilder the screen went.

Liam smirked at that story. 'Madhouse!' he said. 'I don't think we need to worry about Jason dating soon. He's still way too infantile.'

'Silver lining,' said Iris, setting down the half-empty baked-bean can and two sauce-caked spoons she'd rescued from Jase's bed. Cold beans, Billy explained, worked best.

'We tried bananas but it wasn't as fast. We're experimentalling.'

'Peas and beans: the musical fruit. The more you eat, the more you toot,' Iris quoted, despite herself, from a Margaret Atwood novel she'd read a million years ago, when she knew nothing of raising small dukes of orcs. She immediately regretted her burst of rhyme: the boys took it up in a frenzied chant, punctuated by kazoo imitations.

'Calm down, you lot, calm down! Your mother needs a break!'

And it was all right to say *your mother* to them both, because that was the way it felt now: all four of them together, experiencing the normal human zoo moods of trying to civilise Appetites into Persons.

Really, when *was* an up an up, and when was a down a down? Even when Jason had to be grounded, more than once, some good seemed to come of it. Including for his worst offence. Oh, God, the dread that sowed . . . He'd taken a lighter to school and tried to set fire to another boy's lunch *and* science-fair project. Liam and Iris were terrified he was heading off the rails: that despite all the love they poured into the absence of his mum and dad, he was avenging himself on the world.

The other boy, Lou, had copied, Jason said. There was evidence. Originally they were meant to work as a pair. Jase was the only one who'd handed in the first stages of the project: there were dates and the teacher's signature in red as proof. When Lou ditched Jase and said he didn't want to collaborate any more, things compounded. Jase's team beat Lou's at lunchtime miniball, because Jase scored a late slam-dunk. Jason (unadvisedly, yes) roostered, '*Lou! Lou! Lou-zzerrrr!*' Lou retaliated with, '*You're* the loser.

No wonder your dad topped himself. Probably couldn't cope with you. You'd be a shit-mare to look after. Who'd wantcha?' Then he gave Jase a fat lip.

A school-and-family/whānau meeting was called. In Jason's favour were:

1. He hadn't thrown a corresponding punch.

2. He'd taken the lunchbox and the poster out
to the miniball courts, because 'I didn't want to
arsonate the entire place'.

3. The plagiarism accusation held. (The poster
was only scorched by the time the duty teacher
apprehended Jason: he'd spent more time trying to
melt Lou's ClickClack lunchbox.)

4. The comment about Pete and Jase was well
below the belt.

5. Jason's behaviour at school until now had
been impeccable, despite what he'd been through.
His marks were pretty, ahh, average, but he was
known as a friendly and likeable kid. These antics
were out of character.

6. Jase initiated the idea of after-school reparation:
helping the caretaker empty out bins, or vacuum
schoolrooms. Commendable, really.

And, as Jase's teacher told Liam and Iris — out of Jason's hearing — there were several factors against Lou:

1. He had already been suspended once. (For trying to search for 'Big Tits' on the class computer at lunchtime, within earshot of some Year 7 girls.)

2. When asked about the plagiarism, Lou said science fair sucked cock anyway *and* he hated that lunchbox.

3. Lou refused to put money in the headmaster's swear jar.

4. All four of Lou's parents and stepparents had agreed, in *their* school-and-family meeting, that Lou had a bit of an attitude problem.

The up that grew out of that down was that it gave Liam and Iris a chance to say to Jase, as he sobbed through an apology at home, 'No, we are *not* going to send you away. You are *not* too hard to look after. That was never behind what your dad did: Pete didn't die because of anything you'd said or done.' Which, of course, was the question scalding him, until pushing the fire outside his head had seemed the only way free.

After the family debriefing, Jason asked if he could be alone in his room. Would they mind keeping Billy busy? He just —
    'Yes, of course,' they said. 'You take some time out.'
    Which Billy thought was totally unfair. He still thought time out meant punishment. So when Liam and Iris assumed he was contentedly working on a crayoned picture of Doctor Topper's MultiDimensional Suitcase, he was writing a note to Jase, using all the phonetics an extremely verbal and

high-performing five-year-old who still struggled with bs, ds and ps could muster.

bear Jason sum qeoqle are to mean
love from
yore baSikly bruthr Billy
xOxxx

A soft darkness grew in the house, while Jase stayed shut away; thinking through how many wounds? Then, around six, he came out again, hungry, stretching. He read the note, and rumpled Billy's hair. Said nothing, but led his little cousin back into his room and pinned the letter to his wall. Iris made popcorn, hot milk, let the kids choose a DVD from the family shelves to watch while she cooked. Billy said Jase could decide. The ten-year-old settled on a David Attenborough, of all things. She would have thought a smash-'em-up cosmic warlord space-race crossed with dysfunctional family psychodrama would have been more cathartic. But Jase said he wanted to try something new. The boys sat there, gazing at the hillstar hummer from the Andes, the purple-coloured wood star from Ecuador, barely bigger than a moth. Each time the scene shot changed from cave or plant back to bird, the boys muttered to each other, 'Bid.' Or 'Bir-duh.'

Peace. Even keel. A respite from *He's a worry, what should we do, have we handled this properly?* He was going to be okay. They'd stick to their decision to ground him for another week — but he knew he'd overstepped a line, and he knew they loved him.

YOU WOULDN'T SEE IT IN THE PAPER

AND THEN — YOU WOULDN'T credit it. You fucking well excuse Liam's language but you wouldn't see it in the news. If you put it in a movie, people would hit eject. If it was in a book, you'd roll your eyes, then donate it to a school fair. There was a chain of events that led to *oh, hell no*. Because, you see, you take your nephew in, and there are sports lessons, remedial maths and orthodontist appointments, haircuts, how do we keep his trust, and what about geography? Does he know the suits in a pack of cards, or where's Nigeria and what's bacteria, can he swim, who will drive him there, and does he know how much we care?

All that, and just when you think you've got some kind of balance, you hear about your redundancy.

Fan-fucking-tastic.

Which would also be about the time one of the kids changes, too, wouldn't it? Heads into some new phase, so there's your wife incensed, saying, 'Who's going to tell him he can't *call* women that? He can't talk like that. What's he been *watching*?' (As if Liam were responsible for everything screened, ever. Yeah, make *that* guy redundant, right?) 'He's twelve now! You need to speak to him. He needs a man to say it, Liam. Today I've had it up to *here*.'

Liam wondered if he was to blame. How to be a father-figure to a boy who's lost his real father? How to be the man you thought your brother should have been? How to be a family man at all, really, when clearly it's hard enough holding down a job in the media as it is? Such thoughts were uncomfortable, so he replied, 'Iris, I know it's hard. But I don't always know how to say things to him. There's just all that — baggage. Mine, too. Pete *was* my brother, you know.'

'I know; I know. That was off. The boys are just a lot of work at the moment.' A sigh. 'Sorry, Liam. You've got enough on your plate.'

Yes, they took their nephew in and there was all that mess, but they did it all for love. And of course Liam did it all in hope and fear for the boy's future. How would it be for him each birthday, each dark anniversary? So they tried to keep things normal, show him life was still a gift.

And then — yes, we've been avoiding the *and then*.

And then one morning when Liam was in a rush, Iris reminded him: she has a recall mammogram after school. Has he remembered he'll need to collect both boys? But he hadn't *wanted* to think about it, Iris and illness, he'd forgotten, and he has a meeting that afternoon with the bank manager, because Liam and an old (moneyed) university friend down south are taking the plunge into business together.

Since Liam received his redundancy package from TVNZ he'd been treading water, thinking the situation through. With journalism in a slide, he'd had to take on the changes, show some grit. It'd been a difficult time (understatement). Iris suggested a counsellor or life coach but Liam found that mildly offensive. He thought he was quite capable of working things out on his own, thank you. He decided to see redundancy as an opportunity, not a loss. A chance to do something completely different. Go back and try one of the roads not taken, as a favourite poet from his uni days phrased it. (That's how Liam and Iris met, you know. In a literature survey course, umpteen-mumble years ago. Shakespeare, Dickinson, Heaney, Larkin; Bethell, Curnow, Tuwhare, Manhire, Harlow, Cilla McQueen . . . It's not just pointy-heads who like to read, is it? Liam's taxi driver just the other day started quoting Janet Frame. It's a snobbery to assume the shop clerk, the immunisation nurse, or the barista at your favourite coffee place don't read and think as much as you. Or keep notebooks where sometimes *thinking* grows an ivy tangle over the page. Liam used to keep a journal. Once kids came along, though, there was less time for all that . . .)

Anyway. Another road not taken. Liam and his mate Steve are going to try running an adventure tourism operation down south. Kayaks and paddleboards first, then maybe white-water rafting farther afield. The switch will be a gamble. Liam's chest, as he thinks ahead to the bank appointment, grips even as he tries an internal mantra of, *ka pai, carpe diem, ka pai, carpe diem* . . . And right then his nephew says, 'But basketball starts today. It's over at Wesley.'

Liam's concentration jolts, so even though Jase is just a boy, he lets rip. 'Jesus, you're twelve years old now, Jason. Don't you know to give us more warning?'

When Jason mutters sorry, Liam's frustration and tension aren't finished yet, so he ignores it. 'In our day, your dad and I walked and biked everywhere. We didn't get namby-pamby ferrying around.' Before Jason can ask more about his dad and his dad's day, Liam notches up the volume. 'Twelve is time to start showing independence. You can walk to basketball.'

Iris says, 'But there's Billy, too.' Liam solves that with a chop of his hand. 'Right. Walk together. Jase, head over to Billy's class straight after the bell, scoop him up and take him to your game. Iris will be there by the end, if not half-time.' He's already slinging on his jacket, checking for his wallet, fuming: *Trying to pull all our lives together and I still have to deal with this sort of trivia . . .* His impatience tightens in a thick band across his torso.

Afterwards, he wonders. He wonders if his mood had anything to do with it. He wonders if Jason felt the undercurrent of *Sometimes you're a bit too much for us to deal with. Sometimes you complicate things just a touch too far.*

The smash happened at a notorious street corner during the after-school crush: a corner they had always warned both boys about, telling them don't cross there, go the long way down to the pedestrian lights instead. Jason was dare-devilling on his bike, showing off for a new girl at school: trying to get his feet up on the handlebars, palming his basketball from hand to hand, looking back over his shoulder to call out to her, and he went off the curb, into a car that swung too fast around that corner.

Not that corner. Not Pete's boy.

Oh, hell no.

The girl, Thalia, was white as bone when she told the

family what happened. Poor child was pulled out of the school altogether: couldn't cope with going back. And her family just arrived in the country . . .

And Billy? Thank God Billy didn't witness it. For some reason, he'd taken the family rules into his own hands; ran on ahead to the practice courts for Jason's game. Cue another moment of disbelief for Liam and Iris: *I can't believe he made it over that corner on his own.* He waited there, grumpy, watching Jase's team play. When Iris turned up light-headed with relief that her mammogram was all clear, Billy asked, 'Will Jason catch it when he gets here?'

Iris jigged a little. 'If he plays well!'

Billy wrinkled his nose. 'Mum-joke. Where is he?'

'Jason?' She scanned the court. 'I thought he'd be with you.'

'*Meant* to be.'

That's when she felt the first rabbit dash of dread. Stay here? Retrace Billy's steps? Rush home? Call Liam? Call Jason's school?

The fear came too late. She should have cancelled the appointment when Liam couldn't collect the kids. Or Liam should have rearranged the appointment with the bank. They should have made more effort to work out which kids were on Jase's team, so they could call in transport favours on game days.

But the practice was within easy walking distance.

But the team had only just been announced.

But Jase hadn't told them.

But that corner.

All the *buts* butted their sore and sorry heads against the guilt, yet the guilt still stood. It stood, and it steeped, from the funeral through the following disoriented, stumbling weeks. Iris sometimes felt as if the very ground she walked on were flooded with it.

Had Jason been a marked boy? Was the skin between him and disaster thinner once he'd lost his parents? If so, could she and Liam have done more to protect him? Should they have done more anyway, as a natural duty of responsibility and care?

TWO DARK PAILS

BILLY KNEW AND DIDN'T KNOW TOO. First the news made a white buzzing start in his head. Then he cried and cried. He wanted to sleep in Jase's room that night, so he would hear him when he came back.

'Hey, kiddo,' said Liam gently. 'He's not coming back.'

'I know,' said Billy, 'but—'

'Let him sleep there if he wants,' said Iris. So Billy slept in his cousin's bed that evening, only to wake up after a dream where Jase was holding his head and it came off in his hand like a basketball and the basketball broke like a chocolate egg after the first bite. Billy pounded down the hall, whimpered at his parents' door, and for the first time ever Liam let Iris bring Billy in under the covers with them. And Billy was glad and sad and found himself thinking, *What will Jase say? Will he be jealous?* That was one of the thoughts that had walls in it, thrown up like a dead-end in a maze, because Jason wouldn't know. *Dead-end* meant Billy had to burrow in even closer to his mum, finding loose nightgown to clutch and bring up to his nose, hiding his thumb so he could snuffle and suck hard, back down into sleep.

He knew that his cousin's ghost would never come and hurt him but he couldn't go into Jase's room after that dream, not even quickly, in case Jase watched from the wardrobe. He couldn't touch Jase's basketball: even the colour made Billy feel queasy. And one weekend, when his dad said, in a flat kind of way, 'Would you like to go and shoot hoops?' Billy said no. His dad asked, 'Why not, kiddo?' Billy explained: 'It's Jase's ball.' Dad said, 'Billy, Jase isn't . . . The ball's yours now. He'd want you to use it.' And Billy said, 'NO.'

One day, he was meant to be walking home from school with neighbours because Iris was unwell — for a couple of days she couldn't get out of bed and Liam said it was all right, he'd organise things. But Billy ran on ahead. It was very important that he got to the accident corner. He had a powerful feeling that the world was about to go on rewind; knew it from a shiver in the poke-bones of his neck and a strange ringing at the back of his skull. He ran and he ran and he ran, even with Gregor the neighbour-dad yelling *Billy come back*!

Billy knew, he just knew, that Jason would be there. Billy would see it this time. Jase would be on his bike, balancing his basketball, but Billy would be able to shout out. He'd run up, he'd grab Jase's jersey, even pull him off the bike if he had to. It was all going to be okay.

Billy pounded up to the corner, chest hurting, and there was plenty of traffic, but no bike, no other pedestrians. No kids from Balmoral or Wesley. He stared at the footpath, disappointment blurring his vision. A bird hopped out from behind a kerbside wheelie bin. It was a myna, making its squeaky noise as if squeezing a rubber toy to get Billy to take chase. And first of all Billy did want to run at it, throw a stone, because why should a nothing bird still be alive when Jason wasn't? Then it cocked its head and, like a bandit in its yellow eye-mask, looked right at Billy.

'*Bir-duh*,' heard Billy in his head. He started, turned around, but there was no cousin to be seen. Gregor the neighbour-dad jogged up, giving his son Jimmy a piggyback. Gregor looked like he was going to yell but Jimmy said, 'That's the bad corner, eh Dad?' Billy turned to look for the bird and the silent-speech in its eye again, but it was already strutting off. It soared up, white flashes on its wings.

Billy had to turn and walk home heavy with knowing and not-knowing.

'You okay?' asked Gregor. 'You're awfully quiet for the Billy we know.'

'That was a myna, eh?'

'Yep. Horrible things. Noisy. No good for the native birds. They eat their eggs, did y'know that?'

'Yeah. Not all mynas would be bad, though. How can we tell if one certain bird of a whole kind of bird is bad? Maybe *that* one's never eaten anybird else's eggs. Maybe that one only eats scraps and leftovers. Did you ever think about that?'

Gregor laughed at the back of his throat, all phoney. 'Thaaaaat's more like Billy. C'mon. Homeward bound.'

Billy scuffed along, two dark pails of knowing and not-knowing slipping and sliding inside him.

A MARKED BOY?

THEY ALL TRUDGED ON as best they could, of course: Iris and Liam trying to get life back to normal for Billy, as they had once done for Jase. Iris spent the first weeks watching the boy intently for any signs of distress. She walked him to school: there and back. She took his bag for him: there and back. She knelt at his desk to settle him in as he drew peacocks, and bright green-coloured birds, and a wonderfully strange mythical creature with an almond-shaped skull that was part human eye, part bird's head: the tear-duct corner narrowed like a beak; the lashes tipped like head-feathers. She took extra care to see the teacher before and after school each day; volunteered as parent help on all the outings, helped with the advanced reading group; offered to stay on longer each day, but the teacher smiled, 'You do more than your share, Iris. I'm sure you've got things to be getting on with.' That was true. Iris had been letting admin for Whipstitch, her small clothing label, slip. At home, the prototype tunic tops and hoodies were made, but she had to get them off to the machinists; there were already orders to fill. *All right*, she thought. *At least I have tried to do one thing to the limits of what's needed.*

Yet there was a fresh sense of danger at large. She wondered if Billy felt it, too, as he had become very quiet. He seemed younger. For ages, his nickname had been Billy-box, shortened from Billybox-the-Chatterbox; his vocabulary was *theasaurine*, as Liam said: his monologues would wear out the Duracell *and* the Energizer bunnies. As young as five: 'Did you know the first dinosaur to be named was the Megalosaurus? And a person who studies on dinosaurs is a palaeontologist. Palaeontologist. Weird. What's a palaeon? What if a big dinosaur bone came alive and ate you up? You could run and run and climb a tree and throw a match and burn up the dinosaur and if the tree catched on fire you could jump into a lake and if the lake wanted to drown-ded you, first you could build a boat of burn-ded up dinosaur bones. And if . . .'

Yet now, when they called him Billy-box, it seemed to mean the opposite. Billy with the lid on, closed up. He went through a bout of just about living under the dining table: asking for a blanket to be thrown over it; taking his books and Lego underneath; drawing there; only accepting the solicitous phone calls from his aunt and grandmother if he could stay in his table hut.

'Isn't he too big for that?' Iris's sister Carrie asked one visit. She blanched at the mere sight of Iris's frown: it clearly meant *Shut up; this is a hard time for him.*

One week rolled over into another. They kept things quiet and gentle, no big transitions — Liam agreeing to delay the move down south, trying to do as much as he could at a distance from Steve (setting up the website, marketing, emailing, taking calls on his mobile). Iris could have been researching South Island outlets and machinists for her clothing label, but when she was worried about Billy, logistics at a distance felt like too much hard work. It was far more soothing to work on some alterations for friends; to run up a couple of A-line skirts for Carrie; or to meet up with an acquaintance who wanted to commission not her wedding dress, but her 'going away' dress. It was comforting to be in this familiar zone. Relaxing, even, to sketch multiple versions, colour them in, visit a haberdasher, eyes and fingertips drinking in the colours and textures as if she were bread soaking up wine.

With home kept some sort of normal, Billy gradually seemed to adapt and thaw. He lost interest in the table tent. He wanted to go to the zoo every weekend. He wanted in particular to see the birds. He started storing up interesting facts, sometimes writing them down in his spiky, uneven handwriting in a diary. When he tried to copy their cries, Iris found it tolerable, comic, quirky. Even endearing. He was opening up again, taking in the world. If his chirping and trilling was a kind of regression, it seemed so only in the sense you might take a step back for a powerful run up. She joined in, talking as if he were a boy–bird hybrid. 'Fly off to get your PJs? Okay, Mr Finch. Hip-hop, spit-spot.' She waited patiently for him to shape-change: from bird, to cat, to astronaut, to stallion: metamorphosis-boy, kaleidoscope mind, life pouring back in, light through a lens.

What had scared her was silent Billy. Billy trembling like the skin of cold water in a knocked glass. Billy retreating to a life under the table; Billy clutching his cousin's old photo: the one when Jason first visited them, and was holding Billy-just-born. 'Billy's red like a baboon's bum,' Jase had said, 'and nearly as ugly. But *cute*-ugly, eh?' His own mother,

Steffie, had scolded, but Iris thought it was coffee-spittingly funny: considered it the start of her education in raising a son.

Jason was four when Billy was born; Billy was eight when Jason died, so Jason was twelve. Two boys, eight plus four — the senseless maths of grief: what was she measuring? How could the numbers carry the weight of loss?

One day, Billy came home sick from school. When Iris brought him a bucket to have beside him as he lay on the couch, he admitted, 'I had to say stomach-ache at school. They wouldn't have understood.' He pointed, item by item: the windows, chairs, Iris's library books — *New Zealand Gown of the Year; Chanel: The Woman Behind the Legend* — the kick-mark on the wall from when Jase broke the no-balls-inside rule; the twist of old pattern-paper and green thread the cat had given up chasing. 'It's all sad now.'

Iris hugged him. She cried for Billy crying for Jason, as she'd also cried for Liam crying for Pete: grief was packed inside layers of itself.

Still, that day home sick and tearful seemed to be a turning point. Billy wouldn't talk about it the next day. After school he even wanted to hang around after the home-time bell; play in the fort and swing from the bars with twin sisters, who tried to teach him cherry drops and apple turnovers.

These after-school stints became regular. Iris didn't mind, enjoying the chance to catch up now and then with Moira, the mother of the twin girls: an Irish woman who had caught her eye well before they'd talked. She dressed like the young Peggy from *Mad Men*: Peter Pan collars, or bright scarves knotted at her throat; modest vintage skirts, lots of plaid and checks — not Iris's colour palette at all, but the tailoring set a flame of envy darting under her ribs before they spoke. Moira was no demure ingénue in real life. Her quick, ribald tongue and no-bullshit attitude to her kids was refreshing. There was the time she admitted outright to Iris, 'Had enough of 'em. When Sean gets back from Wellington this weekend, I'm gone. I'll let him have a bit of what he fancies — he's a pussycat after that — then I'm off to Waiheke for the weekend. Just me, a bottle of wine, and my book. No *noise*.'

Moira's breeziness helped Iris not to call out 'Careful!' too often as Billy played. Moira rolled her eyes if her girls tripped on the low swing bridge, or tumbled onto the bark chips. 'Don't break your neck while your dad's away. Save it for him!' She'd pick them up, kiss them with an air of cuff-round-the ear, saying, 'Back you go. Never see "princess wanted" in the job ads, do you?'

Despite her eye for good tailoring, Moira dressed the twins in — well — anything they liked. No designer wear; more like torn leggings and permanently paint-stained sweaters. 'Getting them dressed is hard enough without fighting them over their poor taste,' Moira said, as if exhaling sardonic smoke — though there was no cigarette in sight.

Iris asked what it was like to cope with twins, some strand in her wanting to hear it was *heinous* — a favourite Moira word — so she wouldn't feel the ache of not being able to give Billy a companion. She and Liam couldn't conceive again; Iris was too old, now, for medical assistance, and Liam wouldn't countenance adoption.

As Moira answered, Billy climbed to the top of the jungle gym, scanning the sky. Then he stood with his thighs pressed against the bars, and leaned forward, his arms spread wide, face tilted to the sun. Her heart flipped on the spot: *Billy*! But he laughed and cawed; stepped his way down safely.

The pose became a ritual. She began to think of it as Billy's yoga, saluting the sun before it sank into early winter dusk. They had another ritual, too. Every day, on their walk home after farewelling Moira, when they got to *that corner*, Iris snatched up Billy's hand. They balanced on the brink of the curb as if on a diving board; then ran, his arm clutched up to her side. Part of her wished they could blend together completely: a single garment, hidden seams.

All the time, she was waiting. Waiting for the subject of Jason to come up directly: feeling the questions swim under the surface of their intimacy; thinking she should let Billy take the lead. But she didn't want to push. Didn't want to seed more feardreams and night-visits; to dwell on it and risk more darkness than there already was.

What if he had a natural acceptance, a healthy, realistic *in the midst of life we are in death* detachment, and she stained it with her own sadness, the fear that ambushed her daily?

Keep it normal, keep it safe: that was her job. Hardest work she'd ever done; but no reward richer than seeing Billy contented.

She had to try for 'normal' against a constant sense of urgency. Was there somewhere they had to be, some due date — her mind cast around asking, *What is it, what is it I haven't done?* Whenever they got to night-time, and Billy was tucked up safely in bed, she felt the exhausted relief of making it over some finish line. *We made it*, she thought. *Through another day.*

Her small ministrations of worry and love were the

stitches that held everything else together as they prepared for a move between islands. Friends laughed or cavilled about the shift. But Liam really wanted out of Auckland and Steve needed Liam on the spot now: it was going to take at least the two of them to cover the clients who wanted a guide; not to mention all the e-work, phone-work, paperwork. There was money from Liam's redundancy pay-out. They'd sell their Auckland place, and find something decent in Dunedin: the housing markets still practically different cultures in the north and south.

Yet Iris thought the change followed all too soon after their other upheavals.

'That's life,' Liam argued. 'Change is the only constant.'

'You talk like an insurance billboard,' Iris said.

'We can't keep looking back, sweetheart.' He put an arm around her, rubbed her shoulders; reached down to where he knew there was often a knot under her shoulder blade, from where she hunched as she sketched and cut.

She shifted under the pressure. 'We've barely got through everything else, though.'

The silence he left seemed a small, grey, deliberately lobbed thing. Was he imagining her words weighted with it, so they would sink below notice?

She ploughed on. 'Pete and Jase. Don't we need more time to process it all?'

He turned away, pointlessly rearranged fruit in a bowl on the kitchen bench. He chewed at his lip; it reminded her acutely of Jase: *So — am I a norphan?*

'It's not like we'll forget, Iris. We'll be taking it with us.'

'I know, but —' So much was banked up in that *but*. She was also wondering how to manage Whipstitch in the new place. Maintaining contacts here would be crucial.

But other things bothered her, like how would her outlook change in the southern light, living near the wild coastline? Would her ideas still sell up north if her entire sense of colour and fabric altered?

He shrugged, mouth rueful, which she translated as *resigned to life's shit*. Then he said, 'All of it, Iris — it's made me see. If I don't try this now, I never will. I know it's a risk. Let's give it a year. I'll keep my hand in by freelancing now and then. Adventure tourism pieces. For in-flight magazines, travel websites, that kind of thing. Then if things with Steve don't pan out, I can see what journalism work I can scrape up, or —' He tried a Darth Vader voice '— switch to the dark side. PR, or something.'

He toyed again with an orange: fiddling with its stars'n'stripes sticker. Iris felt a niggle of guilt. Rushing to get through the groceries before Billy had to be collected from school, she hadn't bought locally. Threw a coal onto global warming by wanting oranges in a New Zealand winter . . . and so defeated the purpose of trying to go on foot, with her eager-greenie granny-shopping-trolley, the one she toiled with to and fro on days when ecological anxiety jumped onto the back of maternal anxiety. Or was it the other way round? Was it maternal anxiety making her think harder about how to heal the world?

And another thing: when she got the oranges and Billy safely home, he wouldn't eat them. He wanted nuts and seeds and sugar water. They fought about it for a good long time until she convinced him that oh, woodpeckers, orioles, tui, wax eyes, all *kinds* of birds everywhere eat oranges . . .

She wanted straight gin herself after that battle: why did every tiny interaction have to feel like a struggle? Did other mothers have their minds whirling at five hundred kilometres an hour as they weigh up good, bad, healthy, unhealthy, local, global, encouraging selfishness versus treading softly after crisis; the list of angles grew. Did every other mother feel that at some point along the line they'll make grave mistakes?

Grave mistakes. Her mind slung to a halt, and her focus unravelled further. She had a sharp memory of Jason hoofing through the house as he got ready for school, voice deepened as he imitated his headmaster. 'Kuds! Kuds! That's not Our School Stan-duds, kuds! Top button undone? Inappropri-utt atta*chewed*, kuds!' She'd loved his mimicry: it meant he already saw through social follies; was making his own judgements; and felt secure with her and Liam. Had she laughed enough at his high spirits? Had she let him know what an extraordinary triumph he was, really, this joyful boy who could take the mickey, clown about, despite being shunted off to his aunt and uncle? Her mind flicked up an image: Jason's body flung into the air, a scrawl of limbs. She shook her head as if the scene sent burning cinders into her hair.

'Iris?'

She'd lost her bearings. Liam tossed the orange back into the bowl, as if impatient with the whole damn concept of *fruit*. He said, 'I need to let Steve know a date. We'll have to put the house on the market and start scouting for rentals.'

THE QUALITY OF
THEIR SILENCES

THE IMAGES AND ECHOES of Jase left her without any appetite to argue. It must be exponentially worse for Liam. She was waiting for him, too, to discuss it properly, post-funeral. As with Billy, she thought it best to wait; hoped that whenever she hugged either of them, and held it for just a little longer than usual, it said she was here, ready to listen; was already listening to the quality of their silences.

But life pours back in, with all its dear and dreary dailyness: a young boy climbing into your bed far too early, pressing his icy feet against your calves; you know from his cold toes that he's been waiting outside the door, trying to be brave enough to not come in. And when you ask, are you okay? he nods and talks at a tangent to scared, lonely, icy feet: 'It's sausage sizzle at school today, can I have two sausages and an ice-cream order?'

The days slip and teem. There's — can I have money for

Wacky Hair Day; can you come on the school trip to the marae; can we go to the fundraiser; can I take my skateboard for Wheels Day? Fix the broken watch-strap; take the car in for its WOF; finally research fabric wholesalers and even machinists down south; find a real estate agent; tidy the place for open homes; go online to look at rentals; don't forget the haircut, the GP, the dentist, the physio; Billy got softball player of the day, that's great! (Don't say every kid gets it once, that's discouraging.) Billy got an assembly award for his rainforest project, what an all-rounder! A store in Hamilton wants more of my A-line skirts. That's brilliant, Iris — and guess what? The website's up for me and Steve; we're calling the business Float Your Boat. Whaddaya reckon? And we've got four advance bookings. *(Does any of this have meaning? Is any of it what we need to seal over the gap? Don't say that. Say your lines:)*

'We should make the most of it. Celebrate. Would you like that, Billy?'

'Can we go hang-gliding?'

'Eh? *Hang-gliding?* Ah, no, you're probably too young. You'd have to be at least sixteen, I think.'

'Can we go to the climbing wall? Jarrod at school goes to the climbing wall.'

Iris looks to Liam, but her head fast-forwards a horror film. She sees Billy drift high as a lost balloon. She sees Billy as a young man flailing like a scribble on the air, a copy of his cousin, but dark against a blank screen of snow.

Liam picks up on her fretfulness. 'Mmm, not sure. Something that everyone can enjoy would be good. How about — a movie? How about — a meal out? Just a thought. Like I say, we should celebrate these little things.'

'Yeah, we *should*, Dad.' Worldly-wise and sour.

'What's up, Bill-bo? Why say it like that?'

Billy keeps his thumb inside the two halves of *Which New Zealand Bird?*: he's been flicking through to find a picture to trace. 'Because the one truly big thing sucks so much.'

'The one truly big thing?'

Billy looks at his father with such disgust that it's as if their polite, mild kid had said *fucken*. Widening his eyes, he opens the book so forcefully he almost cracks the spine backwards. Then he slams the book shut. He hurls it onto the floor. He flings his arms out, caterwauls, whirls in circles.

'What on earth are you doing, Billy?'

'Kaah, kaah, kaah!'

'That's a horrible racket.'

'Kaah, kaah, kaah!'

'That's enough, Billy.'

'Kaah, kaah, kaah!'

The more they try to quieten him, the wilder he gets — in fact it reaches the point where Iris insists, 'He must have a temperature. It's like a fit. I've never *seen* him like this before.'

Liam's eyes almost bulge with anger. 'This will not be tolerated.' He heaves Billy off the back of the couch, and carries him kicking and screaming into his room, which, after a bout of door slamming and more Billy-caterwauling, Liam barricades with a small hallway bookshelf.

Iris repeats, 'He can't be well.'

Liam rubs at his thinning hair. 'That's no excuse. Besides, we can't even take his temperature until he stops kicking. For Chrissake, he's eight! That's toddler behaviour.'

'He was like that with chickenpox, once, remember?'

'When he was *three*. That looked more to me like a case of little-shit-itis.'

'It's all the uncertainty, Liam. All this change.'

And they look away from each other, as if even the brink of the unspoken is too bright to look at straight on.

EASY-WAY-OUT

THAT DAY, BILLY FINALLY DROPPED the crazy act out of hunger. He knew enough to apologise first, and only then ask for food, but when they said, 'What was all that about?' he repeated, like an angelic automaton, 'I might be coming down with something.'

Liam shook his head, walked away into Bigger Things to Deal With.

Iris fixed Billy a snack. She made a coffee she didn't really want, and sat beside him. She sipped, watched and held back, but then, as she gazed at his picture-of-innocence profile, after weeks of carefulness, she dashed at the subject, as if Billy's fit were infectious. 'Was it to do with Jase? Do you want to talk about it? We can talk about it, you know. Any time.'

Billy plunged his face into his cup. When he looked up, milky-brown moustachioed, he was wary. 'Okay,' he said.

Long silence. Billy seemed to be staring deep into the well of hot chocolate, divining some secret there. Then she gathered from the way he fluttered his lashes that actually he was eyeballing his own reflection.

'Now?' Iris prodded.

'No fanks,' Billy said, false-cute, before ducking back into his drink again.

Kids. They pushed the boundaries but wouldn't be pushed. Often conversation with Billy was like . . . like trying to scoop up a beetle that paddled and battled and scuttled, Dr Seuss-wise; then vanished, down some thin crevice in the floorboards.

'Billy Bug?' she said. 'I know things are weird at the moment, with me and Dad talking house palaver, and moving and things. There have been so many hard changes lately. But I promise things will settle down.' She really truly crossed the fingers of one hand hidden inside the other. And Billy abandoned the milk, shuffled himself onto her knee like a much younger child, pressing his head against her chest. He was far too heavy and awkward for this; but she let him stay there for a moment.

'Mum?' he said. She waited, ready for one of the hard questions: where do we all go when we die, why do we have to die, what does it feel like, can Jase read my mind now like a kind of god?

'Yes, sweetheart?'

'Can I have a trapdoor in my new bedroom when we move?'

Should she be comforted or dumbfounded? She lowered her face to his hair, took in a deep breath of boy-scalp before forcing him off her knee. The familiar, sweet, musky-coconut scent was soothing, so she went for the easy-way-out answer: 'We'll see.' He was momentarily mollified, so she added: 'It's the kind of thing we could think about if you show us a sensible attitude. No more crazy scenes like today, eh?'

Which didn't seem to sink in, exactly. For a week later, off he went, making another to-do.

A TO-DO IS NOT WHAT YOU ARE SUPPOSED TO DO

AT AN AFTERNOON TEA with Moira and her girls, Iris had to admit to her newfound friend that they were moving down south.

'Oh! Oh, I'm so sorry to hear that,' Moira said, and the genuine disappointment in her voice sent a cool drift between them: they both looked down, watching silence fall. Moira tried to dispel it by asking upbeat questions about 'Dunedin, that's south, south-*east* isn't it? I've never been there. Sean says it's like Ireland. Did you hear that, girls? Billy and his mam are moving. Are you excited about it, Billy?'

'Kaah, kaaah!'

'Billy, don't be rude, please.'

'Isn't south where the earthquakes are, Mam?' asked Abigail, one of the twins.

'Not Dunedin, though,' said Moira.

Iris didn't want to talk about the quakes or admit that her utter dread of them was another reason she wasn't at all keen on the move. Everyone would say, Dunedin's perfectly safe; you'll be fine; platitude, platitude, platitude. Yet peril crackled on the air. Newspapers, websites, radio stations, all broadcasting the fear and disruption in Christchurch, just as Liam wanted to head south: how could you not be jangled by it?

Maybe Jason's death had turned up her sensitivity to these things: the daily news-alarms of storms, acidic seas, dwindling species, drought, energy wars, religious wars, civil wars, avenging blood with blood, as if that ever brought the dead back . . . This sense of the world on the precipice . . . was it worse than it had ever been, or was she losing her own equilibrium? What if it wasn't either-or? What if it was both?

Horror tingled even in Iris's fingertips, but the lovely Moira was looking at her with expectant, lucent eyes, so Iris remembered to breathe out. She faked her calm — as easy, it seemed, as faking other things at home, for the increasingly preoccupied Liam.

She cleared her throat, smiled. 'Not in Dunedin, that's right.'

Helping herself to one of the afghan biscuits that Iris and Billy had brought, Moira asked, 'Do you know where you're going to school, Billy?'

'Kaah, kaaah!'

'Billy.' Iris put a warning hand on his arm.

'Not so keen on talking about it?' Moira pinched up crumbs from her shirt, popped them into her mouth. 'Will you miss Auckland?'

'Kaaah, kaaaaaah!'

Billy flung out his arms, jumped up, and while trying to zoom off who knows where knocked the small occasional table where the tray of coffee pot and biscuits, cups, milk jug and fruit loaf had all been as beautifully set out as if it were a birthday. (The sight of the spread had filled Iris's heart with premature nostalgia, knowing she had the announcement to make: no more comradettes-in-the-burbs for the work-kids-house-garden-husband-errands juggle. Though frankly, the way Billy just then hollered and anticked about, they might never have been invited back anyway.)

'Kaaah, kaaah!'

He turned around as Iris remonstrated with him and — drunk on embarrassment, now, was it? Drunk on his own carolling? — accidentally bashed into the table again, this time sending plates skittering and coffee slopping.

'Billy! That is no way to behave,' Iris scolded. He stood in the middle of the living-room making an irritating, insistent *cheepa-cheepa-cheepa*!

'Ah, don't worry about him, Iris,' Moira had said. 'Kids are weird little arses at the best of times.' She helped Iris to mop up the coffee, and they collected the scattered biscuits.

'Billy — *outside*,' Iris said, pointing, her arm at full and furious stretch. 'Don't come back until you've run off all that — that — *bullpucky*.' She apologised, 'Sorry, Moira. We'll go soon. We've disgraced ourselves.' Moira took the plate of biscuits from her, eyeing them for muck. But then she gave a sly, conspiratorial smile. 'We need a drink for the shock. It's nearly five o'clock: perfectly civilised.'

Once they'd opened the wine, Moira had Iris in stitches-of-tears, with her stories about the friend who posted a photo of her positive pregnancy-test stick on Facebook as a way to tell everyone the news, including her husband; or the time Abigail, when she was tiny, asked how the milk bottles got out of the cows; or the other time she asked were she and Caitlin twins because Moira and Sean had sex twice, or because her eggs had two yolks? Or was it the spoom had two handles? 'The spoom?' Moira had asked. 'The spoom that goes with the egg.' 'It's not a spoon.' 'I know it's not a spoon; it's a *spoo-muh*. *Muh*. But does it have a *handle*?' 'No, it's a *sperrrrm* and it has a tail.' 'So how does it scoop up the egg?' Or the time Caitlin decided to make the fish tank smell better by pouring Moira's Christmas eau de cologne into the water. All the goldfish died. 'Like I said,' Moira shook her head, 'they're all mad, so they are.'

When it was time, Iris took her leave, so Moira could get on with her evening. They found Billy contentedly playing outside with the twins, the girls burying him in their sand pit as best they could.

'He's a kneegyptian in his tomb,' said Abigail.

'No,' corrected Billy. 'I'm having a dust bath.'

'Well, as long as everyone's happy,' said Moira, a jaunty pink from the wine high on her cheekbones.

'Can Abigail and Caitlin come to visit us soon, Mum?'

'Can we go on holiday to Dunedin?' asked Abigail.

The women exchanged looks. 'We'll see,' they said, intonation identical. Iris tried not to show how bittersweet that was.

We'll see. A season of we'll sees; days and weeks measured in them. Crates, rubbish bags, moving trucks, petrol-station stops, ferry tickets and crossing a sea of we'll sees; long, uncomfortable drives of them. Billy crammed in the back with luggage; Iris crammed in the front with three cartons of Liam's blessed inherited Toby jugs at her feet, because he wouldn't trust them to the movers, or even to the back of the car. Crammed, though *she* had to argue the case for bringing her grandmother's sewing basket. She swore at Liam when he said it should be freighted with the rest of her workroom clobber. It stored, among other things, her three best pairs of scissors, favourite thimble and measuring tape, a quick-unpick so glossy it looked good enough to suck, and a copper letter opener, decorated with Celtic swirls, which was actually the best tool she'd ever found as a point-turner for collars. *Crap!* she'd spat, wanting to accidentally-on-purpose drop the whole lot of his Toby-yucks *whoops* to the concrete. What a pity, never mind, less to pack. How she wouldn't miss that weird, leery John Barleycorn. *That* wasn't part of Liam's heirloom collection. It was a gift from an old, before-Iris woman-friend of his. Faye Prescott. (Whom Iris found just a little too breathy and solicitous, and who had told her one too many times how *lucky* she was to have a Man Like Liam . . .)

Oh, all the petty arguments about packing and unpacking, *Newspaper AND bubble wrap for the Toby jugs, Iris!* All the hassle and bustle and all the immediate, practical so-called urgencies that mean no time to think, but also no time to let the mind travel too far into itself.

Box on, Liam says, you've got to box on. And Iris the over-thinker, surrounded by bloody *boxes* thank you very much; well of course at one point she wonders if Liam has unconsciously decided on this major transition as a form of avoidance. Maybe he's deliberately created no time to think. Though it's hard in any circumstances, yes it is, with a son like Billy.

He wanted a new bird book for the road-trip down south. A *particular* one. NO, not that one, this one. Expensive, because it came with an actually okay pair of binoculars. He wanted to stop off at every scenic spot to bird-watch. He wanted to talk and talk in the car. Where other kids, surely, would be lulled off to sleep by the engine's thrum, Billy seemed to rev up. 'Is he red-lining?' Liam asked. 'I think we should ban sugar for the next leg of the trip. Doesn't Dramamine make kids drowsy? Let's get some.'

The new bird book seemed to age Billy overnight. He began to talk like a midget professor.

'Did you know that birds experience time more slowly than we do, Dad?'

'Really?'

'Says so right here. They take in more information than we do, so that's why they can choose out a twig from a tree to land on even when they're flying so fast.'

'Huh.'

'Is that why this trip feels so long?' asked Billy.

'Wouldn't it be the opposite?' asked Iris. 'Or do you mean because we're travelling so fast?'

'It feels long because it is long,' said Liam, glaring at the stock truck ahead.

'Guess why some birds only stand on one leg,' Billy commanded, just as Liam was overtaking the fourteen-wheeler.

'Because they're one-legged?' If Iris played goofy, Liam might lighten up.

'No, Mum. It's to stop heat loss. Cooooool.'

'Aren't you getting car-sick, reading?'

'Nope.'

Now Liam scowled at the sight of a horse float. Iris offered chewing gum as a distraction.

'Hey, listen to this from *Which New Zealand Bird?* — I like how he writes them down. Which bird do you think this is? Tw*eep*-tw*eep*-tw*eep*-too-too-too.'

'Too-too-much,' Liam said.

'I like it better than *kaah kaah* and coffee-table collisions, that's for sure.' Iris glanced at Billy in the rear-view mirror. He looked out the window, impervious.

'Eh?' Liam asked. The way he had lately begun to forget their conversations made her (a) worry he'd be a candidate for early Alzheimer's or (b) believe he must think most of what she said was brain-freezingly trivial. Iris tried a trick she'd learnt in a drama class a million years ago: take a deep breath in as if filling the capillaries all the way down to your toes. Breathe out just as slowly. It was meant to be relaxing. Sometimes it just seemed to oxygenate the worries. She carefully pressed *insouciance* into her voice. 'You know, the to-do at Moira's.'

Now, in the car arrowing along State Highway One, they passed a hedge trimmed into the shape of a giant chook with a shrub-sized egg right beside it. Billy cried out in delight, *Look!* Yet Iris still felt both the historical scald of embarrassment, and a tightening screw of regret at leaving her new friendship behind. Oh, well, maybe Moira would visit. Maybe they would be school-holiday billets: Moira and Iris selling inter-island trips to the children as 'fun for kids', when 50 per cent of the motivation was actually sanity for mothers.

She looked at Billy in the rear-view mirror again: he was sucking his bottom lip, calm and thoughtful; lulled at last by the steady rhythm of the car's engine. Maybe Moira was right, and his behaviour was no quirkier than most. The peacock-squawking and flittering about was simply a stage. After all, kids' lives at the best of times were an express-train of phases: each one whizzing past you with a shriek and potent fumes . . . Really, Billy was a natural oxymoron: an ordinary oddity. And it was the defining condition of parenthood that it was hard to think straight or talk properly. Her own discombobulation was ordinary, too — and it was all the more the expected state given all the hoo-ha of upping-sticks from island to island, north to south, loss to loss, no, don't dwell on it, just get on with it. *Move on*, hummed the car wheels. *Move on*.

TIME MUDDLES
AND SLIDES

DISCOMBOBULATION WAS A NEW word for Billy. His mum was using it a lot while they tried to find a house; then decided to rent one; then enrolled him in a new school; then while Mum did the 'screeds of things your father and I still have to sort out'; then when they all went round to Dad's new business partner Steve's place for dinner. They met Steve's children there, and his wife, whom Billy wasn't afterwards allowed to call Posh Hannah. Billy was told off for talking a lot; he was told off for asking too many questions. He was even told off for telling Mum and Dad the things he'd learned about spoonbills after he'd seen *six* of them at an inlet they drove past. He was told off for trying to show Steve and Not Posh Hannah how a pukeko walked and how a kārearea, the falcon, can turn on its back in flight if attacking a bigger bird. He was told off while Mum and Dad unpacked boxes, shoved in plugs, made phone calls; they said his burble in the background was utterly discomBOBulating. Could he please go and try the old trampoline or tree house left behind by previous tenants; could he befriend the landlord's cat that came so-called 'free' with the house?

DiscomBOBulating, discomBOBulating, discomBOB-ulating, he whispered to himself. He liked it. Saying it was like invisible bubbles. It felt exactly right for the way things in the new town bobbled at him and floated past in a slightly unreal way.

Time muddles and slides. The way it does at school, for example, the day he is asked to run a message. He likes his new teacher. He likes the very green and grassy playground. Yet he misses the sounds of Auckland. He misses the slow heat. His tummy feels wrong. He tries not to think about that on his errand, though it turns out he has to go past the bike racks. There is a bike that looks a bit like Jason's, except it has handlebar streamers. In his head he says, 'You look like a bike I used to know.' There is something friendly, horsey, about it. As if it will whinny and toss its handlebars to get the flame-coloured streamers out of its eyes. Billy pats the bike seat, and says, 'Easy, easy. Good girl.' The bike asks, 'What's wrong?' 'Oh, there was Jason's accident,' Billy answers. The bike understands.

Billy imagines parts of the crash, sees it on the screen that sits up to the left inside his head. A small figure does an aerial jump like a BMX hero. Black against the sky, it floats down fast, like the wriggly threads you see when you're tired. Billy tries to make it stay still, but again and again the tiny Tom Thumb leaps and drops. Some people think you can decide what to dream about before you go to sleep. Billy doubts it. He can't even stop his own thoughts when he's awake.

The bike asks Billy, 'Did you go to the funeral?' Billy retorts, 'That's a weird thing for a bike to ask.' Then he feels bad about it because the bike starts to look more like chrome and tinsel with yellow sponge showing through the PVC seat cover and less like something alive.

Billy runs his hand down the bike's metal stem and along the frame as if he could wake it up again. He waits for it to huff, some horse-bike kind of purr. It stays still, metallic. A weird thought arrives: *a bike-shaped coffin of a bike*. Cold pain tingles at the side of Billy's jaw as he remembers events after the funeral.

When the service ended, even when he slowly realised that of course Jason wouldn't really be at the chapel, Billy still half-thought he would silently slip away with them afterwards. Billy thought that once they had the real Jason home again, now that he had died, it would probably be like one of the times Jason was grounded. Like when he was in major trouble for using Liam's credit card on the internet for a game he didn't have permission to buy, *and* for not coming home from a movie when he'd agreed: a super-bad week, followed by a fortnight of no-friends, no-screen-time, no-pocket-money, no-iPod. Billy remembered some of the shouting.

'You've had sod's luck, Jase, you're right. It's not fair that you don't have your own folks, true. But we're trying to do our best for you, and you know what? We actually love you. When you act up, it's like you've thrown that back at us. We have these rules to keep you safe. What if — what if Iris and I started stealing groceries because I was upset about your dad? It's not bloody logical, is it? What if we ignored our responsibilities? Stopped paying for sports and holidays because we decided life's not fair?'

'Don't you like holidays with us, Dad?' Billy said.

Liam had said, 'Butt out, Billy.' So Billy stuck his butt

out and waggled it, which Dad didn't think was very funny. Billy got sent outside.

Jason had been like a turned-down version of himself then: quiet, in his room or doodling; and in the weekends, spending hours building elaborate Lego space stations again with Billy, as they lay on the floor next to the stereo, listening to all Mum and Dad's old eighties and nineties CDs. Sometimes Jase would sing under his breath, 'I'm *ban*ned, I'm *ban*ned, I know it,' then do a Michael Jackson move that made Billy's parents laugh but try to hide it. Billy wished Jase wouldn't do the move, to be honest. Actually, he wished Michael Jackson on YouTube wouldn't do it either. But Billy *had* liked Jason grounded.

Billy had thought after the funeral would be like that: his cousin more exclusively his own. Yet the house was eerily quiet, tidy. There was no Jase to leave his things lying haphazardly around like graffiti tagging his space. He wasn't there to gurn with, when Mum and Dad nagged, or when Mum did her nut because someone had sneaked off with her embroidery scissors. No Jase to talk about the coolest things to stock in joke shops or the weirdest way to get into the book of *Guinness World Records*.

When they moved down south, Jase wasn't there to say it would all be okay and so help *make* it okay, even if in every other way it wasn't.

Billy's head felt as if it would never get out of exactly that kind of loop. Sometimes, he just had to talk and talk to drain off the noise in his head. Sometimes he just had to run and jump and flick and shake.

Knowledge seemed to have that shadow-twin of not-knowing with it all the time now. Like, Billy knew Jason wouldn't be there each day after school. He knew there was no point bounding into Jason's room when he was up too early to wake Mum and Dad. His cousin wouldn't be there to sardine with under the covers, and play fart-ball, or stew up some fart-soup. (They never got away with blowing off in Mum and Dad's bed. Dad said what they did was not only disgusting but highly toxic and very likely flammable. If there was static electricity because of friction between Mum's nearly-a-negligée and the sheets, they'd be fried alive.)

But every now and then, the not-knowing Billy would think, *I'll ask Jase.* Or he would save him a place. Or look for him in assembly when Jase didn't even know Billy had started a new school.

Billy swims up a bit from remembering and realises he's picked at the exposed underlayer on the bike seat. Ashamed, he quickly stuffs the foam crumbs he's pinched back into the gap. He doesn't know whose bike it is: hopes they don't notice. He pats the hole and whispers sorry. He stares at the jagged edge of the rip. It looks like skin and that makes him sick.

A lot of stuff makes him feel sick these days. The world has gone pretty strange. His dad seems to have turned sort of deaf. His mum does this thing where, in the middle of some normal job, she freezes, her eyes wide as a spooked rabbit's. He wishes she would stop suddenly calling for him, insisting on being in the same room, even following him right up to the *toilet*, sometimes. He is *eight*. Nearly *nine*! When she trails him and calls after him in that high voice, his arms and back stipple all over with bumps of new goose-down.

Billy blinks. His eyes feel a bit sticky, sleepy. He is supposed to be telling a teacher in another class that his own teacher would be ready for singing group to start after playtime. It is his day to be Class Helper. He doesn't want to go back inside the classrooms, though.

At the edge of the playground is a monkey-puzzle tree. His mum always says, whenever they see one, 'Hmmm, no monkey in it; that's a puzzle.' He can't help looking for a monkey every time. He ambles over there and startles a small bird. It chitters with alarm, seems to skid on the sky before it soars away. As it climbs higher, there is a pulling sensation in Billy's chest. A wish so strong should have the power of rocket fuel: why can't he fly, too?

He turns, trying to keep track of the bird dot — and then he hears another bird, from somewhere in the garden over the fence. A riroriro. Its song reels and wheels: whenever he thinks it will rest, it bells and pipes again, spiralling, winding, climbing. It sings with rolling, wild joy.

The bird comes into view. It sees Billy. It looks right at him, so deeply into Billy's eyes that for a moment he feels held by its mind. Had the other Auckland bird somehow talked to this one? For it knows things about Billy. There is a calm acceptance: *You are Billy, I know you.* Then it fans away. Billy feels its song in his body the way you feel good dreams still in your blood as you wake up slowly.

That dream feeling. The birdsong brings it back, with pictures, too, that come like the fall of honey from a spoon. There's a dream he started having soon after Jason died. Each time it's slightly different, but on the first night, Billy looked down and thought what a handsome feather vest he wore, then saw his feet. They were talons delicately curled around a branch. A tiny white tuft drifted to his few thin toes. *I am raining*, Billy thought. Then, in the rapid way of dreams, his legs and wings coursed with new knowledge.

He didn't leap — he merely stretched out on the air and floated. Hearing a triumphant cry from down below, *Billy's flying!*, he circled in the sky, song spilling from his beak as if the spool of music helped to keep him in the air. Whenever he woke, he tried to hold the sweet blurred feeling in his head so he would dream it all again . . .

He tries to get it back right now, but the school bell shatters the mood. At the same time, he sees his teacher charge out across the courtyard. Miss Hooper calls him, very annoyed. 'Billy, you were supposed to deliver my message to Ms Johnston. What on earth are you doing?'

His tummy jolts. He tries to make a standing leap for a lower branch so he can swing himself up into the tree. He dangles from it, but—

'Billy! Down here on the count of three. One, two—'

He drops, though his mind hares to and fro. He comes up with a question-lie. 'Wasn't that the playtime bell?' He knows it was, and he also knows that isn't the point.

'Did you give Ms Johnston the message?'

'I was going to, but I thought I saw . . .' His mouth bumbles. 'I thought I saw some rosellas out here.' No he didn't. He feels even more ashamed when the lie works. Miss Hooper looks from tree to tree, then scans the sky. 'Really?' She sounds so happy. 'I love rosellas.'

'Miss Hooper, we could have a bird-feeder in the field. We could put out sugar water and nuts and things.'

'That's not a bad idea. It'd be lovely to be surrounded by birdsong.'

'That would mean tuis and bellbirds maybe. But Miss Hooper, have you ever *heard* rosellas? It's like cleaning windows.'

Miss Hooper gives him a funny look.

'Fast squeaky circles,' he explains.

Then something distracts her: the principal waves from the lower playground. Some Year 4s mill around him, wanting him to shoot baskets with their ball. He misses, then toils up the steps, hands in pockets. 'You're a mine of information, Billy,' says Miss Hooper. 'Now, what exactly did you want me for?'

Ha! Billy sees his chance. He goes from frozen on the spot to on his mark, get set, go: legging it, as he calls over his shoulder, 'Nothing! Just gonna give Ms Johnston that message!'

WORLDWIDE UNIVERSAL
BLAHNESS ON A STICK

AT THE HOME-TIME BELL, Billy worried that for his slip-up Miss Hooper might pop out of the classroom and grab his mother, or tell him to stay behind until his mum came peering in to look for him. But all that happened was that over the scrape of chairs and shoving of desks, Miss Hooper called out, 'Oh, and kids, keep your eyes out for a flock of rosellas on your way home. Wee brightly coloured parrots. *Apparently* they've been spotted near the school.'

When he got outside the classroom he saw some boys from his class turn around. They made chicken wings with their elbows and one of them clucked, 'Bok-bok-ba-*GEK!*' They laughed and started to run, backpacks waggling like tongues. Billy marched past his mum, so she would have to follow him instead of making him put on his hat and coat, or asking Miss Hooper if he'd had a good day. When she caught up, he said, 'I *can* walk home alone now. I know the way. You don't *have* to come and get me.'

'But you're still pretty new here, Billy.'

He looked up ahead and saw a group of girls together:

no mum, no dad. They only lived around the corner, but still. The chicken-call boys were over the road, way ahead, squirting their drink bottles at each other in a running battle.

He whacked a roadside hedge. 'Other kids do it.'

Right on cue, a skinny brother and sister, knees and elbows so knobbly they looked built from K'nex, scootered past, helmets nonchalantly slung over the handlebars.

His mum sighed. 'They should be wearing those,' she said. 'Did you have a good day?'

Dumb question.

'Why the bad mood?'

'It's not Auckland, you know. There's not so much cars.'

'You mean *there aren't so many cars*. Don't start talking like all the other dingbats, Billy.'

As they passed the corner store, a trio of older girls came out clutching paper bags of lolly mix.

'Hi there, what's-yer-name!' said one of them, smiling, and another said, 'It's Billy the Bird-boy.' Billy ignored them and the girls drifted off, already more preoccupied by suggesting sweet swaps.

'Billy the Bird-boy?' asked Iris.

Billy scuffed his shoes. Then he pointed. 'Have they got an invisible mum?'

Iris chewed her lip. 'Okay. Look. We'll make a new deal. Next term, you can start walking on your own. I'll meet you halfway each day until you prove to me that you're mature enough to handle it.'

Mature enough to handle it — blahness. Worldwide universal blahness on a stick. Of course he was old enough. Nearly every other neighbourhood kid in Years 6 and 7 did it: some got picked up by car, sure, but heaps went by foot, bike, scooter, skateboard. By hop, skip and jump. He didn't really know what Mum was so worried about. He was way more careful since Jase, of course he was. He wasn't going to get run over: he *knew* the road rules. Besides, he only had to cross the road once to get home and, yes, it was at a roundabout but did she think he was stupid?

If she was worrying about volcanoes or *asteroids* on the other hand, or . . . well, if it was an asteroid . . . fright swept his skin and Billy started to run. He pushed through another gaggle of girls with Dora and Barbie backpacks. They called him gaynuts but he didn't care because his dad's friends in Auckland were gay and it meant, as far as he could tell, being a good cook and funny and listening to what Billy *actually* had to say and having matching serviettes and tablecloth, whereas Iris said, 'Oh, I'd love to be this fancy, there's Grandma's best lace tucked away, and it'd be so *easy* to whip up table settings for every season, but what's the point you kids muck it all up anyway with your messy eating.'

You kids.

Everybody else seemed to be walking home with another kid. A brother, a sister or a friend. Random angry crazy wetness flew into his eyes and he wanted to run away but he didn't know where to, so he just sprinted as fast as he could, downhill, trying to race his mother's cry *Billy!* out of his ears.

He got way ahead, he could see their house, and he wasn't watching his feet, so even though he saw the roadworks sign on the footpath and the men laying gravel, he didn't see the sign's tripod feet, so he went sprawling onto all the billions of tiny chipped stones. A big burly guy with sunnies, dreadlocks and facial tattoos asked,

'You okay?' then helped him up. He said, 'Oooh, mate, that looks *nasty*,' but Billy was too sore to say thanks and he didn't wait for Mum. He limped on home, crying for real now, throwing his backpack down at the front step and collapsing there on his bum, staring at the thick dribbles of blood on his knee, and hating, hating, hating with a miserable runaway hate.

He heard click-click snip-snap scurrying footsteps and didn't want to look up at Iris, who he was sure would say, *You see, you need to stay with me, if you'd stuck with me you wouldn't be in this state*, but instead it was someone else, saying 'Billy?' as if it wasn't a very good idea to be him.

He looked up, eyes travelling from white sandals with white-polished toenails, to a floaty ribbed white tunic thing that was more like a rice-paper lantern than a dress, tiny white suit jacket and a white fabric rose on a ribbon around the person's throat. Ugh-balls. Posh Hannah. The person married to Dad's new work-partner. She held a folder of papers, clutching them close and standing back as if his blood might be catchy.

'What happened?' she said. Without waiting for an answer, she leaned over and pushed the doorbell, then also rapped on the door.

Billy's mum came hurrying up behind her. When she didn't tell him off, he felt guilty that the hate had got inside him. She just said, 'Oh, Billy, that looks awful,' then helped him up, opened the door and led him to the bathroom, saying to Posh White Hannah, 'Sorry, I'll be with you in a moment. Just go on through to the kitchen, if you like, and put the kettle on.'

The Dettol and cotton wool made him want to kick.

'Stings like Billy-oh, eh?' Such a Mum-joke he couldn't

74

help laughing. She decided there were too many cuts for Band-Aids, so she used gauze and a wind-on bandage, and had to help him down off the bathroom bench because his legs hurt to unbend.

He pressed his face into her tummy.

'Let's go see what Hannah wants,' she whispered, 'swishing her sub-Issey Miyake outfit at us like that.' Her eyes were bug-wide so Billy knew *Issy My-yukky* meant that Mum was jealous, Hannah was a pain, and when Mum had said 'put the kettle on' she really hoped she wouldn't.

Hannah had gone into the living-room and was looking at the family photos on the mantelpiece with a frown. Mum went all stiff-fake-nice. 'I think I'll make Billy a hot chocolate. Would you like a coffee?'

Hannah followed her to the kitchen, saying a long speech about dropping papers off for Liam because Steve left them by mistake at the warrant of fitness place but they needed Liam to blah blah whatever long ramble. For some weird reason Billy could hear a radio jingle about *whiteware, whiteware, 20 per cent off whiteware* in his head and he was concentrating so hard on not walking in a way that hurt that he almost collided with Hannah, who had stopped. Because Mum hadn't reached the kettle. She had stopped. Because plonk in the middle of the kitchen floor was a fat rat. With a chicken bone at its feet. His mother gasped, reached behind them and slammed the kitchen door shut. The slam was like a starter gun: the rat raced the edge of the kitchen, around, around and around.

'Ohmigodohmigodohmigod!' Hannah was saying and finally the rat stopped, in a corner, panting.

'Where's the damn landlord's damn cat?!' Iris shouted at the rat, as if the rat might have done something with it.

'What's the point of having a so-called free cat if it doesn't stop *rats*?'

Hannah shrieked and pointed. The cat-flap in the back door, which led out from the kitchen, was moving. The landlord's cat was trying to head-bang it open, but was finding it hard because its mouth was full. It wanted to bring in another rat.

Now Hannah had one hand over her mouth. Billy thought she was laughing until he realised she had terrified tears in her eyes. She had turned very pale to match her white-wear and the laughing was shaking. 'I'm going to be sick,' she said.

His mum rushed for the cat-flap, locked it and started hissing, like a giant cat herself. The cat wouldn't give up. It kept pushing the rat against the little Perspex door.

'We need to throw something over it!' Billy snatched an empty ice-cream container from the bench and gave it to Hannah.

'I am not catching a rat in that!' she cried, peering into it as if there might already be a rat in there that would creeple-creeple out.

'No, the *cat*!' he said; he wasn't talking about the container, he meant that cats were frightened of water, and—

'What?' said his mum. He hobble-rushed (sore knees) to grab the cold kettle from the bench, and without really thinking properly — though he knew there wasn't carpet so really it would be okay — he flung water at the cat flap, to shock the cat, even though it wouldn't get hit. The problem was the water splattered everywhere, which frightened the inside rat, so it ran at Hannah, right over her peeping toes, and she truly was sick, right into the ice-cream container, while weeping, 'Oh, I'm so sorry.'

'No, that's what it was *for*,' said Billy, and then, 'It's run behind the fridge!' Hannah, shaky and gulping, asked where the bathroom was. Iris, oh-dear oh-dearing, showed her the way, bellowing at Billy, as if *he* was the one who'd brought the rat in, 'Don't you dare leave that door open!' She didn't say don't move the fridge. He thought that if he did he might be able to catch the rat in something — something, something, something — oh, look, yeah the swing-top rubbish-bin-shaped-whatsit they kept on the bench for food scraps before they went into the compost bucket. It was empty — *bonus!* — so he whipped it off the bench, then, making sure not to bang his knees, shoved at the fridge with one shoulder. The fridge was on coasters, so although it was difficult, he budged it just enough to *freaky!* see the rat dart up behind the metal grille at the back. It stopped part-way; Billy knew it was there because its tail dangled out.

His mum called from the hallway, 'I'm coming in, Billy. Keep that bloody animal away from the door.' She entered wearing rubber gloves and carrying a bucket and a softball bat.

'Hannah's gone home,' she said.

'Didn't she want to help?' asked Billy.

'She has murophobia.'

'What?'

'Irrational fear of rats and mice.' His mum looked super-worried. 'That *woman*. She said, "*Vermin* are attracted to unhygienic places. *I* am extra vigilant." She was basically saying I'm *slack*. As if I don't look after the house enough. My God! She'll probably never visit us again.'

'So?' said Billy, thinking *but you didn't really want to give her coffee anyway.*

'It's a bit awkward, isn't it? Given your dad works with her husband.'

'Does Steve have muralphobia as well?'

'It's *muro*phobia, and no, or at least I shouldn't think so, it'd be pretty strange for both people in a couple to — or, maybe not, it *could* be an attraction, some common ground, but — I don't know, Billy, does it really matter?'

'Are you going to bash the rat?'

'I don't know! I don't want to, but — how the hell am I going to — I can't think. Let's get out of here for a moment.' She led Billy from the kitchen to the living-room, still carrying the bucket and bat.

'How are we going to catch it if we're in the living-room and it's in the kitchen?'

'I just need to be away from it for a moment. I can't stand their tails.'

'Is it a phobia?'

'Billy, would you just let me *think*?'

They were in there for a long time.

'Can I have a snack?'

'How can you even want to *eat* when there's a rat around? Oh, *Billy*. Is there anything left in your lunchbox?'

Glumly, 'Probably.' He went to find the bruised banana.

'You better get on with your homework,' said Iris, gloves and bat put aside. Now she was sort of *smacking* clean washing into Dad piles, Mum piles, Billy piles, and jeepers-that-already-needs-mending piles. 'We better just get on with things till I come up with a solution.'

So Mum muttered and banged about with things that didn't involve the kitchen. She went to the spare room, saying she was going to start unpacking some Whipstitch things she hadn't had time to organise yet, though *when* she would get headspace to design for next season, *she* didn't know. Billy couldn't see how he was supposed to know either, although the tone of her voice seemed to mean it was something to do with him. Either him or *Issy-pissing-Miyake*, whoever that was: because he could hear Mum saying that a lot, along with *That woman!* Anyway, it all made his homework look quite easy, so he did that. Then he was allowed to watch TV.

Mum brought out a folding thread-storage case, which was half-empty. She muttered, 'When I picked it up, the bloody thing fell open.' Then she went out, came back with heaps of spools carried in her skirt, like she'd been collecting eggs from crazy-coloured hens. She dumped them on the couch, then started winding up thread and clicking bobbins back in the right rainbow order in the case. His tummy started to rumble again. But the idea of the rat was getting bigger and bigger, and though he'd been quite excited and pretty brave before, the way his mum's face had turned tight made it seem like the rat was pressing all of the oxygen out of the entire house.

'Could it get into the food from there?'

'Oh, God, surely not!'

'If that cat found two rats does that mean there might be more?'

'Probably. There's probably a nest of them somewhere. Foul, foul, foul. We'll have to set traps. We'll call a pest exterminator. We'll call the landlord.'

'Will we have to call the police?'

'No, Billy!'

'But you're acting "Emergency! Emergency!"'

Iris shouted, 'No, I'm not, I'm being perfectly calm. You saw Hannah, didn't you? I'm perfectly calm!'

Because she was shouting they didn't hear Liam come home. He appeared in the living-room with his eyebrows in a shape that Billy thought should be the way to write question marks, so Billy answered, before his dad had even said hello, 'There's a rat behind the fridge and I think we could pull it out by the tail.'

'I'm not touching its bloody tail!' said Iris.

'You said "bloody".'

'Billy! This is an extreme situation! I'm allowed to swear!'

'A rat?' asked Liam, as if Billy had really meant kitten.

Billy rolled his eyes. 'I know what rats look like, Dad. Posh-I-mean-Hannah's scared of them. She was here. She'll never visit us again probably. She's got murophobia. Is that bad for you?'

'Never heard of it.'

'I mean that she'll never visit.'

His dad caught the same grumpy *what-now* look that Mum had worn since Hannah left. Liam went to the kitchen and saw the rat's tail still dangling from behind the fridge's rear grille.

'We'll have to pull its tail,' he said.

'That's what I said!' said Billy.

Liam disappeared.

'What's he doing?' asked Billy.

'No idea,' said Iris through the thumbnail she was chewing.

'This is a weird kind of interesting,' said Billy.

'No, it is *not*!' said Iris. She picked up the softball bat.

Liam came back carrying giant pliers, and wearing the thick leather workman's gloves he used when sharpening tools. 'Leave your mother alone for a bit, Billy,' he said. And then, 'Damn. Can you go into the garage and get the cat cage?'

'The cat's outside.'

'Not the cat, the cage. Get the damn cage!'

Billy squawked excitedly. He shook out his arms, admired their span, tipped them to and fro, relishing the light's sprint across his feathers. He flew off to get the cage.

'Fricken zoo in here,' he heard his dad say. Billy's skull zinged and his stomach shrunk at hearing both parents cuss in one day. He brought back the cage; ears wide open for more unusual events. With the expression of someone not wanting to look, his dad, well, *pliered* the rat by its tail. He pulled and pulled and the rat scrabbled, fought and squeaked then tried to climb up its own tail to bite Dad through the gloves but Dad somehow shoved it into the cat cage, and the rat tried to run out but Mum hockey-pucked it with the softball bat saying, 'Oh, God I'm a wimp — I can't hit it properly, I can't hit it properly,' and it scrambled, but then it stumbled, so Dad could scooch it into the cage with his foot and slam the door shut.

'Teamwork,' he said.

'What *now*?' asked Billy.

'I suppose we better kill it,' said Liam.

Iris rubbed her arms as if she was freezing. 'I don't want to kill anything. Not even a rat.'

'But you eat meat, Mum.'

'Billy!'

'What? You could maybe turn the rat into a purse, Mum. Or a fur collar?'

'Would you like a lie-down, Iris?' said Liam, hand on her shoulder.

'NO!' she shouted. Liam and Billy flinched. Iris left the room.

'Your mum's gone to lie down,' said Liam.

'I know,' said Billy. 'It's the stress.' Father and son looked at each other. 'I'm not stupid,' said Billy.

'Know what?' Liam sighed. 'Sometimes it'd be easier if you were.'

Billy looked at the rat, which nosed its whiskers out of the cage. He regretted the fur purse idea. 'Some people have rats as pets, don't they, Dad? They're on sale at the vet-and-pet shop.'

Liam snapped his fingers. 'Brilliant. We'll call the vet.'

'To sell a *wild* rat?'

Liam frowned, then said, 'They have special injections that put animals to sleep. Help them to die. I'll find out what it costs.'

A strange, happy curiosity that had been slowly un-creasing in Billy at the sight of the thin fuzzed muzzle and the tiny questing whiskers closed down into grey and grey and grey. He quivered, then swooped in a birdline to his dad for a hug to take away the weirdness of what is death, when does it come, who decides, it's only a wild rat, why so upset, what's the matter, why does even the word *die* start this rising dark-water feeling? But Liam was stripping off his gloves, striding off to find the phone: telling Billy, run outside and play, if you've got lots of energy, go and use the trampoline, why do you think trampolines *exist*?

WHAT EATS AT DAYLIGHT'S EDGE, WITH ITS SHARP, RESTLESS MOUTH?

PERHAPS IT WAS THE THOUGHT of a rat's nest nearby, in goodness-knows-whose garden tangle, but Billy seemed to want to be away from home all the time. He constantly asked to visit the Botanic Gardens. He also punctuated all conversation with chirrup and flutter, neck-thrust and swoop. And whenever Iris asked what he'd like to eat, he'd answer, 'Nuts and seeds!' 'What about pasta?' 'Nuts and seeds!' 'What about sausages?' 'Nuts and seeds!'

'*Fish and chips*?'

'NUTS AND SEEDS!'

'I'm sure it's nothing.' Iris and Liam took it in turns to reassure each other, passing to and fro the bothered-by-it-baton. Liam's favourite: 'It's just a phase. Don't be fazed.' At which drollery Iris sighed, 'Things will settle down.'

Once he's had a full term at this school and made new friends, things will settle down.

Once Liam's in a clear routine at work, things will settle down.

Once Billy's exhausted every New Zealand bird book in the children's section of the library, things will settle down.

Once he's watched every episode of Attenborough's *The Life of Birds* on DVD, things will settle down.

Once he's tired of the same outing every weekend, and saying over and over, 'Wanna cuppa tea? Wanna cuppa tea?' to Rocky the Botanic Gardens aviary cockatoo, things will settle down.

And *once* things have settled down, Iris thought, maybe this something, hmmm, what-ish? Grey-ish? Removed-ish? about Liam will pass, too. He's busy. He's pressed. Mustn't add to it. Things will ease.

Yet eight weeks on, things still don't feel quite right. What is it? Their rental place has decent insulation, afternoon sun, a swathe of backyard with basketball hoop, battered trampoline, tree hut, *with* a trapdoor, way-hey, Billy! The house is close to parks and a choice of schools; it even comes with *That Cat*, which despite the ratastrophe, is great, because they'd left their pets in Auckland. So what eats at daylight's edge, with its sharp, restless mouth?

Billy's off at school, Liam's off at work. Iris has fallen way behind on work for Whipstitch. Although she filled all her orders before she left Auckland (just! frantic!), she needs new ideas, should source them in a southern feel. Drop the hoodies and skirts from her line and try cowls? Or capes, with several loose tassels, to reference the gorgeous korowai she'd seen a woman wearing as she strode up to a film première at the Regent? Merino tunics? Sparkly, multicoloured balaclavas — kind of disco Pussy Riot for students dancing in southern winters? She looks through a few favourite websites, then sits with her sketchpad and jars of pencils, but perhaps it's the light in this new studio room. She can't conjure up that addictive sensation: the half-hypnotised, half-hungry state she gets into when an idea pushes through her fingers and onto the paper. She should do a comp-shop; trail through town and see what's already on offer in local boutiques and markets. Though she's still reluctant to think about choosing a machinist down here, or working out whether it would be less risky and more economical to courier prototype designs back up to the Excellently Reliable and Lovely Deidre and her team in Auckland . . . Like a schoolgirl, she writes a beautiful, cursive *shitballs* on her sketchpad. Maybe she could go back to the yoga classes downtown she's tried, mainly to meet people. It's pretty hard to make new acquaintances when you're self-employed.

She *could* suggest buying lunch for Hannah, if she were truly lonely — to compensate for the whole embarrassing rat drama. But actually, something else — the pheromones? The tiny whiff of class difference? The general smugness of Hannah's attitude? The fact that they met through Liam's work, so his obsessions would be in the foreground again, as if Whipstitch were frivolous? Something, anyway, makes the idea unappealing. Desperate. And it's crazy — Iris knows it's quite a bit more than slightly crazy — but just today, there have been aftershocks in Christchurch, it's on the news, and yes, Dunedin's 400 kilometres south of that, but actually — she thinks she'll just stay home.

She's feeling edgy. Can't concentrate, not right now. Can't stomach the hyper-reality and games-arcade flash-flash-flash of TV; everyone else's lives on Facebook look so, what? enviable, and, let's face it, *elsewhere*; she can't even concentrate on that book she's been craving time to read. Could it be that the rest of the house is still in disorder?

So she washes the cups
And she washes the cups
And she washes the cups again;
Then when they touch the rack
She sees she needs to wash the rack
So she washes the rack and washes the rack
And washes the rack again.

And as she cleans the house
And cleans the house
And cleans the house again,
She thinks about Jase.
She thinks about Billy.
She thinks about Chatter-Billy Chatterbox
whispering to himself
deep inside his thoughts.

She shines and shines the bathroom mirror
As if she could shine away the sight of her face.

Does Liam shoulder away the thought of Pete
every day?
How often does he think about Jase?
Does he think about Billy thinking about Jase?
Does he—

Stop it, Iris.

But, no, there's something her head won't finish with
yet . . .

Does Liam think about what Jase thought about his
parents? Of how it would be for Billy in Jase's situation?
Will any of that come into the risks he calculates out on

the water, or when hunting big-river thrills? She dreads the thought of his first trip away, when all his rants and groans about setting up Float Your Boat — the paperwork, the compliances, the GST this, IRD that, OSH and ABA (Another Bloody Acronym), she's actually not that interested (who would be?) — are done. She worries he might decide they have to move again, to Queenstown, say, if he decides sea kayaks and paddleboards in Dunedin are too tame . . .

She lets the water thunder from the laundry tap, imagining herself small enough to be in a boat on its foaming rapids. All too easily she can see a water-spout churn around her, so she turns it off, wanting to shut off thought as fast. She goes to do something very quiet and dry. She dusts and she polishes and tries to sing, 'Here Comes the Sun'.

Under the tune she mulls, frets, puzzles. Hyper-thinks, as Liam calls it: one worry hooks on to another and another, until what started as a single thread is a tanglewood. And lo, the worry makes chaos materialise right before her eyes. Iris finds more dirt, more dust, more boxes unpacked, items misplaced; books and ornaments badly aligned. Three cartons contain Liam's precious, pug-ugly collection of Toby jugs. She'd been leaving the unpacking to him, secretly hoping that the landlord's credenza would fill up, so the chubby, ogling, piratical faces would stay battened down in their hatches. But hey-ho, the credenza was three-quarters empty, and she supposed unpacking Liam's kitsch would be an act of love.

So she sorts the house
and she sorts the house
and she sorts the house again —

She is just about to stop for lunch — it's nearly two, in no time she'll have to walk up the hill to get Billy — but sees a yellow spill. Or an annoying oblong strip of foil, is it? Some rubbish splayed brazenly on the floor; more muck, more disorder. More *will I ever be done with this, will this place ever feel, I don't know,* right, *how can a child not even your own leave this atmosphere of untoward and ice? Once a person gets like this, do they ever again find warm and home and real and true?*

Swearing under her breath, she bends down to snatch up the mess, sponge it or scrub it or whatever else it would take to feel stable (and oh, she remembers badgering Jason about his socks, school bag, general junk strewn around as if he were a boy-nado, *that poor kid*) when her hand's shadow swallows the mark. Her fingers plunge right into liquid gold. She's been trying to clean sunshine. She should laugh, but she sits on the carpet and stares.

A SHORT SPELL

PERHAPS WHAT CAME NEXT was her fault. Perhaps if she'd made it to the school at the usual time, just before the bell . . . but she must have gone into a trance. The honey of the shifting patch on the floor soaked into her; she imagined wearing sunlight; a sheath dress made of molten amber. Now and then leaf shapes shadow-played over the light's border. She fell into an exhausted fugue, and—

It can't be a short spell. She's fifteen minutes late, and doesn't meet Billy coming the other way. Odd. She heads to his empty class, explores his still-new-really school. He's nowhere. Tamping down panic, she hurries to the school secretary at reception. The woman manages to both stay calm and go through every worst-case scenario. She tells Iris to think where he might have gone. Tells her to phone Liam. Tells her that tonight someone will be at the school until five o'clock, and not to hesitate to call, but perhaps it would be best if she goes home, waits for Billy there? If he doesn't show up within half an hour, get Liam to ditch work early and search the streets. 'If there's still no luck, phone the police. You don't have to wait to notify them, especially not for a child.' The woman's garish rocking-horse earrings swing as she says, 'I'm sure it won't come to that. You'll probably find he's gone to a new friend's house without thinking.'

Iris wheels around and rushes back downhill, her heart catapulting. '*Billy, Billy, Billy*,' begs the blood-beat in her head. 'Bad luck comes in threes, oh, no, bad luck comes in threes, shut up. This family is cursed, shut up, this family is marked, shut *up*. Billy, Billy, I'll tear a strip off you, Billy, Billy, I'd never ever hurt you . . .'

She'd left her mobile at home, of course, when she hurried off in a flap of *I'm late!* So it's not until she gets back inside — and finds no Billy — that she calls Liam. She explains. Thank goodness, he understands. He says he'll get on his bike straight away. 'Are you coming home?' she asks, painful tingles in odd, disparate places — thigh, ribs, arm and one side of her scalp; the fears are trying to gather and swarm.

She assumes Liam's silence is fury but actually he's taking time to think.

'No. What I'll do is I'll head to some of the places he already knows. The kids' section in the library, the Botanic Gardens, then that park by the inlet. I'll have my mobile. I'll call you when I'm on the way home.'

She imagines him in profile, chin lowered. She swallows. 'Shall I call the police?'

'If he's not at the gardens, yes. But I'll let you know.' He hangs up.

Something in her heart jams, as if the hands on a clock have snagged. The needle plays over and over. *Billy, where's Billy* . . . For more than an hour she waits, the tingling in her body now like a strange cooling, as if cells are separately turning to stone. She cannot move. Then a phone call electrifies the stalled air. It is Liam, and the unforgiving, frozen moment splits back into past and present. His voice frees the tight cords in her limbs. Oh, so yes, she does so love this man, so she does.

Liam's instinct was right. When Iris was late, Billy had taken it into his clever-nuisance feather-head to use next Friday's sausage-sizzle money (which he'd forgotten to give his teacher) to pay for the bus fare across town. He went right past their new house, all the way along George Street, hopped out, and every now and then asked, is this the way to the gardens? He even lied to one young woman. She asked, 'Where're your mum and dad?' And Billy replied, 'My big cousin and I are meeting them there. But he's gone on without me!' (It didn't *feel* like a lie, he said later. It felt like the way it should be.) The woman must have caught the urgency in his voice. 'Head thataway!' she pointed. Yep, that looked right to him: he recognised the overbridge now, the underpass mural, the pet store in the distance.

The familiarity meant that afterwards he said, 'But it's fine at the gardens, Mum, we've been there heaps.' As if she were worried about the birds. Or even the plants.

Liam and Iris thought he was more *sensible* than that.

His father found him at the cockatoo cage, fingers hooked through the wire, though there were warning signs up saying that was precisely what *not* to do. Billy was doggedly asking a parrot to talk; trying to teach it a new phrase by repeating, '*Help me, Obi-Wan Kenobi. You're our only hope.*' It wasn't for several days that Iris found that funny. The cockatoo was white, a Princess Leia in her flowing robes; and although its yellow head-crest was nothing like Leia's famous coiled side-buns, there would still have been something unsettling, satirical, about its bobbing and ducking plea for freedom, if it had learnt the catch-cry.

Liam jumped off his bike, slung it against a park bench, and went to Billy, speechless with anger, relief and the cross-town sprint. He grabbed him by the shoulders and, Christ forgive him, gave him two hard shakes. 'What the hell's gotten in to you?' There was only a handful of other people around: every adult turned and stared, but to Liam, even the old guy with a walking stick had *that kind of . . . creepy, vacant-streets feeling. Paternal overdrive, maybe.* To Billy, on the spot, he said, very low and false-calm, 'Never, *ever* do that again. You don't go off like that without telling somebody. Anything could happen.'

Billy still wouldn't come until he'd fed his last coin into the donations box for the birds. Even then his hand crept into Liam's trouser pocket, ferreting for change.

Liam yanked his son's wrist out of his pocket. 'Do you *understand* why I'm angry?'

Billy went down into himself. You can tell, said Liam; his face doesn't move, but it's like his eyes draw up a screen. No — oh, I don't know how to put it exactly but it *Drives. Me. Spare.*

But you — Iris wanted to say — can't you see there's a sort of, hmmm — but she couldn't say it then; it wasn't the right time; she was trying to hear the *and then and then and then* of facts; as if, when you knew them, you would know how to break the chain.

Liam had taken Billy by the neck-scruff, turned him around and started to march him home, all the time wheeling his bike along, one-handed.

They walked the entire route. Yes, through town, along the one-way roaring with stock trucks, over the railway footbridge, into the southerly, along the howling waterfront with the sea's grey surge beside the footpath. Billy said it made him seasick to even look at; well, bloody don't then, said Liam, and how am I ever going to get you into a kayak, eh? which Billy conveniently ignored.

'There's a bus, Dad!' he said.

'I'm not putting a bus driver to the trouble of stowing my bike, and I'm not paying for the fare. This has been your mistake and you're to feel the consequences.'

UNREELING

IRIS KNEW THAT WHAT Liam couldn't say to Billy was that he needed to walk off the feeling that a rope was rushing through his hands. Liam was going to cut up rough right there, even when everything was actually okay. Billy was there, he was fine; it was just a lesson. It had been a lesson to them all.

Liam told her he decided to save the lecture till she was there, too — as both back-up and softener: his 'on-the-other-hand' woman. With Iris there, he knew he'd manage to sound reasonable: 'You're too young to go that far on your own without telling us.'

An utterly exhausted Billy dropped his chin, and his eyes took on a hooded I-know-you're-right-but-won't-admit-it look. 'But I caught the bus on my own. So I *am* old enough to do it. Next time I could just let you know first.'

Liam interjected. 'You're not old enough yet, Billy, and that's that.' He waved a Keeping Ourselves Safe brochure he'd dug out of a kitchen drawer, where it had been slung with all the new school enrolment information. 'We need you to sit down and read this again.'

Billy talked to his shoes. 'It's not like I'm a little baby that's going to take sweets and go home with some sicko.'

Iris felt the dissonant shock of the Billy in her head meeting the Billy in the room. Wait a minute. Was he eight, or eighteen?

Liam stared at the ceiling. His lips moved as he silently counted to ten.

Iris tried a change of tack. 'Billy, what was so urgent about getting to the gardens? Why couldn't you tell me you wanted to go?'

He shrugged.

'Is there something about the birds?'

He perked up. 'They usually have a nap in the middle of the day. *That's* why we haven't seen some of them in the weekends. We've gone too early. Some of them like the late afternoons best. I found out today, on Google. I got 100 per cent in my maths extension test, so I earned extra computer time.'

'That's great about the test. But if you'd told me about the birds, we could have gone along together.'

He held her gaze with unnerving intensity, as if probing her for something separate from this conversation; his expression at odds with a dunderhead who breaks basic rules. As, too, was the way he crisply, formally, said, 'I'm sorry,' then slid over to his Lego crate, which he started to jumble through.

Liam hiffed the brochure onto the coffee table. 'I'll need to head in to work early tomorrow to make up for today.' He bit down hard on his words. 'The last thing I need is this kind of wild *goose* chase.'

Snide aside, family pun? Something, anyway, in his tone set Billy right off. Slightly surly now turned into squawking and caterwauling. He was up on his feet, arms waving like a cartoon of mock-horror, scurrying back and forth in circles, calling out in a reedy voice, 'Goosy goosy gander! Goosy goosy gander! Ho-unk! Ho-UNK!'

Iris tried to stop him as he flung past; he wrenched away; his flailing hand smacked her across the nose. She was momentarily blinded; managed to blink away the black and red fizz behind her eyes to see Liam had him by the jersey.

'That's right out of order. Now you're just being an insolent little shit.'

'Liam!'

'Well, he is. Billy, go to your room.'

Billy was half-pipping and piping, half-shrieking and shriking. Iris for a moment couldn't tell which way it would go, tears or giggles, but 'I'msorryI'msorryI'msorry!' he called, and where before he seemed like a kid who needed a good smack (so help her Idealism, that's letting all her own beliefs *right* down), now he seemed truly distressed, as if he had no idea what possessed him.

Hell's bells, her nose was bleeding. Iris plumped herself back down on the couch and seized a wodge of tissues from a box on the coffee table. 'Oh, *bugger,*' she said. Though actually it gave her a blessed reason to rest her head, close her eyes and let a few moments pass quietly.

Liam came back into the room and said, 'Shit. You all right?'

'Feeling Billy-ous.' Trying to make light of this, wanting Liam's hot circuitry of anger to be cooled by patience.

She leaned her head on his shoulder as he sat down and pulled her some fresh tissues.

'Sometimes I just don't know how to handle him,' Liam said.

Iris mumbled through her pinched nose, 'No chapters on this kind of thing in *Dr Spock* or the *Baby Whisperer*?'

'Nor Levy nor Latta.'

'Not on *Ask Moxie*. Not on *Perfect Mom-Dot-Com*.'

'There's *Perfect Mom-Dot-Com*?'

'Probably.'

'We need *Larkin-Dot-Com*.'

'*Larkin-Dot-Com*?' Of course she realised as soon as she asked, so they could say in unison, '*They-Fuck-You-Up-Your-Mum-and-Dad-Dot-Com*.'

She released the pressure on her nose. 'At least we're not having a sense-of-humour failure.'

'I am,' said Liam.

They listened to the house's glorious silence. The bleeding seemed to have stopped. She crumpled the tissues, stared at her hands. 'It's my fault. If I hadn't been late . . .'

'We *should* be able to trust him to walk home from school. He's old enough. He knows the way, should have been more logical . . .'

'It's a different world from our day, Liam. And he's been through such upheaval . . .'

'I think you're babying him.'

She felt a spike of resentment. 'So it *is* my fault.'

Weary sigh. 'That's not what I said.'

They sat woodenly side by side, chess pieces in a house where nobody knew the rules: forwards, backwards, diagonal?

Sideways, apparently: for eventually Liam cupped her knee in his palm. 'He's home safely. We've given him a talking to. Not much else we can do. Tomorrow's another day. We'll let him process all this and talk to him about it in the morning.'

We're the ones who need to process it, Iris thought, though she didn't try to put into words the very real feeling that had been shouldering up behind her attempts at light-hearted. There was an emotion she couldn't name: some two-headed animal, its cold muzzles seeking her ribs, its teeth only just shielded by soft blue-black lips. *Don't*. Like Liam said, hold on. Tomorrow's another day. That's a comfort, or it's meant to be. Don't think, *Oh, hell no, tomorrow's another day*. Okay. Here come the reassurances again. *It's nothing. You're wound too tight. Things will settle down.*

Yet the weeks seemed to swirl, not settle. Liam had equipment to check, meetings, and the first groups of clients, all the while crunching the numbers: Busy^2 x busy^3 = busy^5. Stores up north sent a flurry of emails asking Iris where to return stock that hadn't sold; not her fault, they said; the recession, they said (one of them was closing down); but alongside her paralysis about a new collection, utterly depressing. She went into a spin about whether maintaining Whipstitch at all was a good idea; yet when she tried to talk about it to Liam, their brisk conversations, squeezed into ever-shrinking gaps, felt as fast and furious as Wimbledon finals. They were racing against time, but if Iris stopped to breathe, she wasn't sure what the destination was meant to be.

Nevertheless she hung on. She told herself that all her internet surfing, magazine reading, library browsing, her wandering around the shops, was research — though she hadn't pinned anything new up on her mood-board for weeks. On one particularly bad day, a shop assistant asked her, sharply, if there was somewhere else she could stand, as other customers were wondering about her. Iris had been hovering in front of the thread displays, inhaling deeply, as if the colours were roses and their scents carried contentment. She had to walk away without buying anything; she'd left her wallet in the car by mistake. Embarrassment stung her eyes like pepper.

Yet still she hung on. She tried to make the house warm and well and good. To be a mother who was warm and well and good. To be a partner who was warm and well and good. Cook enticing things. Provide new library books and educational DVDs. Wash, dry, alter and mend clothes. Light candles on a Sunday night; put music on to give Billy a halo of all-of-us-together memories one day. And although the house was rented, she scrubbed tap grouting, washed ceilings, swept cobwebs, vacuumed under furniture, and, when she could, she washed the windows, she dusted,

And she dusted

And she dusted

And tried not to think how dust is predominantly human skin *ashes to ashes dust to dust* and whether any of it would be traces of Jason they carried with them, and where *did* the energy of a person go when they died? Was it naïvely magical-thinking to wonder, if the beautiful foal-like body of a child can become dust, which is still substance, why can't some residual shimmer of the personality remain?

It was yet another thing she wanted to talk about to Liam, but his face was so often . . . shut down. Why, she'd ask the sunlight on the crumbs, the loops of carpet wool, the trees stirring on air outside? She heard her mother's voice, misquoting Tennyson: *Ours is not to reason why; Ours is but to do or die* . . . So she'd try to swerve into something earthed. Practical. Satisfying and *completable*. She sewed patches on the worn-through knees of Billy's trousers, and, as she did, she thought about how lately she kept mislaying or forgetting her wallet. She doodled a tunic top with, in a contrasting colour, one large button-down side pocket (internally divided), and an angular ribbon like a handbag strap sewn across the chest. *Baggy Top*, she could call it. She tried not to think how pointless her efforts were, that none of it would . . . No. She tried to think away wrong thoughts. She truly *thought* they'd tried so hard . . .

SO WHERE HAD THEY GONE WRONG?

ANY SANE PARENT WOULD ask where exactly it had all turned to custard after a day like the one Liam and Billy had when they went back, oh, yes, back to the gardens. Even if they pretty soon gave up on the idea of any easy 'exactly'.

28 August 2011: another date for the family annals. Henceforth always known as That Other Time in the Botanic Gardens, *capitals*. After this dreadful day of Billy-wrangling, when Liam lay exhausted in bed, hands behind his head, he even said aloud, 'Where on earth have we gone wrong?'

Iris pressed one fist gently into his armpit, hand a small animal in a warm burrow. 'Well, Billy's always been — different. Even before Jase.'

Jase, she said, and waited.

Liam cleared his throat. She thought he might finally broach the dark pit beneath everything they said and did these days. He sighed, and said, 'I just keep seeing Billy in the pet shop. As if there's some missing *clue*.'

A clue, a key, then a solution. It really is so very hard

to get to the nub of the matter with a case like this. Billy the boy who felt left behind? Billy the boy with a high IQ and, it seemed, very little sense? Billy the bright-but-bird-brained, Billy the extra-ordinary, was he? Just normal, but more *intensely* so than other children, because he was under extra strain?

Oouuff. Rewind. To the start of this exhausting day.

It had been a brilliantly sunny but chilly southern-hemisphere late August Saturday. So Liam decided to take Billy to the Botanic Gardens *again*, and give Iris a break. He said she seemed out of sorts, needed to relax. Will you JUST RELAX? (You're the stressed one, Liam.) No, listen to me, Iris, no housework, okay? NONE.

'We're off to see the kākā and the cockatoos!' Billy trumpeted, which is all Iris knew of it for hours — and hours. She pottered in the spare-room-cum-studio, thinking that maybe it needed rearranging; maybe if she tried having the cutting table by the *other* window, the kowhai outside would filter her moods. Maybe if she moved Liam's unpacked boxes of *Outdoors Illustrated* into the landlord's garage, there'd be just that much more light in here . . . Her sister called, and they talked for a bit. Iris explained, 'I think brown cardboard sucks in light, Carrie. And it *flattens* what's left. I think if I get the space right in here, the ideas will come.' Carrie hooted, 'Don't go all feng phooey on me, Iris. You've got a plain old-fashioned dose of procrastination. Just *do* it, Dora!' Iris went quiet, then made excuses about having to go. After hanging up, she said to the phone, 'Subtle as a *steam press.*' She needed the therapy of mindless destruction. So she dumped the magazines on a spare garage shelf, *bugger the damp*, and ripped up cardboard boxes until she'd calmed down enough to remember Liam's instructions: Just Relax.

She'd made a coffee and sat down with a library copy of *The Dress Doctor* when the door flung open and banged shut.

The moment she saw their long faces, Billy oddly tousled and damp, she stood up. 'What happened?'

Liam shunted Billy down the hall and helped him strip. He ran a bath, pointed for him to get in, neither he nor Billy talking still (highly unusual). So Iris returned to the kitchen — as if there might be a recipe there: 'What to Do Next: Three Generous Servings'. Liam tracked her down, snatched a beer from the fridge and counted events on his fingers.

1. Coat, gloves, boots and all, Billy waded out to talk to a black swan in the ornamental pond. Liam managed to pull him out before he got past his knees.

2. Billy tried to feed ducks crusts from his own mouth.

3. Billy tried to untie a stranger's dog from a bench because it was barking at the ducks.

4. While Liam apologised to the dog owner, and helped tie the dog back up, Billy went missing. *Again.* (Liam tried to call Iris, but the landline was engaged. Didn't she ever check her bloody mobile?)

5. Anyway. More to the bloody point. After Liam had run everywhere he thought Billy could have

reasonably gone in the time his back was turned, he found him in the local pet shop. Yes, across the busy four-way intersection. When he found him, Billy's fingers were laced through the aviary wires, lips up in a pucker, as if smooching the lovebirds . . .

6. The staff had already called the police because Billy claimed he didn't know where his father was *and* he transposed the digits on his home number so they got a local 'massage' (euphemism) parlour. Perhaps it was overly conscientious of them. But just that day in the news they'd heard about a four-year-old wandering alone on North Road in his pyjamas — locals were sensitive to accusations that the public should have notified authorities sooner. An officer turned up, and when Liam rushed over, the officer said to Billy, 'You had your dad very worried. If you'd disappeared for good, what would he have told your mum? You look old enough to know better, mate.'

7. Billy said, 'He's not my father. I'm a bird.'

8. Billy tried to hook his teeth on the cage wire, grip the links with his toes ('Billy *where* are your shoes!?') and chimp along the outside.

9. Billy was a slip of a kid, but yes, big enough to know better. The cage wall buckled, and wires pulled from their staples in the wooden frame. Billy crashed to the floor. A drinking trough hooked onto the cage wire doused him. The pet shop

filled with lorikeets, cockatiels, cockatoos, finches, budgeriedoos. (Liam's name for them. When he was a child, his father had owned birds.)

10. And there Billy was: damp, crapped upon,
picked out in feather confetti, hoisted to his feet:
a little bruised, but blissed out, because a sulphur-
crested cockatoo landed on his head. The cockatoo
took off, then returned: Billy his repeat landing pad.

There were bloody scratches on Billy's scalp, a nick on his neck, but he was happy, his smile enough to make the pet-shop manager and his assistants assume Billy was a not-quite-right kid. They'd even tried to gentle him with tongue clicks, lollipop promises: 'Careful now. There's a good laddie.'

Simple words for a simpleton. (Huh. Simpleton sounded close to paradise to Liam: as if Billy were a pot-plant person you could take out on the porch, then bring back in, when it was time for food or bed. But Billy: Billy was complicated.)

To the pet-store owner, Billy said, 'I *read* about the sulphur-crested cockatoo today, because we were going to see them at the gardens. Crazy! I've got to write a speech about birds. Some of them have escaped into the wild in New Zealand. Not speeches, I mean, cockatoos. Not many, but some. Most of the freed parrots here are eastern rosellas. You even see them in Dunedin, my book says. Have you seen any? I've been looking for them. Their scientific name is something like spittykai or platy-circus extreme or whatever. I don't know how to say it, the spellings are super-kooky-hard.'

At that torrent, the pet-store owner changed his tune

from there-there, easy-boy-o, to offended and terse. 'Listen, mate,' he said, tapping Billy's collarbone with a knuckle. 'You get your act together. A lummox like you, climbing cages like that!'

The police officer intervened. 'Let's keep our hands to ourselves, shall we? Maybe the boy can clear up the mess.'

The pet-store owner was having none of that: he wanted Billy *out*. But not before he'd taken Liam's address so he could send an invoice.

'I'm sorry for your loss,' Billy said, in a tone that pulled all the adults up short. Was it satirical? Intuitively seeing some long-borne sorrow behind the owner's mood? Whatever, as the man's face purpled with indignance, Liam collared his son and spun him round. 'Right. *Home*, Billy.'

'How old is he?' one of the shop assistants murmured as Liam frogmarched Billy between cat toys and fish bowls. Liam feigned deaf. People often asked, as if a trick were about to be pulled. As if Liam and Iris had hidden a teenager inside Billy. Or as if he might have some upwards-developmental disorder. 'Um, *how* old is he again?'

The question had been asked in that troubled way ever since Billy could talk. Even from when he was two: 'He's got an amazing vocabulary.' And then the frown, waiting for Liam or Iris to explain, because there Billy was still in nappies, hurling food and hissy fits, but also saying 'Reflections' and 'Precarious' and 'Complicated'. If they smiled blandly there was more prodding. 'That's unusual for a boy, isn't it? And for a toddler?' As if the parents should admit, 'Yes. We played him Mozart, Beethoven *and* Schubert, actually, every morning while he was still in utero . . .'

'Oh, *dear*,' was all Iris could really think of to say now

about the pet shop fiasco. When Billy appeared, naked and dripping from the bath, she and Liam shared a *where-the-hell's-the-instruction-book* look. The silence grew too loose and, well, anarchic-feeling. 'Early night tonight, I think,' she concluded: the answer to most evils, they'd learned. They wished. 'Your dad and I are clearly going to need a talk about this escapade.' She gave her son what she hoped was an authoritative frown. Liam copied. They sent him off to find a towel. When Billy's back was turned, Liam made hand-claws, mouthed a desperate, 'WTF??!!' Iris copied that. Billy turned around: it was a real-world version of What's the Time, Mr Wolf? She froze in place and said, 'Bath, book, bottle, bed.' Family code they still used for 'everything's gone to custard, pack him off to his room as soon as humanly possible'.

So when Billy was dry and dressed, they tried to calm everything down with their normal night-time routine. Iris cooked; Liam puttered about on fix-it jobs; Billy was allowed to watch a Sunday-night DVD. '*Chitty Chitty Bang Bang*?' asked Liam. '*School of Rock? The Empire Strikes Back*?'

'David Attenborough,' insisted Billy. '*The Life of Birds*.' Liam puffed out his cheeks.

'Well, if he's *happy*,' said Iris. 'If he's *occupied* . . .'

Liam gave an *I-can't-be-bothered-arguing-after-the-shitty-day-I've-had* shrug.

They let Billy watch a full episode. Iris hadn't timed the meal properly. As often happened these days, she managed to overcomplicate simple things because her mind ricocheted onto anxious sidetracks. To stop herself fretting over the pet shop bill, she'd turned on the radio. Bad move. There was talk of the Christchurch rebuild; there were reports of storms in America; there was an interview with the people of Tuvalu whose homes were threatened by sea-level rise. Unequal unfair irreparable world . . . Were she and Liam running out of natural disaster supplies? How long could they feed themselves for anyway, if . . . ? And if it did come — civil war, starvation — what about cyanide pills? Was that defeatist, or pragmatic? She'd have to check the disaster supplies now, or write another to-do list, or ask Liam for reassurance. (Which would either make him crack some half-arsed joke, or make him angry: as if the worrying were the problem, not the world.)

Tonight, Billy found her smacking her forehead with a roll of tin foil, when she realised she had the oven off at the wall.

'What's wrong?' he said, wide-eyed, fingers fluttering at his sides.

'Oh — nothing. The oven. Dinner's going to be late, I'm afraid.'

'Afraid?'

She waved her foil wand: calm and helpful Glinda, Witch of the Feast. 'Figure of speech, Billy.'

Liam slipped into the kitchen, fossicked around for another beer, then perched on a kitchen stool and powered up his laptop. He still had the slightly wild-eyed look of someone surfacing from drama.

'Speech!' Billy gasped. He scooted from the room, sock-slid back again, flapping his lined notebook and his current reading book — *Which New Zealand Bird?* — carrying his pencil case in his mouth, which he soon spat out. 'Speech, speech! Help me with my speech!'

Oh. The bird talk. He'd had two weeks to prepare for a three-minute oral presentation on a topic of his choice.

It might have been better if he'd only had two nights. The project sent creepers into every cranny of time. Its title was *Chirpy Little Fellahs: New Zealand's Countryside and Garden Birds*. It couldn't just be 'native birds', Billy said; it had to be more specific, so children could 'go home and sit outside and look for the piwakawaka, the redpoll, the goldfinch, the yellowhammer, did you know there are two types of sparrow here, Mum?'

'Ummm — no, I don't think I did.'

'The dunnock or the hedge sparrow, my book by Andrew Crowe, yes Crowe! My book says it sings *"weeso, sissy-weeso, sissy-weeso, sissy-wee"*, and the house sparrow?' Fingers on the book, peering down as if into a marvellous aquarium, he said, 'Their beaks are different and the house sparrow chatters. I wonder if their beaks cause the different sparrow-speaks? Ha, I'm a poet, did y'know it? *I* did. Di-diddly-did.' He flicked his cheek with his middle finger, lips in an exaggerated pucker. As he altered the pucker, the notes his finger played on his stretched cheek scaled higher and lower. The musical interlude didn't last long. 'There's the bellbird — or korimako, you know — the starling, the blackbird, the harrier — kāhu — the plover, did you know the plover can be a garden bird, Mum? Even though I've only seen it, where, what-you-call-it, at the inlet? Is any bird that goes to someone's garden a garden bird? How d'they decide, sea bird or garden bird?'

Such were the small, ordinary domestic onslaughts which made Iris raise her eyes to the ceiling, take a deep breath. Then try to answer, hiding the sick anticipation that ran its current through her — because why feel strong foreboding when *here* they were, at least they had each other, *here* they were, with enough to eat, in a safe kitchen in a safe house with a child asking perfectly valid (if somewhat one-track, obsessive) questions? Under the semblance of being a competent adult, she had to try to not add another worry to the tower of worries. *Was* it normal, this verbal barrage? Better think such thoughts later, in the relative clarity of silence.

TWO SMALL ALICES ON THE EDGE OF THE RABBIT HOLE

THE THING WAS, BILLY had always loved birds. Bird (*bid*!) really *was* his first word, said before his first birthday. The surprise come-and-go of them delighted him: no warning, down from the sky, into the window frame: Look! Arrival! Here! *Bid, bid, bid!* The word rang out again and again, his own one-note call. Miraculous, random, pleasurable IS-ness! She could still remember how it made her, too, see even the humble humdrum brown-coats as personal heralds of joy.

'Mum? D'you know? Sea birds, land birds?'

'Oh, well, they'll each have their main habitat, the place they're most often found. The place they get their main food from, I guess, and where they nest.' Thank heavens he was satisfied with that.

The other children at Billy's new school who have already given their speeches have talked about *Star Wars*, *Transformers*, skateboards, their trips to Surfer's Paradise, their grandparents, their birthday parties, their pets. But Billy — already Billy seems, well, should she even say this? Geeky. Is it because he's gangly, too, with those light, birdlike bones, his oversized feet? There's his delicate, wispy white-blond hair, his pale green eyes, milky pallor. He's not a ruddy-cheeked, nuggetty wee bruiser, not the sort to run around all day after a ball. How does he fit in yet still be his own person? When does nerdy become learnèd, an appetite for knowledge and a prodigious memory socially acceptable? I mean, how many eight-year-olds do you have to forbid doing any more homework, because they're hollow-eyed, they're worried they haven't explained enough, and it's high time they went to bed?

When Iris asked Billy to set the table, he protested, squirming on the stool next to Liam. Who then re-entered the conversation. He had an enviable knack of retreating into a cone of silence when something on his laptop was more compelling than their kitchen-sink drama — but the cone would suddenly lift, and Iris would be disoriented to realise he had been listening.

'No more bird research tonight, Billy,' Liam said, his patience still ragged after the gardens incident. 'You're only meant to talk for five minutes max, anyway. It's not a university lecture, for Pete's sake. It's not a seminar series.'

'You don't mean Uncle Pete, do you? When people say for Pete's sake, who *is* Pete? What's a univearnesty lecture?'

Liam didn't flinch. 'It's just a saying.'

Univearnesty. Ha. Iris liked that: the place of all earnestness. Oh, the Billy-ness of Billy. So smart, so hungry to know, yet his talk still full of accidental puns. He slapped the card of another question on top of the last. 'Why didn't we *all* grow into birds instead of apes?'

There was a pause, as the adults tried to catch up.

'Evolution's complex,' Liam said; then he began what Iris said was a far too *convoluted* explanation.

Billy listened to them banter-bicker, then repeated, 'So why didn't we evolute into birds?'

'Evolve,' his parents chorused.

'Evolute,' he said, 'sounds more complex.'

They smiled. Liam even said, 'I was just thinking to myself earlier today, matey, sometimes I just can't tell whether you're wet or wise behind the ears.'

'Why didn't we grow wings so we could fly? It would be cleverer of evolution if we had our own brains, but birds' wings.'

Iris shrugged, looked at Liam. He'd gone back to his laptop.

'Liam?'

Nope. Cone of silence down. Oh, she was no scientist. Billy's questions made her feel she should go back to school. Although it was amazing how much you could learn about a topic when it hit the news . . . tectonics, liquefaction, peak ground acceleration, seismic lensing; fracking, shale layers, methane gas, potential pollution of drinking water; industrial revolution, carbon, carbon dioxide, seas, the ocean absorbs roughly 22 million tonnes a day, carbonic acid, goodbye corals, oysters, shrimp, lobster, plankton . . .

Her forearm tendons began to ache — she'd been repeatedly twisting her hair into an elf knot. She pulled herself back to the Billy-at-hand. 'Our bodies can't grow wings and still work with our kinds of brains. I suppose, to survive, our ancestors didn't need to fly. We're just one of the strange shapes the life force takes.'

'Life force?'

'Hmmmm. Anyway, no wings will be something to do with what we eat and how we walk. And how we breathe and how we think and maybe even how we talk. The whole entire way we're built.' Billy looked as if her arguments were lacy nonsense.

'But maybe if everything was slightly different, we could,' she said.

Billy hopped right up behind her. 'We could keep evoluting?'

'Mmm.'

'We'd have to have air sacs as well as lungs. Birds use up a lot of oxygen to fly,' said Liam. Ah. He was back.

'How'd you know *that*?' Billy asked.

'Your granddad used to keep birds when I was a boy, remember? He taught me quite a bit about them.'

'What—'

'Hang on a minute. Didn't I tell you to set the table?'

Billy sprung in small staccato jumps over to the cutlery drawer, in a strange and nervy dance as he scatted and skirled, throat straining for song. Yet when they all finally sat down to dinner, he was clearly famished: for the adults were actually able to tackle other topics of conversation while he got stuck into his meal.

Liam said that tomorrow he planned to cycle to the waterfront, where he and Steve had their premises for Float Your Boat. They were thinking of tacking on a small cycle hire and maintenance operation to the kayak and paddleboards gig, given they were right beside the harbour cycleway. They'd thought about kiteboards but there was already stiff local competition, and there was concern that all tourism down south would take a hit after the Canterbury quakes. He and Steve thought some other string to their bow might be good. To encourage locals to use it too they'd have tandems, maybe even a couple of rickshaws or pedicabs. They could hire students to be the drivers, make them wear kilts, or flax skirts, over their cycle shorts. A Celtic-Asian-Polynesian cross. Liam ran a hand through his fringe. They were taking a big gamble on all this. He pushed himself back from the table, hands gripping its rim; stared at the floor as if down a cliff face. Sometimes this whole venture gave him the heebie jeebies. He broke his abstracted gaze. Anyway, Iris could have the car tomorrow, if she wanted to meet recruitment agents. They'd talked about that? That it was time?

'Oh, that's okay,' she said, eyeing her baked potato, which after two mouthfuls tasted like sand.

'You can at least look around,' Liam said. 'See what's there. Even part-time would give you something besides the house to focus on. Help get a network going.'

Her eyes grazed over the wall behind him, then down to the mess Billy was making of his placemat.

'The sooner you've got some sort of secure routine the better,' Liam said.

'You mean we need the money.'

'It's not the main thing, Iris. Lately you don't seem to have been — shall we say — in such a good head space.'

'What do you mean?'

'You've been — you've been obsessing a bit about cleaning. You know, anxious. I don't want you to get too isolated. Don't you think?'

'Ice-oh-lated.' Billy gave a theatrical shiver. 'What is it when a word sounds the way it means?' His hands flourished knife and fork, carving expressive curlicues under his words.

'Actually, it means too alone,' said Liam.

Billy stared at the edge of his plate. 'Mum's not too alone. She's got us —'

'She does *now*, but when I'm at work and you boys are at school —'

Boys. Slip of the tongue, slew of the heart. Iris turned and turned her wedding ring. Liam was watching her. His silence swelled. Why was her solitude the thing he bore down on, instead of his ferocious focus on work, work, work? What was he pushing away with it, why did she feel they never actually talked about the things that really mattered?

She struggled to find a way to say this without sounding accusing. So she was grateful when Billy, fidgeting in his chair, blurted — 'So birds need more air to get into the air. You know what that's like? Balloons! I wonder if you had a lot of gas that you didn't blow off, and you had strong enough arms, could you fly?'

Iris shook her head, almost impressed at the way even a mulling-over sort of boy managed to get farts into the conversation. 'You'd have a stomach-ache with that much gas, Billy.'

Liam joined in the deflection; the let's-not-talk-about-what-we're-always-really-thinking-about dodge. 'The air sacs work more like bellows. Pumping air into the lungs. Different part of the body, mate.'

Iris forced herself to swallow potato. Answering Billy was doing the right thing: responding to a child's immediate needs. But was Billy deliberately diverting them, or did he really not notice? She was the woman in the magician's box, the magician and the saw, all in one. She was always being taken apart, then put back together, with no apparent injury, as far as the audience was concerned. She put down her fork. 'Billy. Do you really want to talk about birds?'

His eyes widened, surprised. 'Yeah?'

So, they obliged and presented him with new bird facts. At each one, he gave a small, interested, involuntary '*huh*': knowledge seemed to physically tickle him as it arrived. He was a funny little munster, all right.

When they had finished their meals, and the adults began to clean up the kitchen, Billy drifted in after them, moving his arms in arcs, graceful, balletic — not a funky-chicken dance — his expression sombre.

Liam emptied the dishwasher, trying to get back on to the topic of good recruitment agents.

Iris swerved around Billy as she tried to put the horrible budget block cheese back in the fridge.

'What are you doing, Billy?'

'Trying to evolute.'

Liam raised his eyebrows: careful, though, not to mock, she'd give him that. 'Doesn't happen overnight, buddy. It takes thousands of years. We need the library. Find you some good books on evolution.'

Billy left, then came back with his coat on, toting the cloth bag they used for library visits. He held it out to Liam.

'Billy, later, I mean. The library's shut now.'

'The univearnesty one isn't. That time we drove past and I asked why all the lights were on you said it's open till eleven.'

'University. It's open till eleven for adults. Not for eight-year-olds at bedtime.'

'Okay, we can go online.'

'No, we'd spend ages trying to wade past rubbishy blogs and—'

'But the BBC or National Geo—'

'Or esoteric academic articles that don't suit you and—'

'But—'

'Besides, we've reached our broadband limit and we certainly can't afford—'

'But—'

'Christ, you're like a dog with a bone, aren't you? Would you give it a rest? I've got things to discuss with your mother and things to do and it's your BEDTIME and I'm TIRED, so—'

Billy's face flared. 'You'd have let Jason stay up later than this when *he* was nearly nine. And besides, why, if *you're* tired, is it *my* bedtime?'

Liam shot some metal tongs into a drawer. 'Because I've had enough of you today, you and your bird act, causing havoc all over town! I've got bigger things to worry about, for Chrissake! I am the adult and you are the child, so *WILL* you *GO* to *BED!*' He whirled, and his elbow clipped the stack of dishes Iris was moving from bench to cupboard. With an explosion of glass and china, the stack smashed to the floor.

'Shit, shit, *shit!*' Liam flung open the back door, banged onto the porch.

They could see him pacing in the light that spilled from the house, his arms akimbo, chin tilted to the moon, as if clenching back toothache. Iris knew this wasn't just about Billy — but Billy, of course, didn't.

Sure enough, he began to cry, and tried to launch himself at Iris. The floor was littered with kitchen shrapnel, and she'd foolishly tried to collect larger pieces in her bare fingers. A painless cut smeared blood over everything she touched. The sight of Liam fighting with himself under the moon; the knowledge that she couldn't protect him; the way Billy bore down on the glass; even, yes, the way his needs seemed to barrel over the adults', made her too terse, too loud, stupid and tearful herself. 'Billy! Think about other people for just one *minute*!'

He paled. Then he started cawing, screeching, flapping his arms in huge slow arcs from kitchen to living-room.

Liam shot back in, as if wanting an excuse. '*Stop* that bloody manic *seagull* act!' He grabbed Billy and propelled him into his room. Not waiting to make sure he was following instructions and getting his goddamned pyjamas on and getting into goddamned bed, he slammed Billy's door. Then he snatched a jacket from the hallway coat hooks, said, 'I need a walk,' and left the house.

Iris slowly finished gathering broken glass and crockery, cleaned her hands, bandaged the cut, took a quick look in the mirror; her reflection reminded her of Dali's melting clocks, with its long, sad lines of middle age. She flannelled away the smear of blood, willing the flood in her head to seep away. She went to Billy's room and said his name. He told her to leave.

Blindly, she went to sit on the couch: just staring, blurred, at a magazine article on — oh, who knew. What prompted her to check on Billy again was realising how cold the room had grown. She found him asleep, under his bed, his face grubby and grey with dried tears, holding his bird book on his chest, thumb marking his place. As she managed to pull his leaden, floppy limbs into bed, and pull the blankets up over his bony shoulders, all her own confusion ebbed. She brushed his forehead with a kiss, hoping its impression would filter into his sleep. *Billy, if we love you as best we can, won't that be enough?*

As she left the boy's room, Liam clicked the front door quietly. A brisk walk was all he needed. His colour was back, his expression hurt yet apologetic. She tried to see the ebullient, curly-haired, slim-hipped, confident young man who'd thought fatherhood would be out there, a carnival ride, jump on it now, biology was just *doing its thang*, why waste the years? He seemed stooped; his forehead showed two wide, pale Vs where the curls had receded; grey glinted in his stubble. His eyes were puffy with exhaustion. She didn't say anything, just went to hug him. He rocked her.

Eventually, into her hair, he whispered, 'Sorry?'

She ran her thumb over his chin. 'It's been a crazy day. We probably just need some sleep.'

He nodded, followed her to the bathroom, then the bedroom, where they lay together, not cupped like spoons, but like knife and fork with a cold, unappetising dish between them. They stared up through the dark, then Liam said, 'Billy — I mean, he *is* just a kid. The aviary debacle *was* his fault, but Billy — Billy's . . .'

All the things that Billy might be gathered in the night. Liam's and Iris's hands crept towards each other. They lay there like two small Alices on the edge of the rabbit hole, both more than slightly unsure, and too unsure to say so.

THE FULL, STAGGERING ONSLAUGHT OF THE KNOWN UNIVERSE

'RAAARK, RAAARK, CHIP-CHIP, TWEETATIT, tweetatit, sweedle, sweedle, drrrih, drrrih!'

'Oh, Christ,' Liam said, from his side of the bed, face dawn-creased, as Billy trilled, super-sized cuckoo, from outside in his tree hut. 'What's our strategy now?'

'Just humour him,' said Iris, arm crooked over her face.

'That's a strategy?' Liam shuffled closer, hand slipping between her knees, resting there, a warm flesh question mark.

With Billy awake? 'Nnnuh-uh,' she said.

'Why not?'

She paused. 'Bed-breath.'

'I can fix that.'

She recalled the sight of him keeping his eyes trained on the moon as if he fought to stop part of himself from falling. She still shook her head. Airily, yet squeezing his hand with her thighs, 'Moment's gone, sorry.'

'Why didn't you tell me there was a moment? I would've brushed my teeth.'

'I didn't know there'd been a moment until I smelt your breath.'

His hand crept a little higher. Deep at the back of her throat, she chuckled.

He stopped then, and lifted up a little on his elbow. 'Hey.' Softly. 'That's a good sound.' They kissed. Liam nuzzled under her ear. 'You okay today?' he said. As if really asking, how bad is the not-okay today? His hand stroked her hip. 'Things will get better, Iris. New places are always strange. New routines.' His hand went back to her thighs, and crept up a little more.

Billy cockadoodledooed.

Liam sighed. 'Passion killer.'

Iris half-laughed. 'Poor Billy.'

'Poor *Billy*? He's the happiest of us all!' Liam's feet slapped on the floor.

Iris eyed the 'this way' arrow of his morning erection. 'Is he just?'

'Promises, promises.'

'Come back, then.' Iris took hold as if gently drawing a horse to drink. Liam raised his eyebrows. Then he gave a small, involuntary, joyous though still somewhat doubting whinny of thanks.

Practised, efficient, married sex has its blessings, Iris thought afterwards, as they descended the stairs together. For then, benevolent with afterglow and wide-awake with aftershave, Liam was able to say, when they saw Billy had made a nest of grass cuttings on the deck, and wanted to eat outside: 'Humour him.'

'Okay.' Two syllables that contained, *yes, and that's what I said, isn't it? But if I say so, and we get started on the* I said–you *said tug of war, then* . . . She felt a hot stab, followed by the familiar tumult as anxiety raced its body-course. Nothing to pin it to: just awash, awash with dread.

As she passed Billy's door and saw his *Which New Zealand Bird?* splayed like an open-winged bird itself, she pretended, for Billy's sake, that the world wasn't burning. That her veins weren't, for who knows what reason exactly, carrying the lava of despair and fear.

'Speech day, Billy!' she called out to him through the double doors. 'Better get some good breakfast into that bird brain!'

THE DRAMA QUEEN GENE

Scene I: The Family Living-room, Early Evening

Iris: [*calls through the window*] Billy, dinner's ready.
[*Five-minute pause. Iris and Liam busy themselves with table-setting.*]
Iris: [*calls through the window again*] Billy, I said dinner's ready.
[*Another five-minute pause as the parents sit at the table, start their meal.*]
Iris: He's been out there for ages.
Liam: Better than screen time.
[*Iris gets up to look out the window.*]
Iris: He must be exhausted. And freezing, where on earth is his jersey?
Liam: He won't be cold if he's bouncing around out there.
[*Iris sighs, goes outside. Liam pulls a laptop sitting on the dining table closer. Iris returns, shaking some of Billy's discarded clothes.*]

Iris: Flung into the flax bushes! He won't put anything back on. Says he won't come in until he knows how to fly.
Liam: He'll come when he's ready. That trampoline's better than a nanny. Keeps him fit and occupied. Brilliant invention.
[*They continue their meal. Throughout there is the sound of trampoline springs squeaking. Billy seems to have started up a call and response. Liam is absorbed in his laptop.*]
Iris: What was that about screen time?
[*Liam scrolls down, oblivious. Iris eventually gives another exasperated sigh, stands at the window. She knocks on the glass, then opens the window.*]
Iris: Billy, come and eat. Come and tell Dad how your speech went today. He hasn't heard about it yet.
Billy: Kwink! Kwink! Kwink! Rosella. *Kra! Kra! Kra!* Kākā.
Iris: I am going to *lose* it, Liam!
Liam: [*mildly*] You and Billy. Both got the drama queen gene, didn't you?
Iris: Billy! For God's sake get inside! You'll either freeze to death or die of starvation. [*Pause.*] Oh, shit.
Liam: What?
Iris: It's started raining. He's heading for the tree house. In his underwear. In the *dark*.
[*She slams the window shut, grabs a quilt from an old armchair and heads outside: too late to stop Billy from turning blue in the lips and fingertips.*]

Call it a myth that chills cause illness, but to Iris it seems too much of a coincidence that, after that, Billy's in bed for several days. He has aches, shivers, a fever: a fever that means at one point he looks at her without recognition, crying out as if a distorted face presses to a darkened window.

Scene II: Billy's Bedroom, Early Evening

Liam: [*sitting on the edge of Billy's bed*] Spot of bird flu, mate?
[*Which bad joke Iris might have forgiven if he'd thought to come home early even just once while Billy was sick. Or if he'd phoned during the day to ask how he was. But she'd had to practically picket for him to get home before seven and give her a break from the house.*]
Iris: [*turning on her heel*] I need a walk.

Scene III: The Dining Room, Early Evening

[*A day or two have passed. We now see Billy with his dressing gown and slippers on, drawing at the dining table, resting his picture on top of the free community newspaper. Liam has cooked so Iris can get a breath of fresh air after another day of Billy-tending. Liam is about to serve up.*]
Billy: If I'd really got bird flu, would I start to turn into a bird?
Liam: No, mate. The virus itself isn't like — like a bird seed. Birds can't grow from it. It's a foreign organism, a germ that makes birds and humans sick.
Billy: Can birds get human flu?
Liam: Not sure. We'll have to look it up. In the meantime [*he unceremoniously dumps rice onto Billy's plate*] cover up before you sneeze on any sparrows.
[*A contented silence: everyone eats.*]

Iris: Good to see your appetite back, Billy.

Billy: [*eyeing the community paper that's still beside his plate*] Can we go to the eco-sanctuary soon? Sirocco the Human Bird's coming. They're starting night tours to see him.

Iris: We'll see, love. We don't want you to overdo things. If you rush around too soon and have late nights you'll get poorly again. [*Iris studies her plate, knife held aloft.*] Liam, remember Pete had that terrible flu, just before Steffie was diagnosed?

Liam: Vaguely.

Iris: I read something online the other day. About post-viral fatigue, stress and depression and rates of sui—

Liam: Iris. *Rates of* isn't an explanation. *Rates of* doesn't mean Pete's case.

Iris: I know, but it's important to be sensible. Given the family history. Given Pete . . . we can't know what factors exactly —

Liam: Sensible's fine, but you don't have to catastrophise.

Billy: What's catastrophise?

Liam: Seeing disaster in every sodding little thing.

Billy: Uncle Pete didn't die from flu, did he?

Iris: No, he —

Billy: I thought he died either from being a selfish bloody idiot, or from being too bung in the head to see straight.

Iris: Billy!

Billy: That's what people said.

Liam: What people?

Billy. Lots. Can you get a kind of flu that makes you crazy?

Liam: Who said those things about Pete?

Billy: Everyone. [*He swigs water from his cup.*] Sometimes

Jase said he hated his dad. Uncle Pete. Really hated him.

Iris: Billy, he wouldn't have meant that. He would have meant he missed him so badly that—

Liam: Who. Said. Those. Things. About. Pete?

Billy: [*whistles a riroriro imitation while making his fork hop, prongs down, across his plate*]

[*Liam sits stock-still. Billy shakes himself, as if rearranging feathers; reaches the end of the musical cascade; starts again,* da capo al fine.

Even when Liam finally moves, his white-hot after-image ghosts there, immobilised.]

OH, POINTED

LIAM DAMN WELL WOULD not get caught up in the family theatrics. Iris with her catastrophising; Billy the boy-sized parrot . . . Huh, they should put *him* next to that Sirocco when the bird did its celebrity tour. Get them to do a double act. People might work out then how birdlike Sirocco actually was. Liam had seen it on TV: bet Sirocco didn't press exactly the wrong buttons on a person, ask braincurler questions and talk non-stop. The other day, Iris said, as a measure of how knocked-about by the flu Billy was, 'Usually he talks so much. But lately it's hard to believe he'll ever turn into a grunting adolescent. Or a taciturn *adult*.'

Oh, pointed. But say Liam took a leaf out of Billy's book, let himself run off at the mouth. What if he said all the things he knew to self-censor? What if. Would they cope, if he let rip?

There was a memory he wanted to shy from. But it was like when you see someone you'd rather not talk to walking straight for you and there's no escape. It happened en route when they moved south. Outside Timaru, they decided they couldn't drive any more. Exhausted, they checked in to a motel. Liam woke at midnight, with a gasp, thinking *Jase. We've left him behind.*

Even when his head cleared, he still felt he'd abandoned his nephew and ditched some chance of making things right with his brother. It hounded him out of bed and onto the motel's balcony. He didn't want to wake Iris or Billy with the savagery of what racked him; didn't want to scare them by letting them see what might be in him, too. He had to walk it off. Found his way down to the deserted waterfront, where he hunkered against a closed-up refreshment shack and waited for remorse to shake him free. The power of it still scared him, how close it was to the edge of something else. Talk? As soon as he thought of Pete, all his focus was on keeping out of reach of a feral, dragging force.

They'd got through Billy's bug; they'd got through Billy's bird talk at school. (All that effort — then the teacher's comment on his painstakingly handwritten, illustrated notes was so *bland*: a terse VG, a soccer ball sticker (eh?) and a 'Wow you sure know about birds, Billy.'

'What did you expect?' Liam asked Iris. 'A Pulitzer? An Oscar?'

At Iris's expression, Billy asked, 'Is there any such thing as "sigh" language?'

Yes, they got through on a diet of banter and bicker and let *that* brush over . . . Bookings at Liam's business, Float Your Boat, were picking up with a spell of calm weather. And the week of nursing Billy through flu had made Iris so claustrophobic that she'd bitten the bullet and made appointments with recruitment agents. She'd finally conceded she had to get *out* more. Part-time work might be the key: she could still collect Billy after school, and distraction might wake her out of her combined fret and apathy, kick-start ideas for Whipstitch again.

Despite the strange sensation of performing herself at interviews — *here I am, very carefully being me* — she maintained a professional veneer. In fact, Iris deferred sweetly to the second 'Intake Consultant', though part of her longed to tell her that her cheap polyester suit was far too boxy for her figure, and she could *see* a triangular iron print on the jacket: so shiny that at first she scanned the woman for others, in case it was some sort of deconstruction/show your workings/visual pun from the designer. If a suit so like a carton could be said to have a designer.

When the woman asked, *And are you planning any more?* it seemed so out of context that Iris said, *Suits? Oh, interviews?* Even as the woman corrected, *Children?* Iris did not crack. She still stuck to her part: Keen and Eager, Highly Employable, until she was 99.99 per cent of the way home.

Then in the car, she felt a creeping, post-interview flatness. So she succumbed to the All American Super Hero-style sign of a video store. A grey sky made it even more the sort of day to escape with a movie. Five. Whatever special offer was on at the moment. Inside the store, Iris's fingers walked along the DVD cases' thin spines, trying to find some title that offered succour.

She flicked through titles: nope, nope, nope, then came across a film she'd seen as a teenager, on TV. With her mother, was it? Or with Carrie, when their parents were out? *Birdy.* The cover image showed a beautiful, lean young man, flesh pale and eerily blue in the light of a cell, as he crouched like a frightened, plucked pullet. He stared at a wedge of sky visible through a high window. She stared at the folded, naked man, trying to remember the plot. A *tristesse* and apprehension she had denied all through her agency interviews now sped up. They spun, pulled tighter, a funnel dragging her into the heart of disintegration.

She walked out of the shop, drove white-knuckled to Billy's school and sat in the car, telling herself she mustn't, everything was fine, lightning wouldn't strike twice. Then, in an out-of-body swoop, she watched her feet propel her from the car, along the street, through the school entrance, and up to Billy's classroom. She tapped at the door, nodded at the teacher and said, 'Billy has a dentist's appointment. Sorry. I'd forgotten. I should have sent a note. Billy?'

He looked confused, but came promptly. Iris pretended not to see the teacher's index finger raised in a *just a moment*! sign. She told herself that the way all the young heads turned and stared meant nothing, nothing. She hurried Billy along; took him home; made him lunch, finding comfort even in his insistence on a bird-dance before he sat down to eat. He fluttered and hovered around the table, hopped from sofa to armchair; then he sauntered naturally to his plate. She was struck afresh by the way the flitting and chirping flared up, then settled: no real pattern to the boy-bird teeter.

Liam had muttered just this morning, after Billy wouldn't brush his teeth, because birds don't *have* teeth, they have gizzards, 'And we thought raising a nephew as well was hard work! At least Jase kept Billy *busy*.'

Iris had paused in her own rush to get dressed in

interview clothes. Sadness filled her, as if he'd loosened a valve, let it run.

'You're right. Jason was no angel. I miss him, though.'

'Do you?' Liam adjusted his watch-strap, started to head for the door.

'You must know I do.'

She fully expected him to keep walking; to revert to the default position *I'm busy, no time to dwell*. But he paused, head bowed. He nodded. 'Still. Billy's different.'

'You know, I was at school with a little girl who thought she was a lion.' Iris folded her nightgown carefully. 'She used to roar and bite when she was upset. Carrie said to me years later, "Sapphire was autistic, but we didn't know what that meant, then. Mightn't have even understood at that age."'

Liam's face looked wiped with shock. 'Do you think we've missed something about Billy?'

'No, but remembering Sapphire made me wonder whether Billy's whole bird act is because he's afraid, sometimes.'

'Of what?'

She shrugged. 'Change. Or, I don't know, just — general danger. Maybe all this talk everywhere about Christchurch. About the Tōhoku quake and tsunami. About . . .'

'We're pretty safe here, Iris.'

'But there are fault lines everywhere, Liam. He knows that, too. He's seen the news, he can use Google as easily as we can.'

'Law of averages. We can't live in fear.'

Yes we can, she thought. *I do. Take away earthquakes, tsunamis and there's still recession, war, fundamentalism, eco-cide, climate chaos, the molten savagery that sits inside us all.* 'But what if Billy does?'

He gave his characteristic shrug and huff: shorthand for *unanswerable*. 'Time will heal. It has to. Just keep things normal.'

She stared, wondering if he was living his life by bumper stickers. Fake it till you make it. Talk the talk till you can walk the walk. Fuck the fuck till you can fuckdiddy fuck. She wouldn't tell him how a Google search one day led her to chronophobia: fear of time. She took an enormous breath in, playing the part of Normal Iris while buttoning her jacket. 'Okay.'

Now, even as she took comfort from having Billy near, she watched the boy with a sense of unease, a taint of the forbidden. When he finished lunch, he said, scowl undermined by the habitual post-snack crumbs on his face, 'Bet you make me brush my teeth even though the dentist will do it all over again in like *five minutes* or something.'

'Actually . . . there's no appointment. I . . . uh . . . made a mistake. Not much point in going back to school now, is there?' She patted the space next to her on the couch.

She might have got away with pulling him out of class. Many were the times when, if Liam asked Billy how school was, the answer was either monosyllabic, or a bird squawk he couldn't engage with. But today, of all days, Liam came steaming home early — his face an arrow of concentration as he clipped into the kitchen in bicycle cleats. He'd forgotten some crucial paperwork and a key to the lock-up for the paddleboards and kayaks; *and* his bike tyre had gone flat on the way home. Sod's law, he'd left his puncture-repair kit at home. He'd had to pump, ride, pump, ride, and a tourist group — a network of home-schoolers from the UK, apparently (what wicked class trips *they* could go on!) was due at Anderson's Bay Inlet. Beautiful out there today:

overcast, sure, but the harbour was smooth as stainless steel . . . He bombarded Iris with all this as he shot around living-room and kitchen, trying to locate the missing items. When he had everything, he grabbed a drink of water, then stared as Billy trod back from the bedroom, carrying a toucan jigsaw puzzle. 'Wait on. Billy's home.'

Iris tidied some library *Vogues* into a neat stack. 'I had those interviews first thing this morning.'

'I know. I thought of calling you to ask if you could hunt for my stuff and drop it off, then I remembered you'd be out. Billy not well again?'

Iris lifted her hands as if she might pluck reasons from the air. 'I — maybe — I started thinking about, you know, having less time with him if I took on full-time work. I —'

'Full-time? It doesn't have to be, if it puts too much strain on everything. We discussed that.'

'Didn't you say the more I could earn the better?'

Liam glowered. 'Anything would help, yes. On the other hand, someone's obviously got to be here for Billy.'

Iris's hands fell to her sides. 'That's what I was trying to do today.'

'He needs a stable routine. He doesn't need you to baby him. He's had enough time off school sick lately. I thought you'd had enough of that, too.' Liam chucked the plastic tumbler he'd been using straight into the sink.

Billy broke the jigsaw apart over his head. Some of the soft cardboard pieces clung together in his hair and on one shoulder. 'Peeta-peeta-pip-pip! I'm a baby bird hatching. Help me, Father-bird! Shell's stuck to my feathers.'

'Eh? Oh.' Liam gave a half-hearted swipe over Billy's head. 'It's off.'

Billy *kaa-kaa-kaaed.* He stood on the couch, his neck

craning. He quivered his arms. 'Baby bird needs more food! Baby bird needs more food!'

'Christ, Billy, you're not *three*. Bloody nuthouse, here, honestly!' Under his breath, although he wouldn't look at Iris, Liam said, 'Think your methods are working?' He turned to Billy and barked, 'You are a boy. Human. *Homo sapiens*. Not a bird.' He gripped his arms. 'An *eight*-year-old boy.' The kaa-kaaing stopped. Billy turned limp and slid to the floor.

'What are you doing?'

'Birds' bones are very fragile. You broke my neck.'

The absurdity got through to Iris. She started to laugh. Liam snatched up his keys. 'I'm late. Can't muck around. See you tonight.'

Billy vaulted up from the floor, lunged at Liam, smacked into him with the heels of both hands. 'You wouldn't even miss me if I was DEAD!' Then he hurtled out to his tree house, ka-ka-kaaing and yodelling.

Liam pinched the bridge of his nose. 'Jesus. Iris, can you talk some sense into him?' Then he was gone, in a click-click of bike shoes, a salt-waft of sea air and sweat.

Iris eventually coaxed Billy inside. That grey-sky feeling lasted all afternoon; even though she let Billy watch DVDs, and she sat near him to sew some fuchsia-coloured buttons on her black winter coat, and a decorative sprinkle of glossy black beads on its collar-tips: a task that would have usually elevated her mood. Today she got through it too quickly and was left apathetic, dissatisfied.

When Liam returned, the volume and sunlight of a completely different day poured through the door. He was all stride and lob: jaunty with a good afternoon. 'The clients loved it! Gave great feedback. Pity they can't send new kids out every year.'

Billy, fresh from a bath, lay on the floor in pyjamas, rummaging through his plastic crate of Lego. Iris sat in an easy chair near him, still listless, flicking through one of the library's *Vogues*, looking at mini-skirts and thinking, *Well, if they're that short, why bother getting dressed at all?* Then, *I must have moved demographics. What a bore.* Liam brought his reheated meal to the couch nearby. 'Whatcha making, Bill-bo?'

'A *Juno*.'

Liam grinned, knowing why the *Juno* was fascinating. It was the first solar-powered spacecraft to travel as far as Jupiter; it had caught Billy's imagination because scientists had placed three special Lego figurines inside it. He'd said, 'Imagine if aliens found them! They'd be, like, "You guys can't talk or move! How did you build a *spaceship*?!"'

'Need me to hunt for any pieces?' Liam asked, through a mouthful of pasta.

'Nahp.'

Liam chewed and swallowed. 'You gonna say hello?'

'We're already talking.' Billy hadn't lifted his head.

'I'm still in the bad books?'

The boy kept raking through for the right-sized, right-coloured piece. Liam moved to the dining-room table and, underneath the Lego clatter, asked Iris, 'Did he stay upset for long?'

She gave a diffident hum.

Liam leaned forward, hands loose between his knees. 'Hey, Billy, mate?'

Billy tilted his head, looked up from under his fringe.

'You know what you said this afternoon? It's not true. I would care if something happened to you. That's one of the reasons we moved here. So I could start a new job and earn money to help look after you. You know that, eh?'

Billy twisted his half-built space probe side to side, examining its buttresses and flaps.

Liam sighed, sat back. 'Actually, I've got news. I guess it helped to put me into a lather today. Growled a bit, didn't I, Billy?'

Billy intoned the sulky rhythms of a sing-song *I dunno*.

'The thing is, Billy —' though he was really saying this to Iris now, assessing her reaction, 'I have to go to Christchurch for a bit. Steve's bought more gear from someone selling up there. I'd rather not have to stay overnight at all.' Meaning he'd rather not go through aftershocks.

Iris nodded dumbly.

'But I'm not up to the return drive in one day.'

Billy looked up: a cautious, interlacing web of glances wove between them all. Liam asked, 'Do you want to come?'

'Couldn't you freight the gear down here?' Iris said.

'Too expensive.' Liam rubbed his eyes, as if tired from the long drive already.

Iris watched her own hands closing the magazine. She had a sense of foreboding, yet didn't want to accompany Liam. 'No, Billy and I will be fine. You'll be focused on work. If you were going back to Auckland, maybe, where Jason's—'

Billy's head whipped up. 'Where Jason's what?'

'Where he's buried.'

He rammed his *Juno* back into the storage box.

Liam set his plate aside. 'Is there anything you'd like me to get you on the trip, Billy?'

'Like what?' said Billy, intonation dulled. 'A bowl of sludge, broken bricks? No thanks.' He picked up the space probe again, and attached a man in an astronaut helmet to it, in a precarious position. 'If you see Jason's ghost you could take a picture.'

Liam frowned. 'What would his ghost be doing in *Christchurch*, of all places?'

Billy gave a sideways, chewing sort of pout. 'Trying to find us. He might be travelling the same way we did, coming through Christchurch on his way.'

'I don't believe in ghosts, Billy. But if they were real I doubt they'd use road maps to—'

'There's lots we don't know for sure.'

Liam crossed his arms. 'That's true.'

'Like scientists don't even know when earthquakes are coming. Or even how exactly birds find their way around the world. And that's something they're *supposed* to know about.'

Liam cleared his throat. 'But science already has lots of solid evidence for those things, even if there are still pieces of the puzzle missing. There's no solid proof for ghosts.'

'Well, so ghosts *aren't* solid, are they?'

'Solid's a metaphor here, Billy. A way of saying.'

'That's what I'll make when I'm grown up. A ghost machine. To prove ghosts.' Billy tapped a red block onto a blue and waited, ear cocked, as if something inside might tap back.

Liam looked at Iris over Billy's head. 'Billy, your cousin's dead. He's not coming back. I know it's tough. But the sooner we all just accept that and get on with things, the better. That sounds harsh, but that's the way it is.'

Instantly the Lego was shrapnel, clattering over the table, pinging off chair, wall and window. 'Kaaa! Kaaa! Kaaa!' Billy's arms beat up and down, he drummed his feet in place, he leapt and crouched, cawed again and ran from the room, out to the deck, up the tree house ladder, where the wind buffeted him, and his pyjamas whipped close to his skin.

Liam massaged his temples. 'I thought we were getting somewhere. Jee-zus, do other kids act out like this, Iris? *Honestly.*'

As Iris headed to the door, the phone went. Liam answered it, then held it out to her. 'Advantage Appointments.'

'*This* late?' But her disbelief was at the fact they'd called at all.

Liam looked chagrined — they hadn't talked about her morning interviews. *Sotto voce* he asked, 'How was it?'

She pulled a face.

He handed her the phone, pointed to himself, then to Billy through the window and, grabbing a folded rug from the couch, left the room.

The woman on the phone apologised profusely for calling so late.

'That's fine,' said Iris, craning to see whether Liam was having any luck coaxing Billy down.

'Two of us are out of the office tomorrow, but this afternoon things just went crazy, so we're trying to sort out placements now.'

'Right.'

'I'm speaking to Iris, with the sewing CV, yes?'

Iris misheard: the so-so CV. 'Oh. I — was it?'

'*This is* Iris Dunningham? Designer and so on, Whipstitch?'

An imperious, offended turn in the woman's voice put Iris into a Tiggy-Winkle-ish fret and pother. She resisted saying *Oh, yes, if you* please'*m*, and giving a curtsey even on the phone. 'Yes-yes, it is.'

'Good. We've got an urgent job with a small clothing

and accessories business. Their help's gone into early labour, but they're on deadline for a contract — a big dinner-theatre production coming up. *Cachet Cabaret.* Basically, they need costume alterations, accessories made, and it also says here — just a minute, oh, bloody computers, why do they always do this . . .'

Iris silently thanked bloody computers. It gave her brain time to act presentable.

'Ah. Here's the right form. They also want someone three days a week, 9:00–2:30 only, to front their shop. They sell new, second-hand, and what do they say . . . reconstructed clothing, alterations service *and* costume hire. Glad Rags. New premises on Princes Street. They'd want to start you in two days.'

By the end of the call, Iris was astonished to see a Post-it in her handwriting, with a start time, an address and the co-owner's name. She felt an inner peacocking. She'd really done it. Going to the interviews had been faking it — but she'd actually waded a few steps through the slow, eroding tide of grief.

When Liam finally brought in a chirruping Billy swaddled in a rug, she was ebullient enough to say, 'Chicken wrap! Good, I didn't get enough dinner!' She play-bit his neck, and his bird-burble dissolved in giggles; and all through bedtime preparations, he was just plain common-or-garden boy. As if it were just the night air he'd needed.

She held back her news until the boy was asleep. When Liam came up from chores in the garage, he held her face in his hands. '*You* look happy — are you actually glad to be rid of me tomorrow?'

'Of course not. But.' She slipped from his grip, brandishing her note like a silver trophy. 'I. Have. Got. A. Job.'

She basked in his confused delight. 'Too *easy!*' He pulled her down onto the couch, and they stared at the memo. They'd grown so used to obstacles, sorrow — it was almost hard to trust the note's simple instructions. Sure, it was temporary. But — should they let themselves feel it? — what a relief. They plunged into a kiss: weeks of talk banked up in it. When they resurfaced, Iris said, 'Such good timing. It gives me something to focus on while you're gone.'

Liam squeezed her close. 'You'll be fine. We'll all be fine. It's only a couple of nights.'

'Yeah.' And desire lifted: pushing Iris away from a niggling sense that there was something besides his trip to talk about; something unresolved. Liam read her quickly, working his hand under her shirt. She couldn't help but whisper, 'Billy?'

'Asleep.'

Things were going *right* for once. Firing all along the fine interior web of nerves: the deep delirium. They tried to ride the moment, but Liam's bloody cell-phone went. He ignored it, but 'Liam?' she asked soon, when it was clear his mind was elsewhere, and they sat together, half-entangled, but a little lost.

'Sorry,' he said. 'Just — distracted.' He kissed the top of her head. She took herself off to the loo, and when she came back, he was packing. She picked up his phone and saw his business partner's name on the screen, along with 'missed call'. 'One thing I won't miss,' she said, 'is how often Steve rings you.'

He gave a wry look. 'Sorry. I'll make it up to you.'

The next morning was a pinball game of — have you seen my sponge bag, where's my homework book, not now, I need the loo! My keys, Iris! Look what I've got, Dad, have you ever seen this? Not now, Billy, would you get dressed? I don't know, I haven't touched them, are there any clean socks? You might have to start helping with the laundry now I've got a job, do you remember *how*? Oh, ha-bloody-*ha*, hardly neurosurgery, is it? So why the — never mind. Billy! Shoes!

The rush sucked them all in; no time to say, *Come home safely*; Liam forgot to say *Good luck with the job* . . . As Iris raced to the shower, she heard the front door bang. It brought a *whumpf* of realisation. She ran out the front door still in her nightgown — which was short and, in direct light, wax-paper-thin. She waved at Liam to wind down the car window. He grinned at her like a loon.

'Be safe,' she said. 'Don't forget: stop, drop and roll.'

'That's for house fires, Iris. Or was that an invitation to come back to bed? Nice nightie.' But his eyes were kind of sad.

'You're meeting Steve in ten minutes, aren't you?'

'Yeah.' He unwound the window more, chucked her under the chin. 'See you in a few days.'

'Okay.' She pushed down the idiot tears, thinking, *the worst has already happened*. She told herself to get on with it: get Billy up the hill to school. Get her head into work mode.

The boy materialised beside her on the footpath. 'Dad gone?'

'Yes.'

Silence.

'You all right, sunshine?'

Shrug. *Chip-chip-chip. Swee-swee-swee-drrrr.* 'What's for breakfast?'

At home again, after dropping Billy off, she began a list: start an internet search for both Glad Rags and Cachet Cabaret. See if there were pictures online of former productions, so she could assess wardrobe standards. Dig out her hardbacks on fashion and costume history, so she could pore over her favourites again. Take them along tomorrow, look prepared. She tried to stop her old, schoolgirl, first-time nerves; to say she *knew* her stuff. She was as sharp a judge of tacks and tucks, hems and seams, pinking and goffering as anyone . . . well, maybe not Marilyn Sainty. Or Margie from NOM* D. But — *phouf. Focus, Iris.*

After ticking off things on her list then going through her sewing room, she decided, *Yes, I need to clean and oil the overlocker and the sewing machine, just in case I bring work home. More urgently, I better get more white cotton and fine nylon thread; must head into Mister Minit to get all my scissors sharpened.* She had her cell-phone recharged, coat and handbag ready, and was about to stride out to the bus when the landline rang. She answered with a snarky, 'Yes?', fully expecting it to be some poor tele-drone, anaesthetised on tedium, telling her they had Experts in Her Area. *Not interested* was already loaded on her tongue.

'Hello, Iris Dunningham? It's Elaine Hooper, here, from Larnach Park.'

Billy's school. His teacher.

'Elaine?'

'Before I say anything else, just to let you know, Billy's fine. He's perfectly safe. But we are having an issue with him.'

A thin, sleeting rain fell inside her body. 'What sort of issue?'

'I think it would be best if you came to the school.'

A KWONK FEELING

BILLY'S WHOLE DAY STARTED with a *kwonk* feeling. Too much hurry-up, do-this, do-that in the morning. He was meant to ask for money for a new maths workbook, but didn't like to ask when everyone was so flap-daddle-panic, as if the motorway might evaporate before Dad got there. Or the shop Mum was going to work at might banish her to Zombie Doomdom if she wasn't all prepared for tomorrow. So he went hunting in his closet. He had a pile of stuff there that he didn't quite want to give away yet. Badges, cards, action figures, old school workbooks. He dug a maths one out of the pile and flicked through it to see how many pages were left. He saw something he'd never seen before. Jase must have sneaked it in at some stage. His cousin had drawn tiny pictures on the bottom right-hand corner of every page. Each one was of a skateboarder. As Billy flicked, the skater seemed to zoom along the flat, then do a flip, his eyes boggling at the top of the jump as he touched the moon, then came back down again, his tongue out and eyes crossed. It was beyond cool. Billy fanned through it several times, a happy-sad feeling pulsing in his throat. When his dad came in, Billy said, 'It must be *really* hard to be a bullfrog,' because that weird throb was too much. And then, 'Dad, have you seen this?' but Liam just grouched, 'Not now, Billy, would you get dressed? Socks ON!' Mum wasn't much better.

'Mum, I found this old book of mine, and—'

'Billy, my head's full to bursting. Are you bleeding to death? No? Okay, so can we just get out of the house?'

It was meant to be funny. But you know, ha-*not*, ha-*not*. Out the front door, the sky was blah colour. There was that sticky feeling in his brain. 'Why does life have to be so — *kwonk* sometimes?' he asked his mum, and she said, 'Oh, *Billy*, you know I don't talk bird.'

Throughout roll call, maths, then the spelling test, he had this sensation of body-wrong. He tried to push down the fidgets. Then, as he started to pull off a clothing layer, thinking maybe it was his fleece, the teacher called out, '*Earthquake!* Under your desks!' From below the gag of his jersey, Billy could hear desks juddering and thundering across the floor. His heart bolted. As soon as he could get his head into breathable air, he fled.

Banging, rattling, the world crashing apart around his ears, he didn't wait: just shot from the classroom door, belted across the school playing field and plunged into a shelter of flax and small bushes. He hunkered there, closed his eyes and just *thought* and *thought* like trying to make it spring from his mind and into the world. He thought about wings or being on a skateboard, vaulting into the sky, far, far away from shaky earth, this terrifying land of lost things . . .

'Billy?' It was Miss Hooper. He could see her shoes,

her ankles, her skirt-hem. 'Billy, it was just a drill.' The bullfrog feeling in his throat came back worse. 'Didn't you hear the announcement in the morning notices? We warned all the children.' He stared at small dirt clusters, felt his panicky breath slow. 'It's all right. Callum and Yuri were being idiots with their desks. Mr Farmer has spoken to them. They're on rubbish duty now. Will you come out?'

He glanced above and *face-palm*, he was nearly looking up her skirt; there were creases on her legs, like she had sort of smiley kneecaps; he wished she'd go away. He switched to staring at one of the shrubs nearby. It was tied to a wooden pole with green twine. He felt just like that. Embarrassment bound him to the spot and he was never, ever, coming out, ever, ever again. The bush seemed to understand. It shook its purple puffballs at him, trembling with shared shame.

'Billy? Come on, now.'

He stabbed a stick into the dirt, thinking *kill, kill,* but if he did, he'd go to prison, so if Callum and Yuri could just sort of — disappear . . .

'Billy?'

Miss Hooper clearly had no idea how huge embarrassment could be. It was bigger than a truck, no, a motorway or a Jupiter moon — some were bigger than ours, a bit. If Billy let his mind travel like this, he might forget where he was. What were the names of Jupiter's moons? He couldn't remember, so tried to think of something comforting. A bird. Start with the *A*s. Albatross? No. Even though they were Dunedin birds. For some reason, the idea of them not touching land for up to three years weirded him out. He *was* a bird person, but still. He closed his eyes and saw a white, slender, wading bird. Skip ahead to *S*.

Today he would think about spoonbills. Their beaks,

their head-crests, the way they swoop their bills through water, checking, checking, down at the inlet. They seem kind. That's nuts, because really what they're doing is killing their food, little fish, insects, frogs, but Billy can't help it, to him they look careful. As if that swooping is making sure everything is in the right place, everything is okay. Like Jason in their old backyard during a game of spotlight, torch beam scanning, scanning, finding Billy safe near the family's recycling bin, both of them stopping the game to listen to the cicadas: that comforting, sizzling sound, as if someone was always cooking in a kitchen that never closed.

He'd been lost in thought, and a movement outside his shelter made him refocus. Miss Hooper's smiley knees were replaced by suit trousers. Billy's scalp tightened. But Mr Farmer bent down, face going red, and said, 'Gidday, Billy. Get a fright, did you?'

Nothing much to say to that.

'Time to come out?'

Nothing much to say to that, either.

'Need some brain food to keep you going?'

Billy listened to his stomach. Nahp. Not hungry. Still shrunk from being freaked out. Nothing to say to Mr Farmer about that either.

'Would it help if I got Callum and Yuri to apologise?'

No.

Way.

Only that came out as 'Skraaaawk!'

'Billy. We need you to come out and join your class. We can't have you sitting out here all on your own.'

Billy wondered if birds can feel embarrassed. Did the ones with scaly faces, like turkeys and roosters, turn red? Or redder?

His silence brought on a shocking thing. Mr Farmer tugged up his own trousers as if he was about to go paddling, then shuffled in under the bushes. It was hard to see all of him because there were plants in the way, but he scooched around to sit down, legs stuck out into the playing field.

'Good place for quiet chats, eh, Billy? Do you come here with any of your friends to play huts? I used to spend hours building hideaways in the bushes with my brothers. Digging, weaving flax, tying together old branches. You ever do that?'

Silence.

'Got any brothers and sisters?'

Silence plus.

A blackbird hopped across the green screen of playing field. Its quizzical, perky head shifted Billy's embarrassment a bit, so he could say, 'Can I go home early?' Which sounded like some babyish Year 1 kid, so he added, 'I think I've got a sore stomach.'

'You *think* your stomach is sore, or it is sore?'

'I think it's getting sorer than before.'

'Sometimes stomachs hurt when kids are upset. Does it feel like you want to be sick? Or are you sad?'

'Feels like I need to go home.'

'Right.'

Billy could see a girl with glasses and pale orange hair running towards them. She came right up, then knelt down, her face a curious, owlish disc. 'Mr Farmer, Ms Fay in the office wants to know how long you will be and did you remember—'

'Can you be a great helper, Jolie, and ask Ms Fay to pop out here?'

'Why are you under the bushes?'

'I am helping Billy.'

'Why is Billy under the bushes?'

'He is . . . doing a project.'

Fear speared Billy. Had he missed something?

'What's the project?'

'Jolie, I *like* the way you are running so quickly to Ms Fay with the message.'

Jolie trudged off backwards, slow-on-purpose, Billy thought. She tossed her thick, pale pumpkiny plait over her shoulder: it seemed like giving the fingers. Billy half-expected Mr Farmer to bark at her, but he just wriggled around then pulled a sharp rock from under his backside. It was weird to think about the principal's bum. Billy realised he had sort of thought Mr Farmer was suit all the way through, which was stupid, but also true.

'What's the biggest thing you've ever eaten?' Mr Farmer asked.

Billy didn't want to think about food, actually. Now that they'd talked about stomach-aches his tummy did feel queasy.

'Dunno.'

'What's your favourite food?'

These were not headmastery questions.

The blackbird — or maybe another one — hopped back into Billy's sightline.

'Shoe,' said Mr Farmer.

'What?' Billy asked.

'*Shoe.*'

Billy looked at Mr Farmer's shiny black lace-ups. 'What's my *favourite —*?'

'Damned blackbirds, they're a menace. I'm angry with

them today because they got into my garden. Threw dirt everywhere. Vandals.'

Billy chewed his lip for a bit, feeling inexplicably sad about the blackbird. 'You know, it probably wasn't the same blackbird.'

'They're all pests. Robbed my strawberries last year.'

'They eat slugs and snails, too, though.'

'Know a bit about birds?'

Billy shrugged.

Mr Farmer softened his voice just the way Dad did when trying to get the cat out of the house so he could lock the cat-flap. Wrong-soft. Billy looked hard at the headmaster. Then Ms Fay called out over the grass. She was puffing from the top-field steps; her arrival made the blackbird chitter into the sky where Mr Farmer's *shoo* had failed.

'You asked me to come and *see* you, Mr Farmer?' she said, in her sing-a-ling-a-sing-song-talking-to-children way.

'Yes, thanks, Ms Fay,' said Mr Farmer. 'Billy's asking for his mother. Might be a good idea to have Miss Hooper call her and ask her to come up to the school?' Then the principal tested Billy, flat-toned. 'Is that what you really want, Billy?' Billy was supposed to say, *No, it's okay now. I'll go back to class.*

But — 'I need to talk to my mother,' said Billy, trying to sound like the man on a TV ad for a crime show, only the man said *lawyer*.

KEY COMPETENCIES — MANAGING SELF, RELATING TO OTHERS, PARTICIPATING AND CONTRIBUTING: NOT ACHIEVED

THERE WAS NO SINGLE WORD for what Iris felt as she churned up the hill. She waited at the school gates for a beat, trying to calm down; wiping under her eyes, which would be grimy with mascara sweated off in her rush: indecorously, culpably. A decent mother wouldn't have to *run* up the hill, a decent mother would arrive looking unsullied . . .

The school secretary recognised Iris from the previous Disappearing Billy episode. She smiled, unflappable, as if there were clear and logical procedures for everything, even frightened boys hiding in bushes.

'Ah, Iris, yes. Head to the playing field. By the climbing frame. Where the wisteria is. See that line of flax and hebes? Poor wee Billy, he's been in quite a state, but I wouldn't fuss. Craig's with him. They're probably having a good old confab.' She spun out of her seat and held the double glass door open. 'When you've got him all sorted, we'll let Elaine know. She'll want a quick word. Righty-ho.'

Then she was back in her seat, hitting console buttons and trilling to a headset, 'Good morning! Larnach Park School!'

Iris sprinted up the concrete steps from the netball courts and ran to the playing field's far corner, where she could see four legs — two short, two long — stretched out from the foliage.

'Hello!' she called, well before she was near. 'Billy?'

Mr Farmer and Billy both sat propped against a low, grey, concrete wall, partially concealed by bushes. As the man shuffled out from the greenery, he momentarily looked as if he wore a head-piece of flax and lavender hebe blossoms. Then he shook himself clear. After dusting himself off, he extended a handshake, somehow underlining the indignity of struggling over roots and leaf mulch. He introduced himself, though she knew who he was. 'Craig Farmer, principal of Larnach Park.'

'We met when I enrolled Billy.' She crouched to the boy's level, tried to find his face in the gloom and bristle of foliage. 'Hey, Billy-boy?' She put a hand on his knee. He scrambled out and clung to her.

Farmer coughed. 'Ah. Of course. Haven't seen you around school much.'

Iris's skin prickled. 'I've walked Billy here often. I suppose you must be very busy. So many people to remember, even at a small school.'

They seemed to be in an arms escalation. Maybe the man was still embarrassed at having been found in the bushes. He seemed anxious to appear authoritative. 'Mrs Dunningham, may I ask — are there any *developmental* issues with Billy that you omitted to tell us when he enrolled?'

'Ms.'

His expression altered as if to say, point to him, not her.

She feigned indifference. 'No. None at all.'

'No.' He rubbed his chin. 'I didn't think so, but sometimes it's best to check. You'd be surprised what parents don't tell us.'

She alternately patted and teased up Billy's hair: stroking, soothing. 'Billy's very bright.' Scepticism darted across Farmer's face. 'He's probably still unsettled, after the last six months.'

A bell sounded, and with shrill, tinkling cries, children in their bright hoodies and popsicle-coloured jeans ricocheted from doors everywhere.

'Unsettled?'

Iris felt anger mount in a huge, glowing lizard-frill around her head. Surely at the very least the man would remember that Billy had started mid-term, if not . . .

'Our family bereavement,' she slung. 'I would have thought that someone in the school might have had the sensitivity to . . .' but she sputtered out of genuine reasons to be angry with Farmer in particular when she saw Billy's teacher approach.

Elaine Hooper extended her hand, too: as if the strange, sideways day called for more formality, a re-setting of boundaries and propriety. 'Good morning, Ms Dunningham. You managed to get here, then.'

Iris masked her confusion by drawing Billy closer. 'Come on, Billy, love. The teacher told me on the phone, the earthquake drill was just a practice. It's all over now. I'm sure the other silly kids who scared you have been talked to by Miss Hooper.' She felt her jaw thrust out: bullish, pugnacious.

You probably weren't supposed to say *silly kids*. You were probably supposed to say something like *the child peer who exhibited a brief instance of poor self-management that may negate targeted personal learning and community objectives and that failed* — no — *did not achieve* our in-school and national standards for inter-individual relations. But Iris was shaking.

'Let's talk in the classroom while the other children are playing. Are you going to come along, Billy? You could show your mum your notebook.'

Billy cooed and chittered, slipping his hand into Iris's.

'A different boy,' Elaine Hooper said to Craig Farmer.

'Good lad.' The principal picked leaves out of Billy's hair with a carefulness that made Iris's outburst seem churlish. Farmer stood with arms crossed now, shoulders hunched a little against the Antarctic wind the hilltop school seemed always to suffer from, even on a sunny day. 'I'll leave it with you, then, Elaine. Happy to chat about things any time, Ms Dunningham.' She nodded, avoiding his eyes. Maybe his odd questions were well-intentioned, though uncomfortably artificial, standard procedure. Like the way one of her Auckland friends, Lata, was always asked in a blithe sing-song by her Plunket nurse, at the end of every visit with her new baby, 'And *no* change to family *v*iolence there?' — as if it were equivalent to, 'Would you like fries with that?' Oh, officialdom was all too easy to satirise, when at least someone, somewhere, was trying to mend a dislocated world.

They headed towards the classroom. As they walked across the netball courts, Iris's hackles were still up, waiting to deflect any slights or stares from other children; but a small cluster of boys shadowed them, and called out, 'Billy,

Billy! Hi, Billy!' He had acquired sudden celebrity status. One said, 'Billy, your *mum's* here!' as if he genuinely thought he were first with the news, even though Billy's hand interwove tightly with hers.

'*Thank* you, Wilhelm,' said Miss Hooper, in a thin-lipped way that sent a force-field around their little trio. The cloud of boys drifted off.

In the classroom, the teacher took Iris to Billy's desk. 'Bring out your Triple T notebook, Billy.'

'Triple T?'

'Targeting the Task,' Elaine explained. 'Billy has a tendency to . . . zone out, don't you, Billy?' She turned to Iris. 'Did you get my email about this?'

Iris's heart dropped. 'About Billy? No, nothing. Just the weekly newsletter.'

Elaine Hooper went to her desktop, saying, 'I'm sure I sent you a message a couple of days ago, asking if you could make a time to drop in after school.' She tapped and peered into her screen, then sat back, pink rising all the way to her hairline. 'Oh. Actually, sorry. It's still in my drafts.' She tsked to herself. 'I *was* wondering — but it's been so busy here, with the reading-level tests, athletics . . .'

'Never mind,' said Iris, reassured she wasn't the only one to have let something slide.

'I wanted to sound you out about how things are at home. How you've been handling the whole bird persona.'

Nervousness made Iris gauche. 'Can it be a persona if it's a bird?'

Elaine's lips shaped a delicate, sour knot. 'So he does act this way at home, too?'

Iris glanced at Billy who, sure enough, was stroking his arm with his nose: preening feathers. But then he pulled back, waiting, the way he might lift a bandage to show a graze was still there.

'Yes,' said Iris, voice strained.

'When does it come up, particularly? I mean, has it been problematic?'

'I —' All of her debates with Liam jostled for air. 'I'm not that sure,' she said. 'I haven't kept *records*.' Another weak joke: it echoed like a self-indictment. Why hadn't she been keeping better track, if she was truly concerned? She'd let maternal anxiety become such a wallowing pit that she actually had a poor grip of the facts.

The women looked at each other in mutual interrogation.

'I think,' said Iris, 'as I said to the principal, Billy's been through an awful lot this year. I've been hoping the bird . . . mania was just a stage.'

Elaine Hooper nodded. 'I've been trying to keep mental notes, but I'm no psychologist. It seems pretty erratic, actually.' The lines in her forehead rumpled into a sweetly stricken horseshoe: upside down, like bad luck. It made Iris realise how seriously Miss Hooper took her responsibilities. She chewed her lip, came back to Billy's desk and took the small 3B notebook from him, passing it to Iris. 'What I have been doing is getting Billy to record the times he keeps to task. Whenever he works without distracting the class, he gets a sticker. Ten stickers on a page earns a reward.'

Iris flipped through the pages of the book. Her skin coursed with embarrassment. Quietly, she tried to say the most constructive thing. 'Look, Billy, eleven stickers already. That's great. What was your first prize?'

Elaine Hooper pressed a hand to the back of her own neck. 'Well, he hasn't actually received one yet. He has to ask for something sensible.'

The bell for the end of playtime cut in to their conversation, and soon door bang after door bang brought in more children, like bursts from an ever-changing jack-in-the-box.

Iris set the notebook down on a desk, while Elaine Hooper carried on valiantly going into more detail about her Triple T scheme, and the past few weeks with Billy. She tried to reassure Iris that yes, Billy was a smart kid, a likeable boy, *when* he settled to things. Yes, she'd been cutting him quite a bit of slack given he was still new here. Maybe they should have talked sooner, as the bird act really had become disruptive, but on the other hand, she was sure it was something that was like, oh, biting his nails. She'd once had a boy in her class who couldn't help pulling down his bottom lip as far as he could with both hands whenever he finished speaking: just an annoying habit, but it drove other kids away. It took time to wean him off it, but with reward systems . . . Anyway, she was sure it would be fine, if they could work on it at school and home: channel it into something positive.

Eventually, Elaine had to turn to the crowd. She held up her palm as if pushing away the noise, and the children melted away obediently to their seats.

'Thank you, Turoa, Shania, Julie-Anne, Hinemoana. And Kyle, well done, sitting quietly. You can see I have a visitor so you need to wait. *Wait.*' Like puppies, some of them trembled and strained on the leash of her commands; surely one small boy even whimpered. Was he really Billy's age?

Quietly, Elaine Hooper said to Iris, 'I'm sorry, Iris, we haven't even discussed whether you think Billy should take the afternoon off — but I think it could help. I want to talk to the others about their behaviour. Give Billy a fresh start tomorrow. If he feels comfortable with it, he can have his say about the drill then, too. Does that sound all right? We'll use it as a lesson in *relating to others*,' she said, mouth an ironic *moue*, as if at last she understood Iris's attempts at joking. Belatedly appreciating what she was doing for her mysterious nervy-bird Billy, Iris warmed to her.

Elaine Hooper picked up the Triple T notebook and passed it to the boy. 'You can start taking this home each day, Billy. Mum and Dad will keep an eye on how things are going with our plan.'

Taciturn, he slipped it into his bag. Iris shepherded him out, hand on the thin ridge of his shoulder. Yet being preoccupied by the very problem of Billy himself — and having him home unexpectedly (what would Liam say, after the way she'd pulled him out of class the other day?) — made her irritable outside school.

'Weren't you told there was going to be an earthquake drill today?'

Shrug.

'Billy, you were, or you weren't?'

'Don't know.'

'If you'd listened more closely, you wouldn't have got such a fright. You have to *listen*.'

He sprinted ahead, but soon used up the energy burst. He started grasping fistfuls of the ferns, poroporo and hawthorn that reached in a tangle over the fence rail beside the steep footpath. Bruised leaves and snapped twigs lay scattered behind him. 'Billy! Cut it out!'

He echoed her: high-pitched, hips sassing, one hand giving a theatrically feminine flaunt on the air as he conducted: '*Neh* neh! Neh neh *neh*!'

She burned in silence, thinking, *Okay, so his only*

problem is he's a little shit. Eventually he slowed down, and his wing-arms folded to his sides. He let her catch up. There it was: the Dunningham jaw, thrust out — like a front-end loader trying to ram the world away. She saw it and thought it a wonder Elaine Hooper hadn't slapped her when she'd shown it herself.

'Billy. Sorry I snapped. I'm really worried about you, okay? It came out wrong.'

He half-scuffed his steps, pushing out his hips with each move, to make his school bag bounce in the small of his back: it signalled *Don't mess with me.*

'Adults don't always get everything right, Billy.'

He gave her a withering *duh* look, then trod on, bag thudding it too: *duh, duh duh.*

'I get that the drill was frightening. Especially with — what was his name? — acting the prat. With the desks and so on.'

'Callum. Callum Longley. He's a total dork. And Yuri Petrovich. Ditto dork.'

She waited for a rusty Toyota Corolla groaning up the hill to pass.

'Did you think it was a real quake?'

He bumped his hand along the pedestrian barrier. Slap, slap, slap. 'A bit. I guess.'

She put an arm around his shoulder, half-expecting him to shrug her off. He let it rest there for a couple of beats. But just when she'd decided that the more she pushed for information the more he clammed up, he folded into her, arm around her waist, sniffing back tears. He mumbled, 'Don't even remember how I got outside. When Miss Hooper first came, I thought maybe it was so big I got chucked out there.'

'That must have been scary.'

His fringe slipped over his eyes. His school bag bumped into her hip, so she took it, slung it over her own shoulder. 'But you're safe now, eh? It wasn't real.'

Topping her words so quickly he can't have been listening, he said, 'I thought if it was like that here then Dad would be dead in Christchurch. Most probably, everybody in Christchurch would be dead. Why does Dad hate me?'

'What?'

He went mute again. Jaw out.

'Billy—' She looked up. Pale and stretched, the sky was ungiving. She found a tissue in her handbag — handed it to Billy. 'He doesn't hate you. He could never hate you. It's just — if he seems grumpy sometimes, there's a lot on his plate. With work, and settling in here, and you know, all the other things. He—'

Billy slipped away, flung his arms up, started to run downhill again, screeching as if scalded. She watched him spin away, a kite that had slipped its moorings in a gale.

I'M SORT OF
THISTLEDOWNY

PARENTING WAS LIKE TRYING to share a swing bridge with cattle who shambled right towards you. Billy was a different child again that night. He wanted warm milk and cinnamon before bed; he wanted stories about Liam and Billy when Billy was first born; he wanted to snuggle up with an old favourite picture-book from when he was small. When she finally said, 'Sleep now, boy-o,' he asked, non sequitur, 'What if Dad died while he was in Christchurch?'

'Dad's going to be fine. Statistically it's very unlikely that anything will happen to him while he's up there. And listen to me. The aftershocks are diminishing. They truly are.'

She was reiterating all the things that Liam had said to her, things that the frightened, primitive spirit in her actually found hard to believe.

He dropped his chin. 'Jason died even though he was in a safe place.'

She paused, consciously biting down *Nowhere's entirely safe*. 'Yes. But Jason — Jason wasn't being careful.' She smoothed Billy's hair, as if there weren't an ache like a deep trench running her core; as if there were one clear, unrepeatable reason that his cousin had died and so other deaths were avoidable. When she could get no more response from him, she said wearily, 'Okay, then. Good night.' But his hand shot out, and he asked, *Could she stay till he was drowsier, and did she believe in ghosts?*

'No, Billy,' she said.

That was evidently unsatisfactory: his hand stayed latched to hers.

'But if you *did* believe in ghosts, do you think animals could have them? And if they could, could they swap bodies with other ghosts, or even go inside live bodies?'

'I said I don't *believe* in them, Billy.' She held back from saying *and I definitely don't believe in talking about them at bedtime.*

'That'd be so freaky. Imagine if the ghost of a rat went inside the body of a — the body of a — *spider*. No, imagine if the ghost of a *squid* went in the body of a *rat*.'

'Billy, that's crazy talk. You're deliberately creeping yourself out. Think about your happiest time ever. Think about — your favourite thing. What do you love doing best in the whole wide world?'

'Flying.'

Iris tried to remember the last time Billy had travelled on a plane.

'I like it best when I'm at the top of a tree, and the tree is like another giant bird, with green feathers. And then I jump from a branch and it's like hatching. Maui was a bird sometimes, did you know that? Miss Hooper told us. And anyway, when I'm in the sky I'm sort of thistledowny but I can ride the air like I'm skateboarding the best half-pipes ever.'

He'd turned babyish on the edge of sleep; perhaps encouraged by her anecdote. 'Wow,' said Iris. 'That's some turbo-booster imagination. Maybe if you're lucky you'll have a flying dream tonight.'

He sat up. 'How'd you know I have flying dreams?'

'You do? I guess it sounded as if you were talking about a fantasy. Or dreams. I used to have flying dreams when I was little. I wish they hadn't stopped.'

'What were they like?'

'Magical. I could travel very fast, and see everything from city lights to miles of green hills. I never landed. Just flew on and on . . . Huh.' She smoothed hair back from his forehead. 'I'd forgotten all of that. It was like having a secret parallel life. Slipping into another world.'

'You know I really have flown, don't you, Mum?'

'In a plane, yes.'

'No. In my own body.'

She laughed. 'Ah. You think you have?'

'I know it. That's how I got outside today, at school. So fast.'

Iris swallowed. 'Right.' She tried to deflect him. 'How many stickers was it on that Triple T book again?'

There was a pulse of silence.

'A micro galaxy.'

'Right, that's really enough jibber jabber. I'll stay in your room for a while longer if you need me to, but only if you shut your eyes and go to sleep.'

'Oh-*kay*,' as if she were the most boring, difficult person he'd ever met. But he reached out for her hand, shuffled down, coverlet over his shoulder, and within seconds breathed the steady rhythm of sleep: going under so fast maybe his talk had been sleep-babble.

She sat there longer. Panic-bolt, flying, animal ghosts . . . You heard parents say, sometimes, of people who went off the rails, 'He'd always been an *odd* little boy, right from the start . . .'

Where did Billy's quirks come from? How strange that an urban human child could get obsessed with animals when the planet's species are dwindling. Could that be a message? And if he is a little crazy, if madness takes the forms of its era, maybe Billy was society saying, *What have we done?* Or Billy was the planet's animals talking in boy-tongue. Billy was a museum of what we might lose altogether.

You think too much, Liam would have said, if he were here. *Why don't you put it all somewhere useful? Take up philosophy. Teach. Maybe then all this thinking would go somewhere.*

You can talk, Iris would have answered: *Mister Straight As in Library Studies* and *Mister Straight As in Journalism. What's an athletic type like you doing with an IQ like that?* And when he'd say, with a smirk, that's *jock*ist, they'd flirt-fight. Pinch, parry, chat-up, deflect. They used to be like that, didn't they? Teasing, touching constantly, any excuse, his hands a careful question, even after all these years, as if her breasts were frightened fledglings. Birds again; was Billy's mania contagious, or did he get his quirks from her?

No answers would arrive tonight to stop this unravelling. Not without the healing stitches of dream.

The first day — oh, and the second, helter-skelter — of Iris's new job went by in a rush. Her new employer, Brandy, was preoccupied with the state of her hospitalised business partner, Leonora. Texts, phone calls and emails seemed to be zapping back and forth, mainly about that. Iris had to constantly ask where X was, where Y, were they planning any new-season Zs, as clients asked? Most customers, though, seemed to be sussing out the new premises, not buying — just as well, as Brandy's instructions about how to use the till were interrupted by another concerned call about Poor Leonora: *No, no more news yet; yes, yes, she'd found a temp, she's here now . . .*

The first set of alterations for the cabaret was ridiculously easy. Someone had made twelve satin bow ties too tight for the male dancers: they'd all been sized on Poor Leonora, but it turned out that at least half the men had necks 'like elephant trunks', said Brandy.

'Do you mean tree trunks?'

'Yes, legs! Poor Leonora should get a laugh out of that, though. I'll be able to say, at least your neck didn't look pregnant, darling.'

Iris cracked on with that job, adding adjustable Velcro straps instead of hooks and eyelets. Then Brandy said there were five Spanish gypsy skirts to run up, and here were the measurements; 'Oh, and can you add this beaded trim to these five bowler-rose,' she said, holding up boleros, 'and to the trouser cuffs on six mastodon trou,' holding up matador pants, 'and tomorrow, first thing, we're having just about half the bloody cast coming back for re-sizing pen-striped suits for the business act.' Iris imagined jackets lined in permanent marker. 'All right, so only three of the cast, but still. They claim that in the fortnight since they were measured they've lost weight from all the extra rehearsals, so it'll be all hands to the quick-unpick. Are you all right, there, Iris, you're looking a bit perspexed?'

Iris had to bite her lip: 'I'm fine,' she said, while thinking,

This is hilarious. Better save her sayings for Liam. At the thought of him, she felt another twinge of fear, as physical as if a needle had punctured skin. *He will be fine; he will be fine. Earthquakes, car crash, muggings, stabbings; no, he will be fine. But how do I tell him about Billy?*

There was a cough at her elbow. As she sat behind the counter, pinning and tacking, she hadn't noticed another customer had finished browsing the racks.

'Can I try this on?'

'Of course! And if it's too big for you — you have such a lovely slim waist — we'd be happy to take it in here: we can do your measurements and whip it up for you.'

The woman looked startled at the compliment. She was in and out of the changing room in a flash, gabbling, 'I'll take it, it's perfect, I don't need a bag, thanks!' She paid Brandy then fled, as if trying to leave before she could catch herself in the act of spending.

'Smooth work!' said Brandy. 'I was giving you the daggers about us sizing her up, when we've got enough alternations to do. But you've really got the knack of that sales-platter.'

Iris fingered at the beaded trim, her own grin taking her by surprise as she thought, *This place is well-named, all right.* The morning zoomed. She enjoyed having clear, defined tasks set out for her, and her hands raced through them. It was helluva good to have adult company outside the house again. She even forgot to eat, and was soon on the bus home to be in time for Billy after school.

The days that Liam was away blurred; she spent them on the hop, unused to the slalom race of transport—work—transport—manage Billy—do the chores—manage Billy—find a moment of quiet before the topple into bed. There, some of Brandy's wackier sayings came back and helped Iris laugh herself relaxed enough to sleep. *Bloody behold. He's the kind of man you have to take with a bar of soap. Oh, she's mad as a meat pie. Look, whoever did that made a complete hand-job of it. We'll never sell it. Put it in the Under $2 bin. Why so quiet, cat got your pyjamas?*

On her second day, Billy was slightly late home. The new job meant that — bloody behold, as Brandy would say — Billy was allowed to walk home alone. (The plan was Iris would get off the bus at 3 p.m. at the bottom of their hill, and they'd meet at the house within a few minutes of each other.) Today when he turned up, she went to greet him with a big, cheesy grin, open arms — but his face was red and sweaty, his blue hoody dragging behind him like a broken wing. He pushed past her, dropped his satchel in the middle of the doorway, and went straight outside.

She trailed after him. 'Do you want a snack, Billy?'

They reached the macrocarpa tree which held the tree house built out of old packing chests. He clambered up the crude wooden steps nailed to the trunk.

'How was Triple T today?'

Billy unhooked the rope that kept the trapdoor entrance open, and let the door slam shut.

All the happy, bustling distraction of the first days at Glad Rags evaporated. She should have phoned the school from work. She should have met Billy at the school gates. She should have made more effort to talk to him after school yesterday. Shouldn't have even *taken* work on . . .

Iris slammed her own way around the house, banging the washing machine lid, compost bucket lid, finding traces of Liam's hasty departure strewn everywhere — including his phone charger — and trying to tidy them away, as if, when the house was clean, her conscience would be, too.

She turned on the radio to try to get her own snit in perspective. There were two items on Canterbury: a report of small aftershocks, and something to do with hearings promised on the CTV building collapse. Right at an important piece of information about the building's original engineer, Billy came tramping back into the house, demanding, 'What's for afternoon tea?'

She turned off the radio in exasperation. 'What's that mood about?'

'Nothing.'

She kept her tone mild. 'That's what boys do, is it? Arrive home without talking, hide in tree houses, then march in demanding food without even saying hello?'

He went to the pantry and took out the baking tin; shook it, to see if there was anything in there. Empty. He tried to reach up to the high shelf where the muesli bars, for school lunches only, were stored.

'You can have crackers and cheese,' Iris said. 'Or a bowl of homemade yoghurt and a banana.'

'Where's Dad?'

'On his way home, I hope.'

'You only hope?'

'He hasn't called yet today. But that was the plan.'

'There were aftershocks in Christchurch again today. Yuri said.'

She frowned. 'Dad would have found a way to call, Billy, if there was a problem. The radio news just said the aftershocks were very small, love. It's going to be fine.' She took the yoghurt out of the fridge, and watched him for a moment. 'Snack.'

'I hate yoghurt.'

'No, you don't. Jason hates yoghurt.' She stood there, hearing the name echo. She fought against the desperate stumble in her chest, thinking, *Don't get lost. Listen to Billy.*

'I can hate yoghurt, too.'

'Oh-*kay*. What do you want?'

'Anyway, it's hate-*ed*. Jason hate-*ed* yoghurt.'

'Why the nasty tone? All I did was offer a snack, and ask how school was.'

'No you didn't.'

She wasn't sure exactly what made her lose it. 'Okay, I didn't. I took away all your things, I locked you in your room, and I refused to feed you!' The urge to slap him grew monstrous. She tried to fling it off the way she would a personal assault, and lobbed the full yoghurt pot over-arm at the sink. A cartoon splatter of boysenberry gloop sprayed the clean dishes in the drying rack.

Billy goggled his eyes, flung up his arms, shrieked and chooked around like a bantam chased by a terrier. 'Kaaa! Kaaa!'

Anger foamed in her at shocking speed. She strode over and grabbed him by the elbow. 'Billy. *Billy.* You can't *do* this every time any tiny thing doesn't go your way! How would you like it if your dad and I ran around banshee-wailing whenever we couldn't handle something? You sound like a totally spoilt brat.'

Reason slid sickeningly from under her. *Liam,* she thought, *This is getting too big. You and I need help.*

Billy screwed his thumbs into his ears, clenched shut his eyes. She dropped his elbow. 'Go to your room while we both cool off. I'll talk to you when Dad's home.'

THE NOT-THERENESS
OF HIM

AND THANK GOD: MARITUS EX MACHINA, Liam's car pulled up half an hour later. When Billy heard it, he drifted to the threshold of his room, sour-faced but, *hallelujah,* quiet.

Liam came through the door, bringing a bucket of small Cookie Time cookies and a box of Black Macs, then went back out to collect three bottles of Cloudy Bay sauvignon blanc: all cheap, irresistible deals, he said, moving from sheepish to watchfully serious.

'Irresistible?'

'Yeah. I just — I'm sick of scrimping and saving. And I figured we should celebrate getting through the last few days. How's it been? Sorry I didn't call. Thought I'd drive all the way, but finished so late yesterday I was fried. Checked into a place in Ashburton. I could've called from there, but I—'

The fight adrenaline from her stand-off with Billy was ebbing away. 'Don't worry,' she said. 'I found your phone charger in the laundry basket. I figured you might have run out of juice.'

'Guess I left in a bit of a rush.'

'Mmm. Sunglasses in the pantry. Shaving gear in the garage. You must have been travelling pretty light in the end.'

Billy shuffled into the hallway. 'Dad, did you just laugh with your *nose*?'

He tried to imitate it.

Liam gave him a quick cuff on the shoulder. 'How're you, wee bruiser?'

Billy rubbed at his shoulder. 'You're the bruiser.'

Liam raised his fists Popeye-style. 'Are you a man or a marshmallow?'

Billy pondered. 'Any other choices?'

Liam pressed his hands at his lower back, then ouffed with tiredness, so they trailed into the lounge.

'Did you spend the whole day in Ashburton?' Iris asked, puzzled.

'No, no. Woke up really late, though. Had to pay for late check-out. And on the way down I did a tiki tour of Kakanui and Moeraki. Went for a dive off Moeraki, actually. Visibility wasn't great, but it's good for paua out there. Nice to have a look around, anyway. I even popped through a couple of the baches for sale afterwards.'

'*Baches?*'

He shrugged. 'You never know. If things pick up . . .'

Billy found a colouring competition that had come with the bucket of cookies, and retrieved his felt pens. He knelt down at the coffee table to start on the pictures. 'I'm giving the monster head-feathers. Nobody else will think of that. I might win for innovation. Winnovation!'

Liam gave Iris a perfunctory, somewhat dutiful kiss, then studied her before dropping into an armchair. There was disappointment in the air — as if the moment had teetered on its heels a little. 'You weren't worried?' he asked.

'I'll fill you in later,' said Iris.

'Ah.'

Pause.

He toyed with keys and change in his pocket. 'Sure you can't tell me now?'

'Walls and ears,' said Iris.

Liam looked at Billy. He seemed completely focused: he was peering down at the small, rapid strokes he was making with purple pen.

'Robins can hear worms in their burrows,' Billy said, colouring the monster. 'I imagine probably fantails can hear when sand-flies take off.' That *imagine*: so elderly.

Liam and Iris exchanged a *yup-you-were-right* look.

Liam swiped a broken cookie from the bucket, glanced at his watch. 'Gosh, it's getting late. What about a bath before dinner tonight, Billy?'

'Some birds can fly with one eye closed and half of their brain asleep. Probably they can hear things in their bath and their sleep, too.'

Liam rolled up his sleeves. 'Run it for you, shall I?'

Billy tossed down his felt pens. 'I'll do it.' He looked his dad square in the eye. 'Thanks for the cookies.'

'Hey, that's okay, buddy.'

Billy got up and stood there with his legs apart, fists balled up on his hips. 'Birds show affection by giving each other food.'

Liam uh-huhed.

'And sometimes, by grooming each other. Their beaks have little nerve endings in them, so they don't just peck, they can be gentle, too.'

'Yup.'

'Sometimes they even regurgitate their food for each other.'

Liam snorted. 'Let's not do that one, eh, Billy? But I can comb your hair when you're out of the bath, if you like.'

Billy twinkled his fingers up in the air and darted off. 'Okay!'

Soon they heard the sound of rushing water. Iris asked Liam to tell her about the Christchurch end of the trip, but he seemed tongue-tied now. She had the vague sense that he was building up to something. Or was his taciturnity partitioning something off?

She was about to ask, 'Liam, is everything okay?' but Billy was in and out of the bath in quadruple quick time. Iris herded him back, so she could scrub the grimy crescent of skin above his T-shirt line. He raced into his PJs, then approached Liam with his comb held out like a small mace. Liam took the comb and gave Billy's hair a couple of cursory flicks. 'There you go. Slick as.'

Billy stayed, gazing at his father.

'What's up?'

The boy's pout gently came and went, as if there were a tiny, fibrous problem on his tongue-tip.

'Off to bed now. It's late. You can read for a bit if you want.'

'Dad! We haven't even had dinner!'

'Oh. Any homework?'

Iris saw then how Liam's teeth were gritted, the hollows around his eyes deepened with shadows. He looked like a man holding up against internal strain. 'Liam, are you all right? Do you need to lie down?'

'I'm fine. Might just need to eat.'

'Right! Oh, right.' She went into a flurry of meal prep-aration while Billy returned to colouring in. Over dinner, Liam tried to eat at the same time as doing accounts, then reading Steve's submission against damming the Nevis River for hydro power. He kept zoning out of their chatter: work sucking him into another dimension. *Cut him some slack*, Iris thought. *He's just got back.*

After the meal, Billy asked if Liam could put him to bed; but the phone went: Steve. *Already.* Iris rolled her eyes at Billy, and he padded off on his own to his room. She followed to find him perched on his haunches in the dark on the bed, his arm curled up as far over his head as he could reach, his eyes screwed shut. He was cooing to himself; a tune Iris half-recognised.

'Good to have Dad home again all safe and sound?' she asked.

He carried on with his wordless song.

'Cooo *ooo* ooo ooo ooo

Cooo *ooo* ooo ooo ooo.'

She stroked his head. 'What would Miss Hooper think of this, eh, Billy?'

'Cooo *ooo* cooo ooo

Cooo *ooo* cooo ooo.'

'She wants you to concentrate on doing things like a boy.'

He refused to move — and so she heaved him over onto his side, pulled the blankets up as best she could; tucked him in. He played deaf all the way: either pretending he was asleep, or that he was so locked into bird-hood that the words of a human mother couldn't penetrate.

She left his room, frustration tightening in her chest. When she and Liam finally had a chance to be alone, they both stood dumbfounded. Chores done, boy in bed, no external clamour of texts, phone . . . the peace was a foreign place.

'Hello!' said Liam, hands up in mock surprise, as if there she was, on a busy street, after years of falling out of touch . . .

He did make her laugh; yet there was still The Conversation hovering. It would bulldoze over everything else, so — let him talk first.

'How did it *really* go in Christchurch?' she asked.

He fidgeted with his keys in his pocket, then forced a smile, gestured for her to come over to the couch. They sat together. 'Full on,' he said. 'Steve was stressing out about a dozen different things, and then there was navigating around the wrecked roads. Poor bloody place.'

She wound their fingers together, marvelling at how blocky and sturdy his hands were: how unfamiliar and *other*, despite all the years she'd studied them, felt them navigate her skin.

He cleared his throat. 'Some things give you hope.' His cool thumb traced in and out of the hollows of her knuckles. 'Small things. Like a library that's appeared on a street corner — an old half-smashed bus shelter people have been filling with books for anyone to use. Then you see streets that make it seem . . . this will never, ever be fixed. Piles and piles of rubble.' He stared at the floor then passed his hand over his face. 'Anyway. We got the job done. Steve's happy enough, I guess.' He rubbed at a mark on his jeans. 'I could do with a beer.' He made to shift off the couch, and Iris said, 'I'll get it.' She fought a small internal tug of war, thinking she shouldn't drink, given it was only her first week in the job. The glossy curves of the Cloudy Bay bottles were too seductive, and she poured herself a glass.

'Cheers,' he said.

'Rough trip all told, then,' she said. 'Here's to it being over.'

'Yeah.' Yet there was something guarded about him still. He lifted his glass to look at the malty fizz. 'How was it here, anyway? Starting at the shop?'

'Work was fine, actually. In a way, it was a break.'

'Eh?'

She sipped her wine, thinking, *Here goes.* Maybe if I tell all first, he'll follow suit. 'Billy's teacher called me while you were gone.' She explained everything, picking up the Triple T notebook from the coffee table.

Liam leafed through the pages. 'That's progress, isn't it? Eleven stickers already. What was his first prize?'

'He asked for gravel paper.'

'Eh?'

'To sharpen his beak and claws. He said that given he's kept inside so much and can't get out to use bark and stones as often as wild birds, he needs extra cage accessories.'

Liam laughed dryly. 'Right. And what did he actually get?'

'Nothing, yet. Miss Hooper says he has to make a sensible suggestion.' She slipped along the couch a little, turned to him. 'You know how whenever we ask about lunchtime, who he played with, has he made any new friends, he says, "There's a game with two guys, it's called Elements, and we have special powers . . ."'

'Yeah?' said Liam, meaning, *Now I do.*

'It's not true. He went to his favourite place when he panicked. Miss Hooper says he often hides in the bushes, apparently happy, but he fossicks there on his own, or sits there peering out, watching the other children play. Last week he started to build a makeshift nest. She's tried to introduce him to children from other classes even; children with "vivid imaginations", she says. But when one little girl, Brianna, tried to pretend she was a bird, too, and brought him some sticks, he flew off and scrambled up into a tree. Brianna couldn't climb that high.'

Liam guffawed.

She set her glass down roughly. 'You don't get it. It's lost its "quirkiness".' She signalled irony quotes on the air. 'Even though I've been, I don't know, gratefully distracted by the shop, when I spun out at him just before you came home —' She wrestled with the words. 'It's been eating at me, ever since the school called.'

His hand lay like a pale, stunned animal on the couch between them. 'I thought we agreed it's just a phase.'

She straightened up. 'That's what I thought before. But now if it's even a problem at school — it's time to get help.'

'How do you mean?'

'Advice, counselling.'

'What?'

'Visit the GP first, I suppose.' She looked at her hands. 'We trust Dr Patel, so I guess we ask her for recommendations.'

Liam said sourly, 'Knows some good pet psychologists, does she?'

Iris didn't grace that with a reply.

'Look,' Liam said, 'if we don't laugh, it's beaten us.'

Iris turned to him. 'I thought I was going to wallop him today. And that's not me. This afternoon, when he was *at* me, I just thought — I can't cope with that bird weirdery any more, on top of everything else. It's too much.' She didn't know all this until she opened her mouth, and now she didn't want to learn any more about her limits.

Iris swore she could feel the new thoughts cascading through Liam. She was the lenient one, the accommodating one. Despite his bluff, *let-me-at-'em* first response to Billy's conception, Iris was the one who had found adjusting to parenthood easiest. She'd even adapted better to having Jason in the house. Many people wondered, was it hard, was Liam's nephew like an interloper? Her sister Carrie asked, several times, did she ever feel, you know, cuckoo syndrome? But she hadn't. Part of her was joyful that Billy had the companion she hadn't been able to give him. Yet it had come from such tragedy, she'd never told Liam of her gladness. Despite his challenges, Jason had an openness, warmth, even a gratitude, that leavened his understandably moody times.

Maybe it had been easier for her because they weren't blood relations. She wasn't scouring his every move for evidence that he was like his father. Liam, though, was always vigilant for signs of Jase going off the rails. So perhaps when Iris hit the wall, the impact was worse.

Now Liam's eyes darted around: looking for an exit? These weren't the roles they played. Where should he stand? What were his lines?

He spoke. 'It's really not just Billy, Iris. You've been in a state of — what — high alert since Jason died.'

They listened to the after-ripples of his name. Paradox: she felt the not-thereness of him so intensely it was as if he were in the room. Her hand floated up, to let the absence trickle over it. Liam clasped her fingers so they folded like a fan.

'You're over-thinking. We've both had so much to deal with — for months now.' There was an uncomfortable lull.

'Let's not make Billy the scapegoat.'

Regret cramped her throat. Unexpectedly, then, he stood. 'I'm tired, Iris. I've had a totally full-on trip. Let's just follow the teacher's advice. Park the rest of it for now, okay?'

Left on the couch, Iris felt very small, very stupid, and consummately dismissed.

HALLELUJAH
HUNGER PANGS

OVER THE WEEKEND, a little distant with each other, she and Liam kept Billy as busy as possible, doing things only a human child could do: kick a ball around in the park, ride a bike, go skateboarding. All was well and good, she thought, until Liam and Billy started an argument, and Billy thought he'd found the clincher: a YouTube video of a skateboarding cockatoo. Liam left the room on a hissed 'For fuck's sake!', and Iris felt she must have missed some part of the build-up — Billy hadn't been that bad just now, surely?

The boy looked bewildered — even more so when Liam reappeared, in shorts, sporting a small backpack. 'Running to the pool for a swim. Save me some dinner?' Iris could tell he was contrite, but still smarting; that he was taking himself off not just to lick his own wounds, but to let Billy lick his. Astonishing how resonant the unsaid can be in a marriage.

She watched Liam leave, wondering about this spill of anger. It didn't seem quite right. She glanced at the clock high up on the kitchen wall, feeling an odd tide of foreboding.

'Mum?'

'Yes, Billy?'

'If an asteroid hit the earth sixty-five million years ago and wiped out dinosaurs, do you think we're overdue for another one, and would we be wiped out, too?'

Grim laughter. Another Billy-shock. Was he a mirror, genetic matter looking into genetic matter? Or had he caught her foreboding like a thought virus?

'It's very unlikely. But scientists are measuring these things, and keeping an eye on them all the time. It's really not something you should worry about. Worrying doesn't do any good, love.' Hypocrite. She should do everything maternal with her fingers crossed. That's what children are ruled by, she thought: not the patriarchy, not the gynocracy, but the hypo*cracy*.

'Can we Google "asteroids", Mum?'

What they needed was permanent safe-search: a Google that only found reassuring facts. 'I suppose so. After dinner.'

'Would birds get wiped out, too?'

'Uuuuhh—' What was the right answer scientifically, what was the right answer Billy-tifically? So many answers to a child's questions had to hold back the full force of the world.

'Mum, are you even listening?'

'Yes, Billy, I'm just thinking.'

'About?'

'What an unsophisticated tool a human is for raising other humans.'

'Oh. Okay. What's for dinner?'

Iris sighed a catch-all sigh.

'Sloppy Joes.'

'What's that?'

'You know. I've made them before. Like hamburgers that can't hold it together. Patties that need putty.'

'What?'

'Mince on a bun.'

'Yay!'

Apocalyptic thoughts and existential crisis postponed by hunger pangs: *Hallelujah*, thinks Iris.

After dinner, Billy asked to play outside, in the weak gold of a clear Dunedin spring evening, its sunlight on ice. Even with him contented, occupied, her concentration on anything but Billy-worry was shot. Iris watched him swooping around the lawn, then trying to leap, body bow-curved, up towards a tree. Lost in thought about him, she jumped at a thin, metallic squeak. Smoke alarm? Some electronic toy with a loose wire malfunctioning?

No. Liam stood there, red-eyed (with chlorine, she hoped, not tears, because if it was with tears, why hadn't he talked to her?). His damp-dark hair was beginning to spring back from where it had been freshly combed. Expectation, guilt, apology and conspiracy alternated over his time-rumpled face in quick succession. From his hand, a large cage swung like a lantern that might light their way out of a tunnel. In it was a yellow budgie, fluttering up a little from its perch.

She might have actually gasped.

Liam looked at the budgie. It hopped as if someone were hitting a piano key over and over.

'But didn't you say you'd never . . . ?'

Liam nodded.

'Since your father . . . ?'

Again the nod.

'But where did you—?'

'Late night at the Pet Warehouse. Special anniversary sale. Got in just as the shop was closing.' He swung the cage a little. 'It was going cheap.' He quirked his eyebrows, then beatbox/scat-mimicked a drum roll and cymbal clash.

Iris betrayed her principles and laughed. Liam went to the French doors and called out, 'Billy? There's someone I'd like you to meet.' He had to repeat and coax: 'Sorry about before, Bill-bo. Can you come here, mate?'

Billy shinned down from the macrocarpa tree, doing without the primitive step-ladder. His sullenness and the slumping, very un-birdlike walk made Iris brace herself for another temper-flare from Liam. At the same time, she noted, *That's a normal boyish sulk at someone who's had a go at him. And that is probably good.*

The birdcage sat atop the newspaper on the dining-room table. Billy saw it, scanned the room as if checking, yes, Liam did mean for him to meet the bird, not whoever brought the bird . . . Then he stepped over, delicately as a heron, to take a closer look.

'Hello?' he whispered. He gave small, squeaking kisses. 'What's your name?' he asked.

'In the pet shop they called it Canary Woof,' said Liam. 'The owner's from London. Apparently, it barks.'

'But it's a budgie,' said Billy.

'Well, it is canary yellow,' said Iris. 'But I bet it never barks. I think your dad's on a bad joke roll.'

They peered at the bird. It narrowed its eyes, as if people were beneath notice. And then, as if a rather hoarse, very old, small, unthreatening dog were woken in the distance, it rasped, '*Rolfe! Rolfe!*'

The family's laughter startled it; its head-feathers ruffled and its wings clattered against the wires: a miniature Lady

Gaga in an animatronic costume.

'Whoops, sorry, little egg-head,' said Liam.

Billy's smile was fit to split itself. 'I want to give it a new name.'

'Any ideas?' said Iris.

'I'll have to think.' Billy's forehead furrowed. The budgie chirruped. 'Oh!' cried Billy. 'He's said it's . . . it's . . .' His nose wrinkled. 'It's hard to translate into English.' The bird was quiet, but Billy held the cage close, cocked his ear, as if detecting something subsonic.

Liam and Iris exchanged a look: *Should we laugh, or are we sinking?* Liam rallied. 'I met the whole family at the store, you know, Billy. He looks a lot like his father.' Iris rolled her eyes: oh-no-I-already-know-what's-coming. They said it simultaneously. 'A chirp off the old block.'

Liam seemed offended. 'How did—'

'Liam. How long have I known you?'

He turned serious. 'So I've become predictable.'

'Your puns have.'

Billy slid a finger between the bars of the cage. 'Can I have him in my room?'

'Of course. If he doesn't keep you awake. We'll try a blanket over his cage, but if he doesn't settle, we'll move him out here again.'

Billy scooched over to Liam, looking up at him a little sideways.

'You got something to say?' Liam asked.

'Oh, yeah. Thanks,' said Billy, lips tucked hard over his teeth while he frowned, as if working out what he'd really meant to say. But he slipped back over to the cage, chattering to the bird under his breath, and pattered off to his room.

Iris turned to Liam, her hands on her hips.

He shrugged. 'I'm hoping it'll help.'

'I know. I just hope he doesn't use it to perfect his mannerisms.' She touched his arm: subtext, thank you.

Liam shuffled bills and junk mail; rattled around for pens in the dump-all drawer; reheated dinner — a one-man pinball machine, trying to head them both off topic. Several minutes lapsed while he sat down to his meal. Iris pulled the paper towards her again, willing herself to give Liam space, not say anything . . .

'I still think we might need help.' Damn. She bit the side of her lip, right into an ulcer: formed by how much unconscious repetition?

Liam played deaf.

'I know you want to "park it", but I'm going to call the GP early tomorrow and make an appointment.'

The junk mail Jaycar catalogue was, apparently, extremely interesting. It seemed Liam was weighing up how important a pre-order of a new single-handled DJ headphone was, compared to an automatic bubble-blowing machine.

'Liam!'

He laid his fork down and raised eyebrows that parodied intent fascination. 'What?'

Iris carefully chose not to flip at how — at how bloody *flip* he could be. 'I really want to make an appointment about Billy's behaviour. And when I do, we all need to be there.'

He stared at her, his shoulders slumping on an exasperated exhale. But then he said, 'Fine. Whatever.'

She huffed out her cheeks. Jesus. Well, it was better than nothing, she supposed. She turned a few pages of the paper.

'What do you think Billy's up to?'

'Learning birdanese, I guess.' Liam used the tone of a man on a diet of pickled onions and tripe. 'Leave him to it.'

'Okay.' Iris actually managed 'okay' for half a minute. Then she said, 'I better go and check.'

Liam watched her tuck her shirt back into her skirt waistband as she stood up.

'Iris,' he said.

'Yes?'

'Come here.' He moved over to sit on the couch. She stayed where she was.

'You're a good mother.'

They locked stares. She gave a small shake of the head.

'Please. Sit down.' She did. He put a hand to her forehead: ran his thumb over the skin between her eyebrows, the way it bunched into a small knot. Her worry-cep, as he called it: big from carrying the weight of the world.

'Look. You're the one going to check on him, right? When he's perfectly safe, in his very own bedroom, doting over what's probably going to be his new obsession. I'm the one trying to get you to come and sit back here,' he patted the gap between them on the couch again, 'shuffle your pretty rump up close, drink another wine, and let me play-act seventeen again. Get in some heavy petting while no one's watching.'

His eyes did seem rather swilly. 'How many drinks have you had?'

He shrugged. 'A couple. Look, I'd let him stay in there and eat birdseed for a day if it meant you'd relax.'

'Looking into each other's eyes?'

'And other things, I'd hope.'

'Talking?'

'We could do that . . . What about, exactly?'

Helplessness drifted through her. 'There always seems to be so much we avoid when Billy's around, and then when he's not —'

'Then?'

'Then there's so much to say about Billy.'

Liam cupped her knee, her breast. She looked towards the living-room door. 'Um, Liam?'

He retracted; cleared the wine glasses away, and capped the bottle.

'Liam, I'll be quick.'

'You're not in the mood.'

'I can try to be in the mood in a minute.'

'Trying to be in the mood is not in the mood. Check on him.'

Iris's spine drooped. Attend to one, offend the other; attend to one, neglect the other . . . family was a push-me-pull-you, it seemed, with as many directions as loves.

She went to the boy's room. She'd just make sure all was well.

Which was when she saw Billy with feathers on his lips. She screamed.

HOP, HOP,
WHAT, WHAT,
PECK SHINY HARD THING

THIS IS WHAT THE BIRD THINKS, decides Billy, although I have to think it in human words:

There is a very large bird with peeled wings and snapped-off beak. Is it hurt? Because its noises are disgusting-ugly, but it is also trying a kindly preen.

Perhaps, Billy thinks, to the bird I'm like the French boy I met on holiday. Accent and cut-up words. So when I copy him, I sound sideways. We chirp in crazy loops. If I were a small bird, and a bald deformed giant honked outside my jail, I would be so terrified I'd poo and poo and then probably die. It will take a long time for him to trust me. I will have to be as much like him as possible before he feels safe.

Billy decides he has to work harder. He will write down dictation in a notebook of everything the budgie *probably* says. He tries to be as honest as possible.

seed seed water water preen preen uh poo uh poo ahh
    tired tired scared scared what, what wings, wings
stretch, wings want,

hop, hop, scared, scared, look, look, what, what, seed, seed, what, what, big bald strange bird, hop, hop, what, what, peck shiny hard thing, it go sing, sing, peck shiny hard thing, uh pooh, uh pooh ahh, hop, hop, what, what, peck shiny hard thing, look, look, same bird, same bird, peck peck, hard bright cold bird hits beak with beak, who's boss, hard bright cold bird looks back, peck, peck, wings stretch, wings sore, want sky want air . . .

Billy bites a knuckle: all of that was still a boy thinking what a bird might be thinking. How could he really, *really* think what a bird thinks, how could he really *evolute* into a bird? One day could a computer read birds' minds?

Maybe he needs to write the budgie's own sounds. Would it help if he could write music properly? Not really, he needs to draw squeaky rubber. It was something like:

Squi squeee squi squi irri irri squirrr squirr skih skih

but there was no actual *s*, no *k*, no *e*, *I*, or *u*. Billy scratched his head. He scribbled, a tangled, skirling zig-zag: diagrams of a constant here! here! now! now!

It was tiring teaching yourself a new language. No wonder whenever you saw a baby it was either asleep or crying.

A feather drifts from the cage. Billy feels its silk. He strokes it under his nose: the tickle is so ferocious he bats it away. He stares at the feather. Imagine if he could gain bird-mind power from it. He sniffs it, licks it, chews it, tries to swallow it, then at the thought that what really eats bird feathers is a cat, he spits, but it sticks to his lip. Which is when his mother appears.

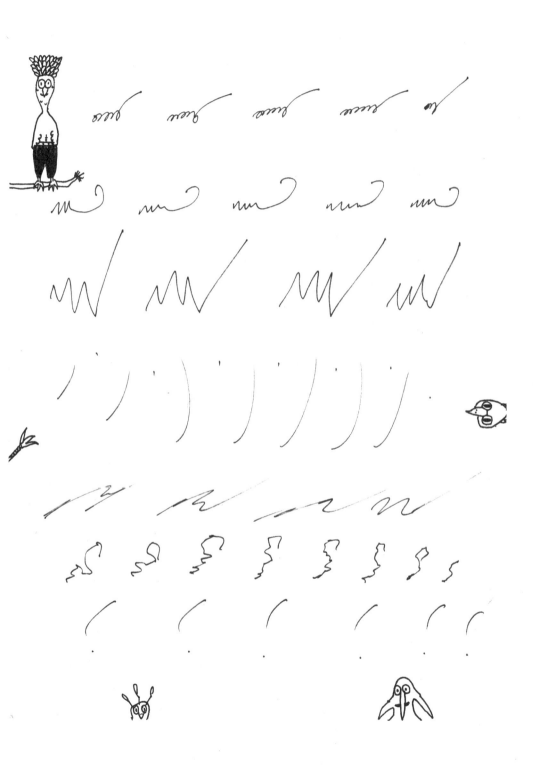

Her scream *Ahhh*! scares him into doing a squirt of wee in his pants.

'Billy! What are you doing?'

He spits again. 'Nothing.'

'Jesus! I thought you were eating Canary Woof.'

Billy feels kicked. 'Mum! I wouldn't eat him. He's family.'

'So everything is okay in here.'

'Yup.'

'You don't need anything?'

'Nope.'

Billy looks at her and her eyes have that burning silvery wetness of when she's frightened or remembering Jason's accident. Feathers creep up from his skin. He tries not to look at his bare arms because whenever he looks, or wants the change too much, the feathers vanish again. He tries and tries, then all at once — he can't help it. He glances down: but the feather bumps are gone. His skin's the colour of milky tea: fuzzed with blond, too sparse to be feathers. He and his mum both stand there. He fidgets in his slightly wet pants.

'Sure you don't want anything? Not even dessert?'

What a relief.

'Oh. Except dessert.'

STRANGE HUMAN WORDS

THE NEXT MORNING for school Billy put on a shirt his mother had ironed for him, an old one of Jason's that she said would fit now. He wasn't too sure about it, even though it was supercool. On a navy background, a skateboarder silhouette leapt, the image repeating in an arc that blipped through bright primary colours. He'd always wanted it. He was the skater, after all, not Jase: Jase had been more into bikes. Billy looked good in it. He took it off. There was nothing else clean, though. He put it back on. He loved it. He stared at his torso, remembered bunting his head into his cousin's stomach as they practised rugby, Jason getting the giggles and shouting, *Tackle, not tickle, y'flea's nuts*!

He couldn't wear it. So he walked into the kitchen to ask his mother if there were other shirts dry yet. At the stove, she turned around with a pan of steaming French toast in her hands: she usually only cooked breakfast if she thought Billy was coming down with a cold. Her face stumbled over its hello. A millisecond later, Billy's dad swung into the kitchen, carrying the empty compost bucket, falsetto

singing an old Ramones song, 'I Wanna Be Your Boyfriend'.
He stopped in his tracks.

'What's the matter, Dad?'

'Wasn't that Jason's shirt?'

'Yeah.'

His dad jerked his head as if something had flown into
his face. 'You looked like your Uncle Pete. Then Jase.' He
waited, as if there was something Billy had to say. A spider
of cold toe-danced across Billy's back, under his shirt. Then
his dad's mouth fell, like a kid's, only Billy had never seen
him cry. Not even at the funerals. Billy felt a rise of panic.
His dad dropped the bucket, turned to go, but wait, wait,
what, what was Billy meant to say? The next thing he heard
was the front door thud.

His stomach turtled. He was the Not-Jason-Not-Pete-
Either. The Not-Jason-Not-Pete-Either kicked itself along
out of the kitchen and back to its bedroom. It wriggled
off the shirt, rolled the shirt into a ball, and pushed that
under the bed. It put on yesterday's shirt. It sniffed under
its arms. Sort of stale. Sort of like — old chicken crisps on
a rainy-stay-inside-the-classroom day.

The budgie gave its strange bark. 'Rolfe! Rolfe!'

Tap, tap. Something pecked from inside the hard dark
rock of Not-Jason-Not-Pete-Either.

'Rolfe! Rolfe!'

The peck was like a perking up. Huh. Billy stirred again.
Not a rock, a roc, he thought. Like in the comic book about
Sinbad the Sailor. I will be a roc today. A powerful bird:
large enough to scare Sinbad and carry an elephant. Or
like pouakai, Haast's eagle, large enough to carry a man.
What had Miss Hooper read them from the school journal
in class? 'The pouakai cried "Hokioi! Hokioi!" while its

wings went *hu-u, hu-u*.' He loved that the wing sound had its own word: *hu-u, hu-u*. Must have sounded like a plane, the bird was so big. Courage bristled back along his arms; his spine stretched into a joyful arch.

'*Hokioi! Hokioi! Kaaa, Kaaa!*' he sang. And with hands like talons he scooped up his school bag. He swooped back into the kitchen, to devour the French toast: easy scavenging. Then he soared from the breakfast stool, strange human words ringing in his ears.

'Wait for me at school today, Billy!'

GIVE TIME SOME TIME

THE GP WAS ABLE to fit in the family the next afternoon. Iris's drive to the surgery was a blur of not wanting to be late, hoping Liam got her text about the appointment, only half-understanding Billy, who had a story about all the other kids painting legends of Maui and the Jawbone, while he did the Bird Woman and Hatupatu. His teacher said, '*That's* original Billy,' and he said, 'How's it original when it's a myth and it's in that book you've read us?'

Trying to pull her mind back from the spectres of her internet search for 'bird delusions' just last night — OCD, schizophrenia, bi-polar disorder, depression — Iris missed a switchback in Billy's chatter.

'Sorry, what? You didn't like your lunch?'

'Not once it fell on the *floor*. It had hair and paper dots from the hole-punch all over it. Gross. I know whose hair it was, too. Even grosser. Hair that's been on *Sally Bateman's* head. I feel sick.'

'The GP's a good place to be sick.'

'Only if there's a cure for Sally Bateman. Nice-ening

pills. Invisible-ising pills.'

'You haven't been at the school for long enough to make enemies, have you? What's so bad about Sally Bateman?'

Billy put his feet up on the dashboard, glaring at his knees. 'I told you.'

'When?'

'A hundred times ago.'

'I get confused about who's Sally, who's Sarah, who's Sandra, and what's the other S in your class? Sione?'

'No, *Sri*-ya, Mum.'

'I guess when you bring home your school photo I'll memorise them all. When I see them after school they all look, brunette, pretty, they all wear—'

'Sally Bateman is *not* pretty. She's a vampire slug.'

'I hope you don't say that to her face. That's hardly going to win you any friends.'

'I will say it to her face, then. It might mean she stops trying to put her slug lips on my neck at lunch.'

'Her *what*?' Iris braked just in time to avoid rear-ending a taxi at a pedestrian crossing.

Billy gave a tired, worldly sigh. 'Sally Bateman loves me, Mum. Totally yuck-balls.'

Someone behind Iris hit their horn and she had to look lively, zip over the crossing and aim for a parking space.

'Were you *smiling*, Mum? How can you be smiling about Sluggy Sally thinking she's in love with me? We're only *eight*. Well, she's nine. But I'm not *old* enough for that.'

Iris pressed her lips together hard, so she wouldn't say, I'm smiling because we're having a perfectly normal conversation about school; because it's amazing how early attraction begins; because Sally Bateman loves you even though you think you are a bird; because you say the most outrageously mature-immature, perceptive-naïve things; because I am possibly on the verge of yet another version of social embarrassment as I take you to the doctor claiming you might need psychological intervention, when actually, you're already coming right, which is to say, you're already being *normally* weird.

'Mum? Sally Bateman is gross! She *licked* my *neck*.'

'Does she know the last time you had a bath?'

'I need one tonight. To wash off the Sally-spit.'

Iris laughed as she parked the car. Outside, Billy reached for her hand, nattering about a miniball coach who had visited school. Happiness nudged her. So what would she say to the GP? *I might be here with a phantom problem. Fancy talking about the weather?*

They saw Liam in his fluorescent cycling jacket, pacing outside the chemist adjoining the doctor's surgery. So. He'd got the text. Points to him. She remembered how they'd argued once about riding a bike to work after Jason's accident. He'd swung back with, 'How can I ride a *bike*? How could I drive a car? When I think about him, and Pete and Steffie, how can I get out the door?' Livid heat in his eyes had made Iris ram tears down.

Billy's head jutted from his neck; he quivered, as if shaking off rain. Cawing, he ran in circles on the pavement, bobbing and lifting. Then he became a smaller bird: flittered to Liam, nuzzled at his arm with his forehead. Liam seemed to be talking to the chemist's window when he said, 'Hello, you two. How's it going?'

'It's been really good,' said Iris, wondering how to convince him. The speed with which Billy returned to bird upon seeing Liam sent her stomach into a cold dive. Evidence? Of what?

Liam put a hand against her back, shunting her towards the surgery. His tension prickled beneath her own skin. If it was this hard to talk to each other, how easy would it be in front of a doctor?

In reception, the attitudes of boredom, defensiveness or submission on the faces of people waiting there underlined her sense of defeat, so there was a strange dissonance when Dr Stavita Patel breezed out, upbeat, calling Billy's name. The other patients must be waiting for other doctors, the practice nurse: a few of them sighed resignedly.

Dr Patel ushered them along the corridor to her room. 'Hello, Billy. Have you come straight from school? Hello, Iris. Gorgeous stockings. What do they call that colour? Pinot Wow?' To Liam, 'Tailwind for biking here?' She spoke with some of her consonants lightly padded; the 'r' richly rolled. It managed to give all her consultations a softly-softly step somehow.

In the consulting room, Dr Patel slipped on a pair of reading glasses that matched her jade-green silk suit. She drew up their files on screen, then spun on her swivel chair. 'Now, what can I help you with?'

Iris left a decent silence: a respectful transition from the breezy good-will of their greetings to the glummer matter of — well — 'We're a little worried about Billy. But I — I just want to say, first of all, that he's a lovely boy. He's a smart, funny kid.' Iris placed a hand on the top of his head.

Liam tore off his reflective ankle straps, unzipped his jacket, each rip and rasp a small detonation. 'He's very bright,' he said, in warning.

The GP glanced from one parent to the other: a speed-reader of the human condition.

Iris clutched her handbag to her stomach. 'We've been

concerned about his behaviour. Lately. Or really — for a while. But we let it pass, because he's had a lot going on.'

Most of it would be in their records, in some form: by implication in the transfer from an Auckland practice to this one; or there would be a note on their files, related to the brief course of sleeping pills she and Liam had asked for, shortly after they arrived, when they were both pretty strung out. She'd mentioned Jason and Pete then.

'I suppose Liam and I have still been, I don't know, upended. We probably haven't been handling it well. You can't help withdrawing sometimes, to protect yourself, even.' She glanced at Liam unintentionally; she didn't mean to reveal the *him* in the *you*. This wasn't a counselling session; the blacks of his eyes trained on her said as much.

Stavita Patel slipped a stethoscope around her neck. 'Remind me, do you have family here?'

'No.'

'Support network?'

'Getting there,' Liam said.

Dr Patel watched Iris, then turned to Billy. He sat arms crossed, legs entwined, scraping one shoe over the other.

'And as for you, Billy — how's school?'

He canted his jaw forward slightly. 'Educational.'

Dr Patel coughed. 'How old are you now?'

'Nearly nine in human years.'

Stavita raised her eyebrows at Liam and Iris. 'Is he having extension classes?'

'Ah — not really, although he's the youngest in his year, so maybe, in a sense.'

She nodded. 'Do eight-year-old boys play sports these days?'

'Some.'

'You?'

'I've got swimming lessons again soon. Unfortunately.'

'He'll have miniball next term. And you love skate-boarding, don't you, Billy?' Iris squeezed her handbag, sure they were wasting time: the doctor's questions were nudging the real problem deeper inside Billy where they'd never reach it. She tried to chase it down again. 'He's very active, he's sleeping well, he's eating well, he's not unsettled or — you know, aggressive. It's more—'

'Billy says he's a bird.' Liam's voice cut the lights: a put-down; a *shut up, woman*. 'It's out of control. His teacher's said so. That's why Iris wanted to see you. But I don't think it's — what — psychiatric. I think it's behavioural, if that's the word. Intentional.' Liam's eyes were so fixed it seemed something was strangling him.

Iris stepped back in. 'We're here for advice on who to see. Would it be a counsellor, or, or, a child psychologist, or —'

Dr Patel adjusted her glasses. 'You're a bird sometimes, Billy, or all the time?'

In his awkward posture, Billy appeared tangled in the wiring of himself. His foot jiggled. 'I'm always like a bird on the inside.'

Iris spoke up again. 'It switches on and off. Sometimes it's when he's frightened. Like at school recently, when he thought there was an earthquake.' Liam gave her a look of crystallising realisation. 'I'm sure it's, you know, not medical, as Liam says. But we want someone to talk to about it. We're concerned.'

'Fed up,' said Liam.

She corrected him. 'We want to get this right.' In her mind, she heard the words, *last chance*, and so, oh, no, here it came, a crying jag. Why here, now, and not hidden away at midnight, with Billy asleep and Liam still in the lounge, watching some smack-'em-up sci-fi that took him so far away he couldn't hear?

'Okay.' The GP poured a cup of water from a dispenser, and pushed a box of tissues towards Iris. 'It's going to be okay. Give time some time, yes?'

Billy's head bobbed back and forward on his neck like a wading bird's and he gave his arms a shake. Liam rubbed and patted Iris's back: but she thought, *I'm not the one who needs this. We've got this all wrong.* Liam cleared his throat. 'Give time some time?' rising inflection, as if learning a foreign phrase.

'A truism, but —' Dr Patel's hands gave a delicate flourish, showing that in the face of it — *phouf* — doubt and cynicism vanished. She tapped her keyboard. 'I'd like to talk to you separately, Iris. If you could make another appointment? I think there's a lot going on here for you.'

Iris took a tissue, wiped her eyes. Her finger and thumb-tips rubbed at each other as if sampling the fabric of the doctor's suggestion — but the GP carried on, skating her swivel chair closer to Billy, squinting at him.

'Billy, can you tell me, have you been having headaches of any kind?'

Head-shake.

'Any other physical symptoms? Any pain?'

Same-shake.

'Has anyone tried to give you any funny sweets or tablets lately, that you've taken and found they make you feel—'

'Drugs?' shot Liam. '*What*? He's only *eight*, it says that in your *notes*! Don't you think we'd know if our own son was on *drugs*?'

Dr Patel blinked languidly, waited for the bluster to pass. 'Billy. Has anyone tried to give you unusual sweets or tablets lately?'

'Nope.'

Iris felt gratitude under the cloudy ache of shed tears. Progress?

'Tell me more about being like a bird all the time on the inside.'

Blank.

'What does a bird think about being at the doctor?'

'Not exactly chirpy.' He gazed at the plastic model of lungs under a poster advertising childhood vaccinations.

The GP couldn't suppress a smile. 'Okay. I'd like to take your blood pressure and listen to your chest.' She worked her ministrations; looked at him over her glasses. 'Hmmm. Interesting. Nice regular, boy-style heartbeat, Billy. About ninety beats a minute. Did you know a hummingbird's resting heartbeat can go up to something like five hundred to six hundred a minute?' She took off her stethoscope. 'You try tapping a finger that fast. Incredible, really.'

Billy looked down at his feet. 'I'm way bigger than a hummingbird.'

Dr Patel compressed her lips again. 'I'll just weigh you, too, eh?' She showed Billy the scales, made a note on his file, sat back. 'Is your mum right about you sleeping and eating well? You seem to be a good weight. No tummy troubles, no insomnia?'

'I'm fine,' said Billy.

'Good. That's what we want to hear.' She entered something on her screen. 'Are you the kind of bird who eats lots of variety?'

'Omnivore. Yes, I'm an omnivore.'

Dr Patel widened her eyes. 'Nearly nine, eh? Not sure I knew the word omnivore at nine. Knew quite a few dinosaur names, though. I was a bit obsessive, apparently. I discovered they were good insults. Spinosaurus was a favourite. Though I also made some up. Jerkodacytl. Drongoceratops.'

Amusement twitched at Billy's face.

The doctor rifled through a desk drawer to come up with several folded A4 leaflets. 'Look, I don't think there's anything terribly concerning here,' she said, warm yet brisk. 'Certainly nothing medical. But — given what you've all been through — I'll just let you know about these people.' She handed Iris one brochure: Springford Counselling. 'They're very good. It's a group practice; they have at least two counsellors who specialise in helping children who have been through trauma.'

The word itself acted like a burn. Iris's and Liam's glances at each other couldn't hold. They both stayed quiet. Billy's stare had returned to the far corner of the room.

'These other groups are good, too. Both still have government funding, believe it or not, so they only charge nominal fees. If you want to go private, though —'

'Nope,' said Liam. 'Can't afford it.'

'Right. If you did decide on anyone else, give me a quick call first. Make sure whoever you choose is registered — but you're sensible, yes? You know these things already.'

Iris swallowed the urge to confess all the times she'd screwed up; smiled weakly at Dr Patel. 'Billy, do you understand what we're talking about? Your dad and I want to take you to talk to someone about this whole — bird obsession.'

As if he finally caught the scent of conspiracy, Billy turned instantaneous verbal spit-fire. 'You have a *human* obsession.

Humans are the sick ones. *They're* the ones poisoning the water and wiping out all the animals and doing horrible things.'

'Billy,' Liam said, in admonishment.

'You all say *bird* like birds are crap, well they're not, there's a lot about them we could learn from. When *they* fly they don't poison up the air. They *grow* their own clothes; they recycle their *houses*. I've seen a starling take apart an old fallen nest to make a new one, *and* it used clumps of old fur dreadlocks too, from the cat next door, that was hilarious. Some birds make better jokes than us, I bet you, like Canary Woof. He knows he's copying a dog. He's cool.' Like a wind-up toy giving its last stutters, he said, volume fading, 'Canary Woof's my parakeet. Dad gave him to me.'

There was a lot of shifting in seats. Dr Patel was first to gather her composure. 'A parakeet. Is that like a budgie?'

'It *is* a budgie. Birds like him are from Australia. They say "budgie" there. New Zealand kinds, kakariki, look different from him, but I've decided budgie sounds wrong for him.'

Dr Patel nodded. 'I see what you mean.'

'Billy?' said Liam. 'Don't say crap.'

There was another awkward pause: like a pothole in the road — thud. Then the GP shuffled the papers she'd assembled. She said, 'I think you're right about the planet, Billy. But I don't think your mum and dad can be blamed for it, eh? I think they're just trying to help you. They love you, huh? Feed you, clothe you, give you pets?' There was a playful sparkle in her eyes as her gaze went to a large, red wall clock. She said, 'You seem to have a lot on your mind, Billy. I'm no expert, but I think sometimes bright children have a tough time, because they *think* about everything more.'

Dr Patel stood. 'It will all be fine,' she said to both parents. 'You care. That's 90 per cent of the work done. I promise.' Already her conviction loosened Iris from some fears seeded by her diagnosis-by-internet, where she'd found pathologies she'd been unable to even mention to Liam. (Delusions, dissociative identity disorder, species dysphoria . . .)

Outside, Liam slipped an arm around her waist. 'How y'doing?'

Billy trailed close behind, peering into a bakery: slowed by the sight of buns and pastries.

'Okay,' Iris answered: all she could say within Billy's earshot.

'Good. Better get back to work. See you round half-six.' He busied himself with bike lock, pannier, helmet. Billy sidled close, face tipped up, fringe falling from his eyes. He lifted his arms.

Insouciant, Liam hopped his bike into the road, arrowing off into his own life: able to separate himself from family concerns as easily as banging shut a door.

Iris watched as he sped round the corner, then she turned to Billy. His arms were drifting down. The look on his face was unreadable.

'Afternoon tea from the bakery?' she asked. He slipped one palm into hers. When she squeezed his hand, then put an arm across his shoulder, it was like touching water and seeing phosphorescence run along the ripples of impact. He smiled as if freshly shone. That was when it broke over her, clear and simple. His arms had been held up for his father.

When Billy asked something about going to the library, 'Can we check out a DVD?', she could only answer with a series of *mmm, maybes*. Her concentration ran another groove and the street's shops were bled of their separateness and definition.

She tried, but she couldn't remember the last time she'd seen Liam hug Billy. Really hug him. Cold air blasted across her shoulders as if a stone had broken a pane of glass between her and the world.

LIKE PROTECTING A MATCH FROM THE WIND

BILLY KNEW HIS MUM AND DAD didn't like his bird-thoughts. Mum said they were trying to find a good counsellor to talk to about them. They'd already *tried* two places, actually. One counsellor was like an angry android, who said Dad wasn't engaging with her and Dad said *Stuff this for a joke, what are we even on this fools' errand for?* And then he walked out. Fun-fun NOT. Then the next place they'd gone along to — his mum wouldn't even enter the building. She said it was too tall and it spooked her after the Christchurch earthquakes. It made Billy feel so weird that he'd almost flown in front of a bus. He got a heck of a fright, so Dad didn't need to yell but he did. And then his mum and dad did some hiss-talking while blocking the pavement and it was *so embarrassing* because a kid from school saw it. Then, even worse, his parents started kissing in public, and Billy really, really did not get that at all, because he'd *thought* they were fighting. He'd tried to fly down the street again, then, and went so far that Dad gave up on him and stormed back to work. When Mum finally caught Billy, she said his punishment that night was no Canary Woof in his room.

It felt way-down-deeply creepy to know that people wanted to change the way you did things.

He watched Canary Woof twitching and nibbling in his cage. If you asked Billy, Canary Woof was the only decent person in his entire family. The only thing he'd ever want to change about *him* was telepathy. If they could think to each other, Woof might teach him how to fly.

When Dad came home for dinner that night, not long after the day there had been all that wacko angry kissing in the street (adults were *nutballs*), he heard his mum say she'd found another family counselling place for them to go. The walls here were thin, and when Billy had his door open, it was like he was hiding in full view — he could hear nearly everything. It was sometimes a mega-pain (he'd rather hear his own thoughts) and sometimes super useful.

His mum said she'd visited the GP again, to ask for more counsellor names. She'd had to explain what had happened with the other two, even admitting that one wasn't suitable — because of the tall building. More weirdness. Then his dad said, 'You made it sound like *Billy's* phobia?'

Long pause.

'So why didn't she recommend this group before?'

'I think she felt that it was more necessary now. Maybe.'

'So what sort of counsellor?'

Then they said stuff Billy didn't understand, about *sigh-kiterry* whatever and *don't medicalise this* and *just nervous tics* and *worst-case scenario*. Their voices were two trains coming closer, about to roar right over you. What he did understand was that his mum was on the yes-let's-go side, and his dad was on the let's-not.

Mum said, 'No. It's not just that kind of thing. They offer services for all kinds of issues. Post-adoption, divorce, bereavement.'

The talking stopped. For a minute Billy thought, *What? Divorce? Please don't let it be divorce. Then — wait, I'm adopted? Then — oh, no, I know I'm not. I've seen the birth photos, which I super-much wish I hadn't. Maybe we're going because Jason was semi-adopted?*

His parents' silence grew. Something sharp and unbending was happening underneath.

'I spoke to a receptionist, then one of the medical staff on the phone. It sounds really open-minded.'

'Whatever happens, I'm telling you now, I'm not putting him on drugs.'

Billy wanted to spew. *Drugs?*

'I've already *explained* that, Liam. You're not listening. No one is saying we'll have to. This is about how screwed up we've become as a couple and a family since Jase died. Billy's not himself. He needs more from you. You're so — aloof. You've pulled back from him. It's like — sometimes it's like you've walked away.'

Billy's heart was a trap that had just set something free. There was a lifting, a feeling of getting lighter. But his dad said, 'Total bullshit. You're blaming me, but take a look at your own attitude.'

Billy held his breath.

'*Listen*, Liam. Can't you *hear* what I mean?'

Billy took Canary Woof from his cage and cradled him in his hands like protecting a match from the wind. He left his room and tried to sneak through the living-room to get to the tree house. Mum was crying. She dropped the laundry basket, Dad tried to grab her, but she shoved a chair between them.

It was all Billy's fault. He belted out to the tree hut, scrambling up awkwardly, Canary Woof still held in one hand. 'It's okay,' he whispered. 'We're climbing the tree. You like the tree.' Missing Jason came on in a freak gale. He wanted him here, so they could shinny up and keep look-out together. They'd harvest the macrocarpa cones that fell on the hut floor and ping them at the window, to break up the fight. Or Jase could take him on a bike ride to the park. Without him, and without friends here yet, Billy always had to go with an adult. It sucked.

Through the doors he'd left flung open onto the yard, he could hear his dad's voice raised even higher. 'Iris! Storming off won't help!'

'Hypocrite!' yelled Iris.

There was another swollen silence from the house then, and Billy sat trembling, breath racing, skin sparking, the warm ball of Canary Woof in his palm. He felt the bird's small twitches as its head peered side to side. Mum came back to the living-room — Billy saw straight in, from where he crouched at the tree hut window. She had handbag, car keys, a small day-pack.

'Where are you going?' shouted Dad.

'I can't put up with your withdrawal any more,' she yelled back. 'I need a break!'

Dad bellowed at her, 'Walking out won't resolve anything.'

Billy pointed Canary Woof at the house, as if he was a remote. '*Pi-kew-pi-kew*,' he whispered. 'Rewind. Say that again about Billy needs more.' But the Mum and Dad movie kept playing.

'Liam, I can't think straight when you go at me like that. I just need space to think. I want to be alone.'

Mum was leaving Billy, too? The hot sparks along his skin got worse; the ache underneath also. He pressed Canary Woof's forehead gently to his. He tried to let his own skull open like curtains that could let light in. Then came the strangest thing. Like drifting awake in a warm bed, he knew that Jase was nearby. Hovering, kind, patiently waiting: Jase was *there*.

It was as if, after all the trying and wanting, a lock had finally come unstuck. '*He's here*,' Billy whispered. Then: the next strange thing. Canary Woof thought his thoughts to him. Billy set the bird onto the hut floor, where he hopped and fluttered before carolling rapid, piping song. Then came a great change: a thickening and a surging along Billy's chest bones, a current along the bare skin of his legs, a tickling in his nose that became a soaring, cloudy lightness in his head.

Billy clambered out the hut window and slid along one of the tree's thick branches. Somewhere deep in his mind he heard the phrase: '*and he felt his heart leap*'. Up, out, launched: all in a moment of hope, Billy flew.

PART
TWO

ROUND-WAY-WRONG

THEY WERE LUCKY. BLOODY LUCKY. It wasn't concussion. There were no broken bones. Whoever had built the tree house had some common sense and hadn't placed it as high as they might have. Billy had only a sprained ankle, a hen's-egg-sized, peacock-coloured lump on his forehead, and stitches in his thigh, which he'd slashed on a twig. (Billy thought luckiest of all was that Canary Woof had stayed in the tree hut, the whole time they were fussing over Billy. So when he insisted — okay, screamed — that Liam run back and check before they went to the doctor, sure enough, he scooped him up and put him in his cage. The bird was too tame, it seemed, to want to go far. 'Poor wee blighter,' Liam said, 'lost his opportunity.' Iris snapped at Liam. 'Perhaps he's *happy* with Billy, Liam.')

Then it was off to the Urgent Doctor, lickety-split. And what do you know? 'Small world,' Iris said.

'Small town, anyway,' their own GP answered, her cheeks sucked in, as if irony were a pastille. Liam's face said he'd like to pull up the floorboards and hide under them. Iris agreed, it was disastrous: they'd become a problem family. She apologised. But Dr Patel gave a dancer's wave with her elegant hand. 'It can go like this, sometimes. When children are under five, I have mothers in and out nearly every week some winters, then I don't see them for months. Even years.' Gracious of her, Iris thought, not to point out Billy was hardly a toddler.

Maybe it was yet more luck that Dr Patel was on duty. They didn't have to say anything more than, 'Billy tried to fly.' And she just got on with it. She packed them off for X-rays; but Billy was sent home with just a Tubigrip bandage round his ankle, and instructions to avoid vigorous sports for a few weeks. Dr Patel's parting words, before they left for the X-rays, were, 'And good luck with the CMHT.'

'Is that like an X-ray?' asked Billy.

'No. It's an abbreviation,' said Iris.

'What for?'

'Crackpots Must Have Therapy,' muttered Liam.

'*Liam.*' Iris snatched the car keys from him. 'Go to your favourite bloody place. Do some after-hours work. You're not needed here.'

That turned him quiet.

Steve phoned the next morning when Liam was running late, but Iris said Liam didn't want to talk: he was feeling very subdued.

Really, everyone was *subdued* after Billy's fall.

Billy looked it up in *Word Splurge: The World's Biggest Ever Illustrated Dictionary*, which his Aunt Carrie had sent to him, along with a collection of Horrible Science books. *Subdued* seemed a good possible spelling word. It sounded like the opposite of overdue: so he thought it meant 'not ready to go back'. That would fit with why he was allowed two days off school and why neither Liam nor Iris went to work, either. He didn't hear Mum mention taking a break away from Dad again, phew-times-a-billion. But when he found *subdued* in the dictionary he figured it was like the quiet before the storm, coming after the storm. Which seemed about right for their round-way-wrong family.

That's what he called them all, when they finally met the new counsellors in a giant wooden villa that Iris agreed wasn't too tall. She also tried to cheer up Billy's dad by saying, 'It's on public health, Liam, you'll be glad the assessment's not costing.' But he seemed to think she was picking a fight. 'Do we have to argue *right* before we go inside?' His mum looked like she wanted to cry again, and Billy's stomach cramped. He wished he could shove the bad feelings right out — like — huh. Like an egg, but an egg that he wouldn't ever help hatch — because if it did, the bird would be a nightmare.

'Do you know why you're here, Billy?' asked the plump nurse who did most of the talking at first. Maybe the doctor was shy? She had a shy smile, with a tooth that peeped out over her bottom lip. Like an egg tooth.

'Because we're a round-way-wrong family.'

'Wrong way round,' corrected Liam.

'Round-way-wrong is what a wrong-way-round family *would* call itself,' double-corrected Billy. Liam gave his puff-cheeked sigh.

'We're interested in everyone's point of view,' the nurse said to Liam. She had two voices: one for Billy, one for his parents. Like the way some birds use one eye for near, one eye for far. Interesting.

'How are you a round-way-wrong family?' asked the doctor. She got it right. That was interesting, too. And she wasn't that frightening at all — though Billy knew that his dad in particular was scared that she'd give him drugs. With a needle, *supposably*, otherwise he couldn't think why his dad'd be so freaked out, given he always took pills for headaches. Or said, when Billy couldn't sleep, that he wished there was something *safe* they could dope him with.

Iris dug her nails into her arm, which always made Billy wish he knew how to fix things. 'Do you think we're round-way-wrong because you're a bird in a human family?' she said.

'No. Because we're a family where a boy would *want* to be a bird.'

Everybody swapped glances. He knew by now that if he said *that* out loud, Liam would say, 'You notice too much, Billy. Can't you be a normal, dreamy kid?' He must be a wonky, wide-awake kid: otherwise they wouldn't be here.

The doctor tilted her head. The more he looked at her, the more she seemed like Canary Woof. He was glad those other counselling places hadn't worked out. She had that tooth, a sharp little chin, dark shining eyes, a thin and pointed nose, a long blonde ponytail, and do you know, she truly wore feather earrings. Okay, not canary yellow: dark blue. But still. They spun and drifted when she turned her head.

The nurse — he was allowed to call her Trisha — was the opposite of the doctor. She reminded him of a wholemeal scone. The doctor, who they said to call Jenna, had nice appley sorts of breasts: pretty, and it was okay to notice them, the way you would her ponytail, or her earrings. The nurse's breasts, though, were huge. It was hard not to look, but it felt like you were staring, even when you weren't. Not the sort of thing you *said*; Billy wasn't completely bonkers! Though if Jase was here, and Billy said, 'That nurse's breasts make me feel weird,' he'd understand. There were some music videos like that, and Jason knew when Billy wanted them turned off.

His mum said his name.

'Sorry?'

'Why wouldn't you want to be a boy in your family?'

His fingers throbbed, his shoulders tingled, and he tried and tried not to, not *here*, but he couldn't help it. He swallowed a cluck, and gave a little wing-shake, to shimmy off nervousness. 'Nothing feels right. Not the way it used to.'

His mum bowed her head and his dad crossed his legs very fast and Billy knew he'd said a terrible thing. He fidgeted, but when he tried to stand, his ankle hurt, and he remembered he was supposed to take it easy. He jiggled the other knee, flapped his elbows. He tried his thinking trick: the one that often helped him sleep. He listed the coolest things about birds he could think of — racing to remember as many as possible before anyone asked him another question. It wasn't an easy trick to get right: sometimes, he could build himself into another panic about not remembering enough.

Billy calming down

1. The great grey owl has ears of different sizes — asymmetrical is the word — a.s.y.m.m.e.t.r.i.c.a.l. Its ears are so good it can hear rodents in their burrows under the snow *in the dark*! That's how scientists know it's the owls' *hearing* that's so amazing, not their eyesight.

2. A book Billy found said there is a bird called the Lord God Bird. Really!! It's a kind of woodpecker. Its other name is the ivorybill. Boring, boring. What's something else interesting?

3. There's a kind of kestrel that can find the voles it likes to eat by seeing UV light reflecting off the vole's pee! Truly!

4. Most birds have a thing called a brood patch, skin where they lose feathers before they have to start keeping their eggs warm. They use it to control the temperature of their eggs. It's their very own egg-lectric blanket!!!

5. Birds used to be dinosaurs. Yes, way!!!

6. Hummingbirds can fly backwards.

Billy's heart slowed its frantic paddling.

The doctor, Jenna, started talking to his parents about what they might need from the 'health team'. She said it would be a good thing if Billy had some sessions alone. Later they would bring the family together, and talk to Liam and Iris separately: if need be. Liam was the colour of a concrete wall. Billy wondered if he wanted to be sick. But he nodded so maybe he'd done a quick look around, couldn't see any needles, and thought it all sounded less terrible than he'd expected? The doctor and nurse just seemed pretty much like ordinary people: the sort you'd see hurrying along the street with their shopping, stopping to say hello to friends. His mind drifted off to an argument he and Jase had once, about a girl at school, and what Jase called her *junkie folks*. Jase had been pretty nasty . . .

'You look worried,' the nurse said to Billy. 'Is something bothering you?'

'Um, are there going to be any needles and drugs?'

Liam gave the *don't-say-any-more!* look. Iris started twisting her watch-strap.

The doctor's peeping tooth tucked away; her smile vanished. 'Sometimes children who see us do get given medicine, Billy, if they're behaving dangerously. Hurting themselves or other kids, say, or maybe if they're so scared they can't even leave their houses. But usually they take medicine just the way you would for a fever: they drink it or swallow it.'

There was a stretch of quiet, during which Billy watched sunlight paint a white line on the wall as it came through a gap in the Venetian blinds. It looked like the swinging perch in a cage. Billy pictured Canary Woof and he felt brief warmth in his stomach.

Dr Jenna looked at Billy. 'What do you think about jumping out of the tree house? Do you think that was behaving dangerously?'

Oh. So Mum and Dad or maybe Dr Patel had already told her about that. Maybe on the phone?

'Mmm. Yeah. A bit.' He was embarrassed. 'But I'm never going to do that again.' He squirmed. 'I worked out I can't fly just like *that*, of *course*. I did a stupid thing but I'm not *actually* stupid.'

His dad coughed and his mum looked teary-eyed again, *great*. The nurse pushed tissues closer to the table edge. Seemed like whenever they went to a doctor his mum needed tissues. He'd always thought doctors kept them for people with colds, but maybe not. He tried to cheer her up. 'I mean I don't *actually* have wings. I don't even have real feathers. Not even those little filoplumes. Have you heard of filoplumes?'

His mum sniffled.

'They look like little grasshead thingies. I know it wasn't exactly smart. You might say it was bird-brained, only it's not the kind of mistake a bird would make. Unless it was flightless. And anyway, I think that's rude to birds.'

Liam pinkened. 'Always had the gift of the gab.'

The nurse, Trisha, smiled: eyes turning into little raisins. 'It's wonderful. Talkative is great. It's a real treat for us.' Billy was baffled. She bobbed her head at him. 'I hope there's nothing else that makes you worried about coming here. This is meant to be your time. When you visit us, we're going to just hang out in the activity room for a while. You can use anything you want in there, and we'll talk when you feel like it. It's not a test; you can't get answers wrong. Nobody here is going to get angry with you if you don't want to say much.'

He felt his mum's hand on his knee. 'Does that sound all right?' she asked.

He wondered if he should claim to be too old for it: but it depended, didn't it? On what was in there. Table tennis, iPads or pinball? 'I can have a look.'

'Sure. We can do that now, but we'll start regular sessions properly, say . . .' the nurse flicked through a diary that had pages crinkled and busy with writing, crammed with extra pinned-in memos, stickers, bookmark, pressed flowers '. . . on a Thursday after school. Four-thirty. Does that fit in with everyone?'

Iris and Liam conferred, agreed. It was okay for a first meeting. At least nobody yelled at him, and Mum didn't *actually* cry, though Dad did still seem locked up in that way he had.

Trisha and Dr Jenna said there wasn't time to use the activity room properly, but it might be good to look at it. Some of it was for total babies: sand trays, water trays, dolls, blocks. He was pretty disappointed there wasn't a computer games section or anything. But there was a train set, Lego, modelling clay, paints, and shelves of awesome figurines: colourful models of just about anything you could imagine. Pirates, knights, dinosaurs, princesses, warriors, farmers, milkmaids, mothers, fathers, children, Vikings and animals: all kinds of animals. Including owls, flamingos, tui, swans, woodpeckers, peacocks, kiwi, bantams, pelicans, and sparrows. So he nodded when Trisha said, plenty to do in here, then, on Thursday?

'Yup. See you Thursday.' He looked up at the ceiling. 'The tenth.'

Dr Jenna grinned; showing all the other now-not-shy teeth. 'A mature and organised young man,' she said, which meant that when they'd all said *nice* to meet you, thank you, goodbye, and they were outside, he reached for a hand from both parents. 'They don't think I'm a total weirdo.'

His mum accepted and squeezed his hand. A few beats later, his dad said, 'Not so far, kiddo.' Then he zipped up his jacket, searched for his wallet and keys. 'Do you have any cash, Iris?'

Billy fanned the fingers and thumb of his empty hand, trying to cast a swan's shadow on the footpath. *Flightpath*, he thought, but his hand couldn't get it right.

At first Iris was disconcerted that Billy was to have initial sessions without her, and that the nurse and doctor would report back with strategies, ideas and, surely, revelations. These she half-feared, as if Billy might enter some dark inner coal-cellar, coming up to report horrors, deep psychic affronts inflicted unknowingly. She was so used to accompanying him to dentist, GP, barber, shoe-shop, shepherding him through all small trials and initiations, that she couldn't stop questioning him when he finished his early sessions.

'Was it good?'

'Yep.'

'Did you all talk much?'

'A bit.'

'What else did you do?'

'Nothing much.'

'Draw? Play with toys?'

'A bit, yeah.'

It was as if so-called talk sessions cured him of talk! Yet after the couple's own first joint session, Iris realised how hard it was to summarise the territory covered.

For a start, she took several, hectic beats to understand what the doctor was really saying when she heard *borderline Asperger's, itself very hard to diagnose in certain, sensitive children of high intelligence. And of course sometimes indications fade with maturity,* and then *dissociative disorder, actively disputed, we're cautioned of course not to confuse it with normal childhood imagination* . . . It appeared the consultant meant that Billy's early sessions had been partly framed to rule out such conditions.

'So, he's *not* borderline Asperger's?'

'No, no.'

'And he doesn't have dissociative disorder?'

'As I said, it's a very unreliable conclusion at the best of times, but no.'

A thin, vertical line between the doctor's eyes deepened when she used a diagnostic vocabulary. She seemed to be immensely cautious: as if she felt she had to overtly tick off all possibilities for them. Yet it still left Iris with a chilled sense that Billy's behaviour sat outside normal boundaries. It seemed to mean that although he didn't fall into any of the recognised, accepted categories of disorder or syndrome, there was still something they couldn't put their fingers on.

The doctor recognised Iris's bewilderment: 'Billy's an absolutely gorgeous little boy. Some of this uncertainty, you know, is the very nature of assessing children. They're mercurial, changeable, beautifully mysterious, perpetually unusual creatures. They're . . .'

'Forces of nature!' Trisha said. 'It's like, like putting a magnifying glass over a snowflake, sometimes. The very act of examining it can melt its shape.' She often closed her eyes as she talked: as if her own words sent out intense brightness. 'That's why I love working with children. There's always going to be that touch of mystery.'

Jenna frowned, waiting for Trisha to finish. It was a tiny flash of friction, perhaps, this sense that the doctor had to let the nurse 'run' for a bit.

'Anyway. We say all this to reassure you, honestly. Trisha and I both think that we're dealing with a bright, sensitive boy who's been through several stresses, and who's using his bird imitations to self-sooth. A private language. It's a retreat in a way, yes; but it has an internal logic.'

Trisha nodded, looking down at her clipboard of extensive handwritten notes: Iris found it somehow comforting that she wasn't skimming her fingers over an iPad, a laptop.

'Logic?' said Liam, meaning, *prove it.*

A KINDA TROPICAL,
JEWELLED HEAVEN-BIRD

BILLY THOUGHT BACK to his first private session. The consultant and the nurse were both there when he went in to the activity room.

'I'll be here to get you started,' said Jenna. 'Trisha will probably take over later. Just have a look around,' she said. 'See if anything interests you.'

Disdainful, Billy trailed his fingers in the sand tray. It was for little kids, but part of him wanted to remember what it felt like. The dry spill over his fingertips stirred a memory of kindergarten, Matchbox cars, making hills and tunnels and someone pouring in water to make a river but it all turned to gloop: sand soup, with floating cars. He told Trisha and Jenna about how he hadn't liked the kid who ruined the layout he and two other boys had been building. Now he tried pouring water in from the water tray with a small plastic teapot. The sand swallowed it up. He poured some more. It made a kind of soft, collapsing clay. Clay. That pinkish-brownish clay that pattered onto the top of Jason's coffin. *We commit his body to the ground; earth to earth, ashes to ashes, dust to dust.* He rammed at the sand to drive the words out of his head. The sludge in his palms started to form a shape. That calmed him down. He patted and moulded it, to make a sand igloo. It was a little hard to see what it was: maybe it needed a person in it, so that you could tell it was a building.

He looked around for the collection of figurines, and found a miniature boy. He put the boy in the sand house. He patted the sand over the figure: buried it. He found a toy double-decker bus. The bus drove over the mound. A small, green parrot figurine hopped over to the mound, then flew away in a whistling arc, to be replaced by another boy figurine. Gradually, all the bird figurines flew down, gathered in an irregular circle, and watched as the boy figurine made little downward jerks of its body. *I'm late*, it said. *Too late.*

As the first bird curved back into the air on a smooth parabola, 'Too late?' asked Trisha. Billy had almost forgotten she was there. He wished she hadn't interrupted; it was good to watch his hands float out there with the figures, very interesting to be here and not at the same time. But embarrassing, now, to find himself acting like such a baby in front of other people. He sighed, blinked, brushed off his hands, stood up.

'What else?' He fingered a rack of costumes, dress-ups: all too small for him. There was Lego; there were baby dolls; other construction blocks. After being sort-of-caught at the sand-box game, he felt awkward about most of the toys. There was the tiny village and zoo of other figurines: depleted of birds by his sand-theatre, but it had police, firemen, ambulance workers, doctors, elephants, princesses, clowns, seals, dogs, cats, fish: the colours as strong as a new box of paints. They made him want to *do* something. Then

he saw there were some white cardboard folding shapes —
houses, buses, cut-out dolls; blank cardboard masks, blank
sheets of paper and card; there were art supplies: Sellotape,
craft scissors, paints, pencils, crayons.

'Can I use these?'

'Yes, of course. What would you like to make?'

He shrugged, but pointed to the blank half-face masks,
the pens and oil paint. Trisha checked her watch. 'Go ahead.'
She brought out another box, full of sequins, stickers,
ribbons, lace, feathers, Styrofoam balls, more card, sheets
of shiny construction paper, glue and glitter.

'Wow,' Billy whispered. He sifted through the box,
gloating over the feel of beads and coins.

It was as if the mask gathered the materials and colours
to itself. He shaped a beak from card that he covered in
gold foil, then used masking tape to attach it to the empty
human-faced shape. He wanted to conceal the join quickly:
found oil paint that would work on both surfaces, and
in swift strokes of gold and green blurred beak to skull.
Pounamu green glitter; forest green sequins; a flash of gold
or scarlet here and there like the beech leaves that fall to the
ground in the bush; dyed green feathers.

'What a beautiful creature,' said Dr Jenna.

'Gorgeous colours,' agreed Trisha. 'Can you tell us
about it?'

'Mmmm. It's a kinda tropical, jewelled heaven-bird.' He
studied the mask at arm's length; worked out the best way
to add head-feathers was to make tiny slits in the top with
the craft scissors, insert the feather's pale spine through,
then tape it securely on the underside.

'A heaven-bird. That makes me very curious. What's a
heaven-bird?'

Billy tilted the mask to and fro, watching light hopscotch across the glitter, sequins, foil. 'It can leave the stratosphere, fly up to where we can't ever see. It knows everything we can't. A heaven-bird is pretty much whatever you want it to be, really.'

The doctor's tooth perched on the edge of her smile, enjoying the story. 'What questions would you ask, if you were a heaven-bird?'

Billy chewed at some solidified glue stuck to his thumb, gave a small, sour spit. Then he stroked one of the feathers. The grooming helped something inside him lift its head. 'Does Jason forgive me?' The women sat still. He tensed, like waiting for a slap, and Billy felt his face go hot and sad, so he slipped the thin elastic band of the mask around the back of his head, and nestled the mask in position. This place was weird. It made him say things he wanted to snatch back and hide.

The doctor was writing something down, in a sideways slope; she was left-handed, but curled her hand around so that it looked as if she was cradling the pen.

'Forgives you?' That was Trisha, reminding him to Target the Task, ha *ha*. He thought for a while, maybe for too long, because Dr Jenna held out a palm, with small brown beads clustered in it. She made puckery noises just the way he did when offering Canary Woof birdseed. He play-pecked, then sat back, as if the seeds were tasteless. Dr Jenna let the beads tumble into their small container. Then she whistled. He whistled a two-note reply, and they all sat, as if watching the circles the notes left on the air.

'No. *First* I would say sorry. And *then* I would ask if he forgives me, or is he still really angry? And is that why Dad's angry, too?'

Dr Jenna dabbed a finger along one of the mask's head-feathers, and Billy felt a happy shiver even though it wasn't his feather. 'Why would a lovely, heaven-bird-boy like Billy Galbraith have to apologise?'

Wearing the mask made his body feel different. He felt stringy but strong, downy and light, airy but brave. He pukekoed around the room in high, stretching steps. He bent his elbows so his arms made stubby wings: but that was wrong. Too jokey, too cartoony. He flag-fluttered his fingers as his arms stretched out; he beat on the air for a while, spinning in place. Yet the sorry in his stomach sat in a frozen lump made of tears and cold breath. His wings folded around his body, and he fell back into his chair. The mask was knocked up as he slumped with his chin towards his chest. He pushed it up to sit like a cap on his head. He crossed his arms tight, holding each side of his chair with the opposite hand.

'You don't look so happy now you're not the heaven-bird. You look as if you're tying yourself to that chair there, Billy.'

He nodded.

From one of the craft-storage baskets, Trisha brought out some index cards, with a felt pen. 'It seems to me there are lots of things a boy could be feeling after someone he loves dies. Sometimes it's hard to give names to feelings, but we could try. We could try to name at least five main feelings kids might have in general, and draw pictures of them here. Would you like to be in charge?'

Babyish idea. Billy shook his head.

'I'll start, then. I think kids can probably be happy — which I'll draw like this.' She drew a simple, round, smiley face, and gave it a few spikes of short hair. 'Or they can be—'

Billy gave an elderly sigh. 'I'm not some little five-year-old. And it wasn't just *someone* who died. It was *Jason.*' The very sound of that sentence set off fury. He slammed his hand down on the table. Once, twice, again. He picked up the craft scissors, and stabbed slits in a piece of card. 'Why *(stab)*, why *(stab)*, why *(stab, stab)*? Why can't we talk about the real him? Every time I try, something stops it. People even get up and walk away. Or they *talk* away from it. Even you!' He grabbed the index cards from Trisha, snatched the pen. He started scribbling circles. 'Of course I'm *angry*,' he wrote *angry* underneath the jagged-toothed face, 'and *sad* and *lonely* and *scared*.' He scrawled a face and a word for each one, hunkered down and stared at them. 'That's only four. What else am I? Well, I'm not super-happy. Sometimes I'm, what, bored. Sometimes I'm *bored* because there's no Jason. To talk to, to do stuff with. That's five feelings about Jason.' He flung up his arms. 'That's me talking about my feelings for Jason.' He dropped the pen on top of the cards.

He felt awful for coming out with all that. Dr Jenna wrote something down. Her left hand curled to the right around the pen, so it seemed to race away from the notes about him. He'd had so much to say, but now, in the silence, he remembered the times *he* hadn't wanted to talk about Jase either: or not in the way other people did.

Once the doctor's pen had stopped moving, Trisha straightened herself up in her chair. 'I don't think you're stupid, Billy. But sometimes, with kids who've been through tough times, we have to take things slowly. That's why I thought I'd use the cards. It's not because I think you're a baby, or unintelligent. Quite the reverse. I don't think I've ever met such an articulate nearly-nine-year-old.' She picked up the cards Billy had drawn on, tapping them into a tidy pile. 'We just try different things to see if they suit different people, you know?' She cleared her throat. 'If I'm listening to you properly, Billy, you say you feel all these things about Jason,' she flapped the cards, 'but you're also feeling guilty. That's a pretty complicated feeling. I'd find it hard to draw.' She started to doodle a spiral. He wasn't sure if it related to what she'd said. 'Do you think you're to blame for something?'

He pulled the mask down over his face again. He could only see a slice of the room through the eye-holes, and his eyelashes brushed uncomfortably against the inside of the mask. Trisha waited. Actually, Billy sort of liked the way she could leave long silences. It made it seem there was plenty of time in this room. It was the opposite of the way he usually felt about time. Mum and Dad so often rushed things: hustled him off to school, chores, homework, or Dad barked him off to a bath. Through a small top window, he could hear the whirr of a bus slowing down and a dusky, cooled song from a blackbird, as if it was giving news that night was coming. Somehow, not seeing everything properly helped him to hear clearly.

You'd think that seeing only a slice of the world would make him panicky; instead, it was reassuring. It was like the way his scarlet helmet with the yellow flames made him feel flash on a skateboard. The mask meant words could come out with armour on. Must be, because now that he was finally asked the worst question, the story appeared, crumb by crumb.

'I was supposed to meet Jason after school,' Billy said. 'I did wait for him, outside the gates. And he did come to pick me up, on his bike.' He looked at Trisha and Jenna.

He half-thought they would guess; frowns turning their mouths thin. But they waited, calm and expectant. He itched, because he knew that he hadn't told the whole truth and nothing but the truth so help me God if there is a God which is very hard to tell, because It just won't talk to us, will It?

'There was a rule. We were supposed to walk to Jason's game together, because Mum couldn't pick me up.' He started tugging at a corner of blank paper on the table. 'So I kind of did what I was supposed to.'

'Kind of?'

'Well, but then Jason saw Thalia.'

'I haven't heard anyone mention a Thalia. Who's she?'

'Some girl he had a crush on. They texted each other. They'd pretty much started to be boyfriend and girlfriend. Sometimes she walked part-way home with us.'

'Were you annoyed by that?'

'Yes,' he sighed.

He had crumpled up the piece of paper and tried to smooth it out. It was stupid that it bothered him, but he wanted to take the curl right out of that page again. Back to the way it was.

'Jase would only want to listen to her, not to me. But I had stuff to say. They held hands and I even saw him kiss her on the cheek once. Sick-making.' His mouth pulled downwards. Bodies are weird, he thought.

'What happened then? Do you want to tell us?'

'Jason started being a dork on his bike on the way to basketball. He was jumping over potholes, bunny-hopping on and off the footpath, even going on the wrong side of the road, skidding round and turning back. Thalia was telling him to stop, and laughing. I got really mad. It was like, that doesn't mean *stop*. That means "it's funny and I like it". As in, *keep going*. They were both being dumb-arse. All girlfriendy and boyfriendy and they were only *twelve*. So I ran ahead to the practice on my own.'

'And the accident happened after you left?'

His bottom lip twitched, and the word came out too high. 'Yup.'

'Do you think it was your fault, because you didn't stay?'

'Yup.' Then it was like what his dad called a southerly buster. It felt so sudden, but of course, when he thought about it later, it wasn't. It had been coming for months. Moving towards him like *The Wizard of Oz* twister, gathering up junk, litter, dust, schools, birds, bikes, children and cars and whirling it all into a snarl of words and tears; a wet, salty, snotty jumble.

'I might have said, "This is the bad corner, you have to wait." Or if I'd stayed and said, "Stop being a jerk, you're not supposed to do that," he might have listened. Or anyway if I'd stayed with him I might have been able to talk to him while he was lying in the road. Held his hand and kept him here. Like held him onto the earth. Maybe the Jason part of him would have stayed down here. But I've never ever said.' He vaguely heard one of them say, *it was not your fault*, but he was busy gulping and stuttering another mess of words. 'I went back there on my own one day. I was going home with a friend, when Mum wasn't very well. She had to stay in bed, from crying.'

Billy had to swallow. Trisha handed him some water, but he shook his head. The doctor and the nurse waited, then Jenna said, 'It must have been hard to see your mum so upset.'

Billy sucked at his bottom lip. 'It's kind of weird. I used

to think sometimes she liked Jason more than my dad did. Even though he was from my dad's side.'

Billy shrugged, changed his mind about the water. He took a sip, but it tasted soapy, so he gave it back.

'You were talking about going back to that street corner, Billy?'

'Yeah. It looked like I was in a dream. But I was just waiting and feeling wrong, and a bird came along. A bird.' He stared at them to see if they understood. 'A bird could still be where Jason wasn't.'

Then Dr Jenna's hand was on his back, rubbing and patting and he hiccupped, which made him give a weird little laugh. 'It's like you're burping a baby,' he said, and then, 'I'm cry-laughing, does that mean I'm mental?'

'No, not at all,' Trisha said, 'and I don't much like calling anybody mental, anyway. I think it probably means you're feeling a hundred different things at once.'

There was more snuffling and trying to breathe normally. It took a long time for that to happen. Maybe too long, because when his head felt a bit clear again, the doctor said, 'You're pretty worn out, Billy. I think that's enough for today. We'll see you again soon, though. Talk some more about this?' Which he didn't answer because he just wanted to find Mum and he also just wanted to lie down right there, and working out how to do both made him even tireder. He put an arm over his eyes, to make his own small night.

TRANSLATION 1

A tree hangs out its plum-coloured signs.
Birdsong inside a boy's skin.
Light writes the earth's Esperanto.

SWITCH-FLIP

BILLY WANTED IT TO BE like the story where someone says 'Open Sesame': his crying outburst to Trisha and Jenna should have been the thing that rolled the stone away from the cave. Now that he'd said it all, couldn't Mum and Dad get better, too?

He described the stone and the cave idea to Dr Jenna, when he was frustrated that they all had to keep visiting, and things seemed stuck. She said she supposed the trouble was, when that stone was rolled away, you still had to go inside the cave. *Phhffft*, Billy sighed, but all he could do was wait, while the adults talked it out.

On the first family session after he made the bird mask, Trisha and Jenna encouraged him to tell his parents about the day Jason died. When he did, even Mum and Dad said, 'It wasn't your fault, Billy.' Jenna said, 'Did your cousin always listen to you?'

'Nahp.'

'So if you *had* said stop, would he have stopped showing off to Thalia?'

He thought for a while. 'Most likely he'd have called me dog's breath or numbnuts and carried on.'

The doctor tucked her peeping tooth inside her mouth, as if a smile had escaped accidentally. His mum gave a strangled noise, but his dad just rubbed the knees of his jeans, like he was itchy.

'You know, Jason was supposed to be sticking with you, too. Maybe another way of looking at it is that he should have followed you once he saw you weren't hanging around. But nobody blames *him* for what happened, do they? He was a child and it was a mistake. What's happened is terrible, but, Billy, nobody was to blame.'

No blame, Billy. No blame. He let the words soak in, waiting to see if they felt true, but then, *then*, Iris crumpled, saying, 'I still can't help thinking if only I'd gone to get them that day—'

Liam cut her off. 'We've been over this, Iris. You were at your hospital check.'

Billy wondered if this was just what dads were meant to be like. Then he wondered if he'd be like that when he was a man. Did he have to be? What if you didn't want to be like your mum or your dad? Was there some third person he could be? Where'd he heard that before? Oh, that's right. Miss Hopper said stories could be told by the third person. Could life be lived by the third person, too?

'And what was Jason doing for Thalia?' Dr Jenna asked. 'Trying to cheer her up, you said: trying to make her laugh. What a lovely kid. What a warm, caring boy he still was, despite everything he'd been through. You must have been so proud of what a good job you'd been doing with him.'

Iris's eyes filled silvery-green. It was the look of all the times she'd hovered around the classroom too long, or that time she came to pick him up for the dentist when there was no appointment, the *I'm-so-lucky-I've-still-got-you* look. It made the whole world seem on the point of falling over the edge of itself into space. Billy tried to hold it back, but there it was: the skittering, downy sensation that spilled out of his head and spread. 'Kaaa! Kaaaa!' He whirled up from his chair, battered around the room, spun on the balls of his feet. Liam said, 'Christ, here we go again.' And Iris said, 'But *Billy*, it's all been getting so much better!'

Dr Jenna asked, 'Billy, you want to fly away now?'

'Kaaa!'

'Billy!' his father remonstrated. But Dr Jenna dropped her clipboard and pen, grinning.

'What a gorgeous bird! How high he can go!' She sprung onto her tiptoes, unwinding a scarf from around her throat. She held it at two corners, let it billow out behind her, a blue sail, as she skimmed and twirled around the room. She cried out, 'I'm playing, too, Billy! Fly, with me!'

Liam slumped down, his hand covering his eyes. 'Jesus *spare* me.'

Iris watched Billy, her hands so tightly clenched they looked sewn together.

Billy zoomed and leapt; jumped onto a chair, arced and dove down. 'What sort of bird is your mother, Heaven-bird?' Dr Jenna called. Billy stilled. He perched on a chair, hid his head under a wing, and peeped a high, weeping note. 'What sort of bird is your father?' Billy stalked around, the bully seagull in a pack, rubbery neck craning and bending again as he ululated at everyone he eyeballed, before he strutted off to stand in a corner, his head preternaturally swivelled around so that he glared one-eyed at whoever dared move.

After a few beats, Dr Jenna said, 'Okay,' let her scarf fill with air, then drift down. She knotted it back around her throat and returned to her chair. Billy's seagull pose ebbed, too, and he stood staring midair. 'Can you come and sit down again?' Dr Jenna asked him. He shuffled back.

Liam jiggled one foot so the floor started to shake. Iris pinned a hand to his knee.

'Can you tell us what the Heaven-bird would want to say, Billy, if it could talk?'

He exhaled. 'This has turned stupid.'

Liam tilted his metal-framed chair backwards, then promptly let it fall forward again. 'He *flick*-flacks like this,' he said. 'How the hell can you tell what's going on in his head? And how exactly is prancing around like a circus act going to help?'

Dr Jenna concentrated on Billy. 'Your mum and dad have agreed to listen to you today, Billy.' Ignoring Liam's exasperated whistle, she said, 'Is there something you want to say to them?'

'Well. Yeah.' Billy yanked at his sleeve-cuffs. 'Is it always going to be like — is it always going to be, *and they all lived saddestly ever after?*'

His parents looked at the floor.

'And I know *saddestly* isn't a word, Dad, so you don't have to nut off at me again.'

'I wasn't nutting off, I—'

Switch-flip. Billy kicked at the leg of his dad's chair. 'Yes you were! You're always angry with me for who-knows-why. Not for doing anything wrong. Maybe you just don't like your kid.'

'Don't be ridiculous, Billy. I—'

'I didn't mean for Jason to die. I loved him and I hated him, and sometimes he was just there. Like — the walls.

Sometimes I didn't even think about him, but everybody acts like —' Billy shoved his hands deep into his hoody's front pockets, and stretched it too far. He'd run out of steam. He pulled his cap down over his head, crossed his arms, and slumped low in his chair. 'Oh, whatever. Fricken *fricken*.' He made a face. 'Whatever *fricken* is.'

All the adults looked at each other.

'Do either of you want to respond?' asked Jenna.

Iris's voice sounded as if it had a crack in it. 'Everybody acts like what?'

Billy didn't move.

'We both love you, Billy. Because you're Billy. We —' Her eyes changed from sad to something else. '*Liam?*'

Billy mumbled into his chest.

'I beg your pardon?'

He lifted his head, looked Liam straight in the eye. 'Why are you so angry with me all the time?'

Liam blinked, colour draining from his face. Everyone watched him. Then he looked like a different father. It was horrible, like something alien was pulling at the skin and they couldn't see what. And he still didn't say anything.

Iris clasped her own upper arm, as if she'd been punched. 'He's right, Liam. I feel as if you're annoyed with me all the time, too. Angry and distant.'

He started to shake his head, but then sat there, blank.

Iris couldn't wait: like poking at a cat with a stick. 'It's not just what you say, there are other things —'

'It's not you,' Liam blurted to Billy. 'It's not.'

'Do you know what it is?' Jenna asked.

He looked at the ceiling, as if he'd put in eye-drops. His fists were clenched.

'I don't, I don't think I've been — I've just been —' The

fists balled on his knees tightened, knuckles white through the skin. 'I've been keeping it together, that's all. Holding it all together for everyone, you know? Just — holding it.'

'Looks angry,' said Billy. At the same time Dr Jenna said, 'What do you think would happen if you stopped?'

His fists sprung open. 'Shitstorm.' He shot Billy a glance. 'Someone's got to keep it all running. Someone's got to work.'

'But I've started working again,' said Iris. Liam's voice wheeled on over that.

'Someone's had to keep a grip. Keep control. Otherwise — we'd all be lost. Everything would be lost.'

Face wary, Iris said, 'But you're allowed to *feel*, too, Liam. Going cold on us doesn't help.'

He looked at the wall, jaw working hard.

'It's not weak to mourn someone,' said Iris.

'Billy started flipping out with this crazy bird caper; you'd been winding up tight as a top — what am I supposed to do? Head the same way Pete went? If I weep and wail and do what *I* want to do, where does that leave you?'

Iris sat with her mouth open, as if an answer were glued in her throat. Then she nodded.

Jenna spoke up. 'I don't think that being honest will hurt Billy,' she said. 'It might make him less confused. Kids might seem to be able to bounce off events as if they haven't noticed them, but they're often highly attuned to undercurrents. And Billy's particularly sensitive. I think he's found his own way of translating the subsonic stuff into his own language.'

'*Subsonic stuff*. Is that your professional, technical opinion?' said Liam.

Jenna straightened in her chair. 'I'm avoiding professional jargon, actually,' she said, in a voice Billy's cousin would have called *pissy*. 'Look, this has been a long session. I have another family to see soon. Next time we could start to talk about the changes you'd each like to see. In the way—'

'Oh, change the fucking world,' said Liam. 'Change the fucking universe.'

'*Dad!* You said the *soap* word!'

Liam's expression gave its strange alien twists again. 'Sorry, but none of this will bring Pete and Jason back.'

There was a densely packed silence.

'Well, *duh*.'

'Billy,' warned Iris. Liam stood up.

Jenna said, 'Liam, I'd like to have a private session just with you. We'll book it at reception.'

Liam was already making for the corridor, as if he hadn't heard.

INTO THE RAPIDS

A WEEK OR SO AFTER THE family weep and wailathon, *so help him*, Liam coasted down the drive on his bike, straight into the garage. Iris would be clock-watching, but now was as good a time as any to oil the chain, pump the tyres, tighten the brakes, fix the brackets on the rear-light holder . . . He swore at his pinched thumb, which throbbed with accusation when he let the wrench slip. This wasn't procrastination, all right? If he didn't get it done now, when bloody would he? He heard Iris moving around in the kitchen above the garage. He sighed, looking at his shelf of Allen keys, screwdrivers, wrenches, tyre irons, spare inner-tubes. *Once more unto the breach, dear friends, once more,* he muttered. *Something, something, imitate the action of a tiger.*

He stalked upstairs, trying to remember where he'd left the laptop this morning, after Iris had pointed out the day's date.

'Hi, sweetheart?' she said. Already questioning him, for God's sake.

'Hi.' He went to the sink.

'How'd it go today?'

He ran himself a glass of water. 'I postponed.'

'You what?'

'Had too much on at work this afternoon, so I cried off.'

'Ironic phrase, don't you think, Liam?' she asked, poison-tipped.

'I'm not the spill-all-to-strangers sort. Talking to cushions, or whatever amateur experiment they'll try. Dance with the bloody scarves.' He saw the squared-off, blunt expression on her face. Something in him teetered.

'Look, Liam. The "play" angle was clearly for Billy. They're trying to put him at ease. They're not going to get *you* to colour in, are they?' She shut the pantry door, dumped a container of flour on the bench, then stared at it as if she'd forgotten why she'd taken it out. 'But you know what? Quite frankly, you haven't been the talking to *anyone* sort for a long time.'

'What do you mean?'

'That's partly what this —' she gestured: meaning the field of tension between them '— is all about isn't it? I've talked this over with Jenna. She thinks that at least some of the . . . insecurity, this constant anxiety, isn't just to do with Pete, Jase, the move. When you're this closed up, I feel unsafe.'

'All this *feeling* wank!' he muttered.

She booted a cupboard shut, then turned to him with her hands on both hips. 'If we don't fix this, Liam, we're looking at a deal-breaker.'

'What's that supposed to mean?'

'I can't live like this. I can't live with someone who's not talking to me. *Really* talking.'

He started to dismiss it, and she said, 'I mean it.'

Her voice, a shift in posture: it was like a strobe seared the kitchen. The way all the curves and lines of her fitted together; her thick, electric auburn hair bunched, with one tendril sprung from her hairclip; her creamy, untanned calves reminding him of the taste condensed milk left at the back of his tongue. It pierced him with unexpected desire, fear, shame and long-brewing grief.

'I can't stay with someone who's not being honest.'

He flinched. How did she — 'Honest?'

She dropped to a kitchen stool. Trouble shadow-played over her face now. 'I don't know what else to call it.'

'Look —' His mouth was dry; his pulse sped up. 'I'm not sure what you mean.'

She stared at him, the fatigue on her face peeling back as if some realisation edged near. 'Liam?'

He turned away.

'What's going on?'

A black orb blotted across his vision. 'Nothing.' He turned back. 'It's nothing.'

'Looks like a pretty heavy nothing, Liam.'

He'd persist with a fudge. Not exactly lying. Then, involuntarily, his mouth said, 'I saw Faye. At a service station in Ashburton. On the way back from my trip to Christchurch a few weeks ago. Faye Prescott.'

What had he done?

It wasn't a name they'd spoken together in years. But he saw he'd hardly needed to say her surname. He couldn't seem to stop. 'We had a drink together.' As if this were the worst part of the confession and he could get away with a half-truth. He should have known that wouldn't fool Iris. In the early years of their marriage, she was always better at poker than he was, even though he had to remind her of the rules before nearly every game. Faye Prescott: she was — the woman from his past who wasn't, really. For reasons he'd never fully understood, she'd been just a friend, and Iris had sometimes expressed suspicion about that. 'Always?' She read him too well. 'Nothing's ever happened,' he'd reassure her, when they had all lived in Auckland and Faye sometimes dropped by, or she and Liam had coffee, or once or twice an after-work drink.

Nothing had ever happened, true: but there was an unspoken tension that made her more dangerous than a genuine ex. With Faye, there was still a coiled bolt of energy stored, or working against itself, somehow.

'And?'

'And —' He felt an internal stutter: an engine that wouldn't turn over. All the *ands* were too barbed for him to say: *and* it had been a relief to see someone who wasn't constantly asking him for something, judging him, finding him falling short. *And* it was good to see someone who had once known him and Pete at their best together.

'Liam.'

That was what he'd dreaded. To hear Iris's belief in him corroding, when it wasn't like that; he did still love her, he would always be there for her, she and Billy were top priority. Morality said so, common human decency cried so: this protesting hinge of love still said so. So why was he sweating?

He had just — wanted respite. Had tried to steal it; needed a break from the strain of work, Iris's worry, the eroding sorrow about Pete and Jase that he couldn't give air to if he wanted to keep home-life sane. He wanted someone to listen to him without blame, confusion and fear behind everything. He wanted rescue sex: straightforward lust and its welcome ache answered. Don't anyone dare say *typical male arsehole*, because after years of suppressed attraction, Faye said she wanted it, too, as much as he did, though she was just as scared.

Could he tell Iris he'd begun to think it was actually possible to desire and care for more than one woman at once? Something had made him call Faye as soon as he reasonably could after Pete's suicide. They'd met for a coffee then, and she'd listened, quietly. That was all he'd needed then. She had moved down south, just before the big quakes, but had flown up to Auckland not long after Jason's funeral. She'd called and tried to see him, but although they couldn't meet, he knew she understood.

He couldn't tell Iris. Couldn't explain it, couldn't hurt her any more than she had been already. Why did it have to be so complicated? She must know how she exhausted him sometimes, with her ability to stack anxiety ever higher. He'd wanted an oasis of time, outside ordinary life. Light-hearted, painless fun. A private retreat. Everyone needed privacy, didn't they, even in a marriage? Was the only place you could have it, once you were married, in your head? He'd wanted to see if he could forget, for a moment. Go back to an old self. Soak in uncomplicated affection.

That was naïve, to believe it could be uncomplicated. And yet — at first Faye seemed to understand. Slightly older than Liam, serene; she was married; had her children very young, so two were already grown and gone from home. A third child, a girl, she had lost when the baby was under one, many years ago now. She'd once confided how this sat in the corner of every other thought. It was there, always. Even under the warm, sliding glow of a second beer in that

Ashburton garden bar, he realised his attraction was split with contradiction. He wanted playfulness, but also wanted to sit alongside her subliminal sorrow.

After the drink, they hadn't slept together. But perhaps that was just chance. The coincidence of meeting in this small southern town, of all places, made them both a little wild, loose, before they'd even finished the first glass. Faye's husband was in Auckland at meetings; the move to Ashburton from Christchurch after the quakes had been rough on them both. People say you can run a business from anywhere with the internet, but Faye missed her old friends; the buzz of a bigger place. The quakes had really made her think, maybe too much sometimes. About things she hadn't achieved. She'd spread her hands on the table, reaching out to grip the edge near him. He decided he wasn't sober enough to drive; she offered to take him to his motel. He moved some of his gear from his car to hers, planned to collect his vehicle in the morning. When they parked up at the motel, the office was closed, the hotelier nowhere to be seen. 'Would you like to come in?' he'd asked, trying to find out what was happening between them, genuinely not knowing what she would answer. She said, 'I'd have to leave before six tomorrow.' The need for sex redoubled, a current tripping him. His hand at the back of her neck, one thumb gliding her nipple; her hands up under his shirt, then at his belt. Then someone who sounded half-cut knocked at the unit door. Liam and Faye pulled back, instantly sober, all the risks fully exposed; she was shaking and apologetic, all that enviable, restful poise and equilibrium gone. He tried to be understanding, though after she left his nerves were so charged up, he couldn't sleep. He watched a blue movie on the motel rental system; hands trying to conjure her up again; coming to afterwards, so to speak, with self-loathing, bemused by how insistent lust had been.

He and Faye had texted and talked on the phone every few days since. He'd grown so confused that he looked for 'affair' in an online dictionary, to see if they qualified, even without sex. The guilt he felt right now seemed evidence enough.

He sat next to Iris on the other breakfast bar stool and steepled his palms up over nose and mouth: mask or prayer. 'I'm sorry. This has all just been such a screw-up.'

With preternatural calm, Iris said, 'What happened?'

He had the sensation of seeing the room through a porthole, and simultaneously, objects seemed to detach themselves from surfaces. Just stress, he told himself. He tried to suck in air to stay grounded. 'Nothing actually happened.'

Stonily, 'A Bill Clinton nothing, or a genuine nothing?'

He gave her the precise details. 'We kissed. Fondled. Nothing more. Talked.'

He wanted to take *that* word back the minute he said it: her eyes seemed to burn him.

His head rang with the effort behind the quiet.

Then Iris started talking in a monotone, as if narrating subtitles to their last year together. 'So all that withdrawal, all that preoccupation, all that *guardedness* and distance . . . it hasn't just been in my head, has it?'

He felt nauseous.

'Did you talk to her because you couldn't talk to me? Or is it the other way round?'

'What?'

'Have you not been talking to me because you were talking to her?' She said it as if it were a simple, clear-cut equation, but in his mind it looped and snaked. He rubbed his forehead.

'She wasn't us. That's why I talked to her. It was just — a breath of fresh air.'

'How can you *not* think we need help? Is this something you want to fix, Liam?' Then as he tried to drag the leaden weight in him up with words, 'I'm sure this is all connected. I mean, so maybe Faye is an outsider you can talk to, but —' She inhaled an odd laugh. 'I'm not sure whether to be furious with you, or relieved that you *can* actually still talk to someone. I'm not sure whether to be grateful nothing happened, or whether, or whether — *fuck*, Liam.' The last words were barely audible, but he felt punched.

He swallowed. This swerve, her focused anger, was bizarrely energising, cleansing. Why? Because here it was, in the open. The monster, Infidelity, had come out of its lair: this was what they had to slay. He put a hand on her arm, ready to agree to any terms, but now Iris was standing, hand over mouth. She left the kitchen, and he heard her in the bathroom, dry retching. He pressed his fingers hard into his eye sockets, trying to stop the spinning. There was the sound of running water, a handle turning, her tread upstairs, the old floorboards creaking almost as if she were rocking one small, sleepless thought back and forth, back and forth. He wanted to follow her up, have it out, get all the answers *now* — but he couldn't move.

TWO THIN, RAINY PEOPLE

THE STAND-OFF LASTED DAYS. Their conversations wore the barest skin of civil. Then Iris found a screed of handwritten birthday lists from Billy. They were on his bed, under his soft, crumpled, flannelette Big Bird pyjamas and a pile of Tintin books. His birthday was still more than six weeks away, but he'd already been brainstorming. One page was headed *Party,* and it gave a list of games and outing choices. There were also the names of several children Iris had never heard of.

There were multiple versions of the other list, *Presents,* as if he kept resolving to be tidier:

1. Mum and Dad talk to each other again.

2. Lifelong membership of Orokonui Ecosanctuary.

3. An iPod that can record birdsongs.

4. New cage toys for Canary Woof.

5. A friend for Canary Woof. WARNING: must not be a bird that would eat him. Check type of beak etc. first.

6. Software to make birdsong into English.

7. Chocolate.

She gathered up the lists, taking them out to Liam like pale rags of truce.

She handed over the pages. His face showed an habitual impassive *I don't care, you can't hurt me, I don't love you if you don't love me*. But when he read the lists, the careful indifference evaporated and he met her eyes, the first time in days.

'We talk,' he said, half-heartedly.

'I don't think even you buy that,' she said.

Liam swept a hand over his face. 'Sit down?' He moved from the dining table to the couch.

She sat at the settee's far end, knees turned away from him. He rested a hand near her. 'Insults aren't going to help.' Silence. Then, in a stripped-out tone that revealed how much internal grinding over the issues he'd done, he said, 'Pulling together for him is more important than either of us, Iris.'

She knew that; had thought it herself a million times. She couldn't put Billy through another crisis. Liam cupped her knee. 'I need you to forgive me.'

She took his hand off. 'I need you to come back to counselling.'

He didn't refuse — but within moments, the arguments cycled back around again. Iris couldn't quite believe that 'nothing else' had happened. Her harangues pushed for graphic details of *kissing* and *fondling*.

'Iris, stop. Are you doing this to torture me, or yourself?'

'I have to know. Protecting my sexual health is a *human right*.'

She relished that look on his face. It said: this wasn't the anxious, frightened, over-thinking woman he had been married to since their nephew's death. She was molten, re-formed in a crucible of anger.

He stood. As he made for the doorway, she said his name.

He stopped. 'All right. We kissed, I held her breasts, she put her hands under my shirt, and . . . Iris, please. Don't. It's not worth it. It's not. This is why I didn't want to tell you. I didn't want to hurt you over something so stupid . . .'

Hours were swallowed by a dark, spinning tunnel.

At last Iris agreed: she would stop. If Liam (a) would neither see nor even contact Faye again and (b) would at least *try* further sessions with Billy's counsellors.

When they called them *Billy's counsellors*, Liam found it easier to agree.

You are so messed up, Iris said — not only at home, but also in their first joint session in the aftermath. There, she added *pissing-well*. *You are so pissing-well messed up.*

'Hang on,' Jenna said. 'Yes, you're angry, Iris, and you have a right to be. But Liam has agreed to come back, so you have to step up, too. This needs to be a bipartite peace.'

It took weeks for her head to stop reeling. (Weeks — and, one day, the satisfying sensation of using the heavy rubber mallet they used for bashing in tent pegs to smash the fugly John Barleycorn Toby jug from Faye Freaking Press-Twat to little bits of china-dust. Break up my marriage? *Thwack*. Break up my marriage? *Thwack*. It was tempting to smash them all, but Iris restrained herself, parcelled up the detritus and put it out with the rubbish without telling Liam.)

An *affair* wasn't what they had come to counselling for. 'I'd call it a symptom,' Jenna said. 'Of what else has gone wrong. I don't think the family has been able to let everyone come to terms with bereavement in their own way.'

The doctor laid out some pictures that Billy had drawn during private sessions. The one that snagged Iris's attention was of a boy with wings, sitting on a swing, legs kicked out at peculiar angles that were in part mis-shapen from not getting the perspective right, in part zany and carefree. Below him were two thin, rainy people done in black smudges, clownish, sad bobble-heads dominating their torsos. Even their hair matched, in long weepy-grey threads.

Liam picked up the pictures, held them out, like someone reading X-rays.

'We've got to get some sort of balance back. My guess is that Liam's flirtation with Faye is telling you how far things were out of kilter. And it was a flirtation, Iris. Not an affair.'

'Pretty extreme,' she retorted, her eyes wide with *excuse me?*

'It doesn't have to mean breakdown and break-up. Not if you're willing to see it as a symptom.'

After that first couple-session, Iris found herself brooding, not over Faye and Liam, but over Billy's drawing. Perhaps because it wasn't what they'd discussed, it sat as an unresolved knot. Instead, they'd started up on any number of large, difficult themes: desire, trust, power, loyalty, secrecy, fairness, even, gawd, *character* traits. Exhausting rather than cathartic, when it wasn't Shakespeare, or

Tennessee Williams, but her own psychodrama-whirlpool.

Maybe she kept coming back to Billy's monochrome painting over the weeks because there was something in it she hadn't understood yet. It was like a phrase in a translation that wouldn't unlock. She was missing some idiom. Our sadness turns him into a bird? He's removed from us? Wants to leave our screwed-up marriage, while we're still stuck in its grey? Often, while she was engaged in some mundane task, or walking to work, or on the edge of sleep, or even when her stomach would start its sad contractions over thoughts of Liam and Faye, the picture came back to her. She wanted it to speak, to tell her the answer to its riddle.

On one of her days off Glad Rags, the image slipped back into her head as she walked uphill to pick up Billy after school instead of waiting for him at home. Liam was still overdue a solo counselling session; he'd claimed that booking one three weeks away *wasn't* procrastinating. Billy had already had three more appointments: said he'd started to like them; would only tell her they 'talked about things', or 'just goofed off today', or 'had a picture talk, you know, talking with pictures'. When she asked directly, 'Was it about Jason? Was it about me and Dad?', all he said, tongue probing his cheek in concentration, was, 'Sort of.'

There was some lifting of shadow from him, though. He reverted less often to hysterical *kaaa, kaaa, kaaaa*! Still plenty of pretending to fly, though; early morning warbling and whistling; obsessive chitter-chatter about 'that blessed bloody budgerigar', as Liam said. Yet his talks with Jenna and Trisha seemed to be winding something back into place for him.

Toiling up the hill now, wondering how Liam's first private session would go when he finally turned up — she saw the boy's scribble of his father sitting in the client's chair, opposite Jenna, rather than the real Liam. At school, she tried to shake off an eddy of anxiety, yet when Billy burst out of the classroom, she said, 'Hey, Billy? I've been thinking.'

He goggled his eyes. 'Did it hurt?'

'Ha, *ha*. No. I — ah —'

'What?'

'You know those pictures you did for Trisha and Jenna?'

'Hey, there's David.' He cupped his hands around his mouth. 'David! Hi David, bye David!'

'Hi Billy, bye Billy!'

He nodded, chest puffed out. 'That's David. We played at lunch today.'

'You *did*? Great!' She braced herself. 'Was it — about birds?'

'Astronauts. And it was cool because it was just us in the top of the fort.'

'Oh. Really? That's — great. He's not in your class, is he?'

'Nope. He's a year ahead, but we found out today we're both in the jungle scene in the school production. We had a practice this morning. And we both got *totally* bored.'

She felt as if she were walking beside someone else's child. What was it she was going to ask him about? Some mood had evaporated, some concern . . . She tried to keep him talking, thinking it might bring back the missing question. 'It's a boring play?'

'No, everyone's just so slo-o-o-w. They, like, have to be told twenty zillion times what to do. So we've got this code. We do Angry Birds. Like the game? When it's really bad, he goes like this —' Billy made two fists and pulled one away from the other slowly. 'Then he goes *pikewww*! And I go *aaaahhhh*!' Billy's arms wind-milled, then he shot ahead of Iris. When he circled back, he said, 'That's me being the Angry Bird aimed at Mrs Gresham. Which is pretty funny, because when she frowns she looks just like one of the pigs from the game. If she notices us, it's points to her. If she doesn't, that's points to us. So far we're winning.'

Should she dance because he'd found a friend? Risk dampening his sunny mood by saying, *I hope you're not getting into trouble and disrupting the other kids*? Say it was *interesting* that he'd found a companion in an older boy? (Did it mean Billy was seeking a replacement for Jase; or did it mean nothing at all?) As she shuffled all the shambolic thought-cards in her head, Billy rootled around in his backpack and thrust a notice at her.

'See!' He crowed. 'School production! This tells you all you need to know about all the blah-de-blah.'

'What sort of part do you have?'

'Not telling. It's a surprise.'

'Won't you need help to learn your lines?'

'Nope.'

'I don't mind. And I could help to sew costumes, too!' She felt a flutter of excitement.

He stopped in his tracks and leaned over a little at the waist, making googly eyes again. 'Nope. Because then it won't be a *sur-pri-i-i-ise*.'

Her mouth gaped, but he carried on in jaunty little skips now and then. She scurried to keep up. 'But Billy, you do know I'm *actually* a seamstress?'

He started a theatrical *I-can't-hear-you!* hum. They plodded downhill, past the small set of local shops on either side of the road. A twiglet of a woman in pink puffer vest, walking a natty little dog in matching pink coat, overtook them and stopped at a mail box. The dog went into a yapping fit, flinging itself to the end of its lead. As Iris and Billy drew past them again, Iris admonished it, channelling some of her Billy-bewilderment. '*Drama* queen!'

Billy rolled his eyes. 'That's exactly what I *mean*. I don't know why they say "Mum's the word" for keeping quiet,' he said. 'It's not true for *our* house.' He grinned, then ran to catch up with a boy on a scooter. Iris trailed behind, a little bamboozled, a little abandoned, but also, for a moment, a little happily *schtum*.

ONE ROBIN

THE DAY OF HIS FIRST SOLO SESSION with Billy's counsellors — okay, the *family* counsellors — Liam dodged Steve, saying Iris had to work and Billy wasn't — ah — too right in himself. Steve said, 'Oh, no, not this pukefest that's going round?' Liam evaded that: the truth being that Billy was at a mini school camp that had come up on them all before they knew it. He pulled a face and said, 'Kids, eh? So, I'll need to take tomorrow off.' Broadly speaking: all true.

A trio of uni students had booked in to try paddleboards for the morning, so he knew that Steve wouldn't be doing odd jobs in town: no likelihood of bumping into him as Liam made his way to his appointment. Steve would just have to leave the answer machine on and hope no casual clients turned up.

When the morning came, Liam didn't exactly tell Iris he'd taken the day off either. She asked, 'Isn't today your meeting with Jenna and Trisha?'

'Yep,' he said, adding, 'oh, and I won't be on my bike.

I'll take the car in for its warrant of fitness.'

He drove across town and up into the city's surrounding bush and hill trails, going just a little too fast, burning rubber on the corners, as if the quiet and emptiness that the borderlands promised could dissolve in a change of wind direction. When he parked at the base of the Pineapple Track, he shouldered on a day-pack and jogged up the trails for more than two hours, trying to clear his mind of the anti-mantra *fuckwit, fuckwit, fuckwit*: or at least reach the overtired place where he couldn't hear it so acutely.

Back at the car, streaming sweat, he sluiced himself with water from his drink bottle, towelled down and changed. He drove, over the speed limit, back to town. He barricaded the surface of his mind from the accusation that he'd run late so the session would be short. And so there'd also be less time sitting in the car, where trepidation tracked him down, catching the scent of his faults when he was at rest. With his limbs moving, his lungs thrashing, his body worked like a bilge pump, bailing out the rising flood of noise in his head.

As he walked up the steps towards the consulting rooms, noting the ache in his calves, he felt a bolt of panic. Had he prepared properly? The motion-sick plunge in his stomach was like the recurring nightmare where he was in a massive river gorge and cave network, with clients who were clueless about the outdoors. In the dream, he'd left behind life jackets, headlamps, food, compass. Horror's dark seep showed that the clients weren't clients, but his family. He had to get them to safety and . . . He patted his pockets, *wallet, keys, cell-phone,* get a grip. He looked up to see Jenna waiting. The blood smarted in his cheeks. She smiled. 'Good timing. I was coming to find you.' She led him to the consulting room, with its rainbow posters, its shelf of plastic figurines, the leadlight decoration in the window where sun and hills beamed in fiery panels. There was a patchouli scent on the air. Jenna turned down music she'd had playing on her computer. He tried to conceal the cynical smirk he could feel twitching up by asking, 'Nice. What is it?'

'*The Lark Ascending*. Vaughan Williams. Talking to Billy reminded me of it. I pulled it up on iTunes yesterday. Makes referencing papers less onerous.'

It was the most she'd ever said about herself; he felt suspicious, as if she were too consciously trying to relax him by shifting the hot spot. Pressure inside his chest increased; he lifted his chin: *let's get on with it.*

He sat down, crossed arms and legs. His suspended foot started an edgy jig. He wanted to reprimand it: *Sit. Wait.* It stopped for a bit. As soon as Jenna spoke, it was off again, wanting out, wanting to walk.

'Liam, I know you're here reluctantly. This isn't meant to be an interrogation.'

He felt a pang of chagrin: that was a bit too on the nail.

'This is meant to be a chance for you to have your say. It can be a one-off if you want. I thought there might be things you'd find it easier to discuss without the rest of the family here.'

The sense that there was somewhere else he was meant to be, urgent work to get on with, boiled to the surface. He plunged forward in his chair, then felt too close to her, so yanked himself back. 'Look,' he said. 'I just want this whole deal over. I want Billy sorted out, and I want to get on with my life. I made a mistake with an old friend. I'm not proud of it. But Iris and I have agreed that we'll try to let bygones be bygones. We're doing okay. It'll take more time, I know. But what I want now is for us to get Billy back to being a normal, happy kid. So I can —' he saw her eyelids flicker '— get *on* with things.'

The small frown had come back. 'What things?'

The music had stopped. Her question sat on the air like a bald crag. He could see no way up or around it. The obvious answer was work. Earn money that would build a fortress around his family to keep them from harm. *Harm.* He swallowed. Looking at Jenna's expression, hearing the answer in his mind's ear, all the *things* fragmented. The idea that money might be the brick house that no wolf could blow down seemed idiotic. He examined his palms until the silence felt airless. He lunged in another direction.

'Can I ask something?'

'Of course,' she said.

'I've only ever really yelled at Billy once or twice over this whole bird thing. I've tried pretty hard to keep a calm exterior, you know? Plus, through all the other drama we've had, I keep thinking, I shouldn't let rip in front of him, none of it's his fault. So — what makes him think I'm angry with *him*?' Exasperation sent him backwards in the chair again. 'And how does pissing around with this bird act help?'

'He seems to behave that way less often with me, now.'

A muscle in his cheek twinged. He was so wound up . . . Jesus, he was channelling Iris. He inhaled noisily. 'True. It's the same at home. I'm not saying you're not helping.'

The doctor smiled wryly. Then Liam blurted, 'What've he and Iris said about me?'

A pen teetered between two of Jenna's fingers: signalling her indecision. To say, or not to say? 'I'm Billy's *dad*!' he brayed, then wished he could haul it back on a chain.

Tip-tip, tip-tip.

He wanted to grab the pen and turn it on her like a pointer: *See here, this is the problem!*

'They've both said a number of different things. But one that really struck me made me want to ask you about physical contact. How you show affection.'

Liam's chin snapped back: '*Uh.*'

'I think — to answer one of your other questions — the bird act is complicated.' She doodled circles within circles; as if it helped her pare detail from detail. 'Billy's been mourning, of course, but I think he's also been affected by Iris's constant worrying. Her anxiety has been impinging. He's been absorbing it, acting it out. Releasing it. So the bird act's been protective. But it's also ended up winning him some concerted physical attention from you. He's said a couple of times that you've collared him, held him down, when you've been fed up with his bird displays.' She chewed her lip pensively. 'Iris claims that you haven't hugged him since Jason died.'

Liam glowered. When Jenna glanced up, he found himself altering the hardness in his face, discomfited. She was unperturbed. 'Being a bird is also a place of safety. It's a kind of retreat, yes? Into fantasy. It's not delusion. I think it's been a kind of translation of everything he hasn't been able to talk about, despite his lovely chatterboxiness. To use a *non-technical* term.'

Liam rolled his shoulders.

Jenna let the moment pass. 'I think, in a way — it was self-rescue. Then it became a habit.'

Jenna talked all the way through his tears that leaked involuntarily. What a relief that she did. What a relief that she didn't say, *There, let it all out, this is what you needed,* hippy-dippy bullshit. What a relief that, actually, there wasn't complete surrender. He hadn't lost control. What it felt like was . . . just coming clean. Who'd've guessed? He cradled his head in his hands.

'Do you need a tissue?' Jenna asked.

'Sure.' He swiped a fistful of Earthcare (yeah, right) from the box. 'Waterworks,' he said factually.

'Yep,' she replied. He shot her a look, but there was no mockery.

'Thanks.'

'So is all this a shock, or does it make sense?'

He sucked his bottom lip, trying to keep in the shakes. 'Both.' Even when he felt calm travel through him like the first effects of a pint, still he had to wipe at his eyes, his nose; was reminded of those small cuts that won't be staunched. 'I'm actually okay,' he said to Jenna. She moved the tissues closer.

'So tell me about this distance between you and Billy,' she said.

He used a few tissues, then clenched them into a ball. 'It'll sound facile,' he said. 'Transparent. But it doesn't feel like that. I mean, that's not the way we live it.'

She waited.

Would this be easier with a man? Or if he were religious and could go to a priest? Would any of it be easier if he had an overarching belief that there was a higher purpose to all this mess, sorrow and difficulty? Would there be comfort in believing there was a grand plan, somewhere out there? He heard her heater ticking. The wind picked up outside, and several leaves sprung at the window: scarlet, yellow, green, like the paint-coloured hands of small children doing prints at kindergarten. He felt absurd tenderness for them.

'Where have you gone, Liam? You're looking very far away.'

'Nowhere.' Which was true. Looking deep into the nothing, the nowhere, the pointlessness at the end of it all.

'Sometimes you just have to ask why we keep going, don't you?' He'd said it as if it were one of those phrases a shell of a man would trot out along with the weather. Bit chilly, call this spring, at the *end* of the day, at the *end* of the day . . .

Jenna frowned, the pen back up to her mouth. 'How long have you felt that for?'

'Ages. Since my brother killed himself.'

She nodded, face seamed with concern. 'A terrible blow. Did you talk to anyone professional when that happened?'

Liam pushed the ball of tissues into his eyes, one at a time. The darkness he saw bruised red. Jenna gave him a minute or two.

'No,' she answered for him. 'I see.' He heard the rub of fabric as she shifted in her swivel chair. 'Before he died, what would you have said the point of it all was?'

He blinked up at the ceiling to clear his vision again. The scalloped plaster edges were like giant meringues. Which seemed the epitome of pointless right now, too. He shrugged. 'Adventure. Extending yourself. Family. The here and now.' He shrugged again. 'All very well when the here and now is good. But when it's not —' He massaged his temples. 'Are we getting anywhere with this?'

'I think we are. It's not comfortable. But I think we are.'

She pulled the sides of her suit jacket across her chest, getting down to business. 'I'm trying to connect the dots here. One of the things in that list was family. Given how much your brother's death affected you — why has there been this remove from Billy?'

Liam dropped his head, letting his hands hang between his knees. Again the default shrug. 'It felt like the tipping point. It all seemed so loaded. Shit, I don't know. I've really only just been keeping it together. I couldn't help — every time I see him, I think of Pete at his age. They're so alike: it's easy to confuse photos of them at the same stage, even. Then I think about how low Pete must have been. How ill, really. None of us understood how bad. Then this dark tsunami comes and — then it's me caving in, but I can't do what Pete did — I have to beat it. I want to get through all that and just see Billy again. You know? There's been all this — shambles and fear in the way. Like there was no clear, uncomplicated, *unadulterated* love any more, because . . .' He heard his own words. He sat for a while, waiting for the sting to fade. 'We failed Pete so badly. We couldn't keep him alive, and then we couldn't even look after his son for him. All this *shit* in the way, and Iris so tense it was stifling — I never felt as if — I never felt as if even a simple hug was safe. Or the truth. Or could undo it all.' His hand chopped on the air. 'I don't fucking know.' Jenna poured him a glass of water from a jug. 'Rinse and spit?' he asked, but she looked impassive, as if to say, *Don't be evasive.* He drank.

'You'd lost your connection to Billy somehow,' Jenna prompted.

'Partly I just — didn't want to let myself go in front of him. You know what it can be like. You stop the fight and — floodgates. Who knows what falls apart then? I've said it before, anyway. Iris was struggling. Billy was struggling. Someone's got to be the rock.' He wanted to expel all those wasted days. 'It's all screwed up. Trying not to hurt Billy, trying not to let on how confused I've been, but . . .' The sentence dangled as if it, too, hoped Jenna would fill in the gaps.

She tilted her head, listening to something out of his ken. 'It's not all screwed up. We might need more sessions for you to talk about Pete. And Jason, of course. If not with me, I can suggest someone else who would help. But look.' She leaned forward, and for an awkward moment he thought she was going to take his hands. 'The most important thing you've done is agree on giving everyone a chance to air things. There isn't any single person or action to blame, Liam. And beating yourself up isn't going to help.' She reached for another glass of water on her desk, took a sip. 'But I wonder — you said, much earlier, that you just want Billy sorted out. You want to get on with things.'

He waited while his heart did a couple of strange erratic beats as if it stood up in his chest to shake itself free.

She looked straight at him. 'Grief doesn't work like that. Perhaps now, more than ever, we have a tendency to think there's a checklist. A couple of steps to take, buttons to press, and it'll be done. Buy the easy guide online. Watch the DVD. Take some pills. Get the app. Sure, even get a couple of counselling sessions, and here's your happiness licence, your bill of health, everything's up and running again.' The sourness was discomposing. 'But it's not like that. It took you how many years of loving your brother, and then your nephew, for you to know them as you did? There's no quick fix for such losses.'

He closed his eyes and held his breath the way he would if lowering into a winter sea. Bear with it. Let the numbness rise.

Jenna spoke again. 'There's something I want to ask you. I remember thinking, very early on in our sessions, when you all came in and "the bird act", as you called it, was problematic for you — I remember wondering, why don't they just run with it? Why don't the parents just — join in?'

He looked up at her through eyes as dry and raw as if coated in sand. He was thinking, *The boy's got to the point of trying to fly and you're asking why we're not joining in?*

'Of course you'd been through huge change.' She watched him again. Then softly, so he found himself leaning forward a little, 'I've said to Billy, yes, it's okay to feel bad things about your cousin. Jason wasn't perfect. Nobody is. And it's okay to have fun again, despite everything that's happened. It doesn't mean you've forgotten him, or you're not showing respect. Maybe that's what you need as a family. Give yourselves permission— ?' The phone on her desk rang, startling them both, and she looked annoyed. 'Sorry,' she said. 'I'm not supposed to get any calls during a consult. I'll let my voicemail get that.'

He swallowed. 'That's okay.' He glanced at the wall. 'Is your clock right?'

She swivelled in her chair. 'Oh, yes, it is. I'm sorry, Liam, we've run over time . . .'

He shook his head, confused: days might have passed, or seconds; he'd lost all bearings. ''S okay. Wouldn't make much more sense today anyway.'

'There's a lot more we could talk about, if you wanted to book another session.'

'See how we go.'

She responded — but with no more ceremony he walked out into the world. He'd been pummelled. The air on his face was a cold yet welcome rinse. He was still guarded, sceptical about talking to a stranger about home. Perhaps this weightlessness, then, was relief at having carried out a duty; having it over. But — like burrs hooked to his clothes — some of Jenna's phrases clung on.

Grief takes time . . . He just hadn't realised how long that would be. Pain creates its own eternity . . . No, 'Pain expands the time.' He'd quoted that to Pete, when Steffie died. Galling to realise how, back then, he thought he understood. Not knowing how to say the right things to Pete, he'd dug around in old books. The search had led into memories of his final-year English teacher, Mr Kirk, reciting poetry and snatches of song, flipping from source to source so half the time you never knew whether it was one of The Greats, Leonard Cohen, Bob Dylan or even Kirk himself, if you let yourself trail off into thinking about hot pie for lunch, cricket practice . . . He hadn't thought of Kirk and his Greats for aeons. Of course they'd called him Captain, and sometimes Scrape-'em-off-Jim (but only ever out of earshot) . . .

Why was he tunnelling around that far back, when this was all about Pete, Jase, Billy? Something drew him in deeper; some warm disturbance. Old Kirk. Liam remembered meeting him again by chance when Liam was at uni, but wishing he'd chosen some kind of outdoor career training. Even then, he had fantasies about adventure journalism . . . They'd bumped into each other during the intermission of a show. Liam had been in a bad phase, actually: ditched by his first true love, an MA theatre studies student who'd decided what she called 'his post-Anglican reserve' didn't fit with her Italian roots after all. He'd gone to the show alone: half looking for Nina, really. Surprised to see Kirk there, he'd bought him and his colleague a small bottle of lager at the theatre bar. They all drank fast; soon Kirk was praising Liam to his friend, saying he'd been known around the school for good citizenship, always having both feet on the ground, a solid kid you could trust in a crisis. 'We knew you'd go far,' Kirk said. 'Eh?' asked Liam, thinking Auckland's no long haul from Wellington. 'Far into the good and right life for you.' Maybe Kirk couldn't take his drink, he'd thought, but next the old boy was gripping Liam's shoulder, and saying, eye to eye, that line: 'Pain expands the time.'

It seemed like the conversation had run off its tracks, but Kirk said, 'Things will come right, son. There'll be another. The heart's extraordinarily elastic.' Liam said — what exactly? Nothing, probably, too stunned to realise Kirk had seen straight into all his numbed answers, maybe the way his gaze kept roaming around the room as if Nina might be there; his glance once snaring painfully on an attractive woman with similar dark looks.

He'd felt his awkwardness then like extra bones angling through his skin; but Kirk continued to grip his shoulder, and quoted some other lines, the gleam in his eyes a mixture of mischief, self-parody, friendship, wisdom. Liam had looked up the quotations afterwards: Dickinson, the loner. Somehow he wouldn't have picked that. He'd grown obsessed by her poems, their strange, halting sorrows, those long dashes, that seemed to mean there was still so much not said. Another one returned now, effortlessly:

If I can stop one heart from breaking
I shall not live in vain
If I can ease one life the aching
Or cool one pain,

Or help one fainting robin
Unto his nest again
I shall not live in vain.

The theatre bar scene had lain dormant all these years, waiting for its moment to make good. Kirk's strong grip on his shoulder, at a time when his whole body had ached for Nina, stupidly lust-sore, had returned him to himself. A moment of human touch; the older man's perceptiveness; Liam had been inarticulately grateful.

He had not asked and asked, since his brother's death, *Why did he do it?*, because he felt he knew the answer. Pete's reasons grew from the relentless hammer of asking himself that other cruel question, after losing his wife. *What's it all for?*

The pace of Liam's walk seemed to fall in synch with fragments of Dickinson's lines, rolling through them again and again. A thought treadmill.

THIS MARRIAGE IS BIGGER THAN BOTH OF US

END OF THE WEEK, and Iris was working extra hours for Glad Rags because — deep breath — she needed her mind taken off home. Or rather, the empty home. It was good news, it really was: Billy had been chosen to train as an Activity Monitor for next year at school. He was off on a three-night Leadership Camp. It was a new initiative at the school. Selected children went to train at the Whare Flat scout buildings. Iris hadn't really wanted Billy to go, but Billy was desperate-keen. She'd talked about her reluctance with Jenna: offering her a string of reasons. Jenna nodded, as if each one were valid, then said, 'Iris, you have to start loosening his reins. I know it's hard, but it will be better in the long run. It's a taste of independence. He talked to me about the camp, actually. His ebullience was so — Billy.'

Iris nodded.

'And how wonderful that the school thinks he's reliable enough.'

Iris pulled her cardigan tightly around her. 'But all Activity Monitor means, as far as I can tell, is handing out sports equipment at lunchtimes, tidying the sports shed, and making sure children play fair. I don't see why on earth they have to take them away for training. It sounds so bloody — military.'

Jenna laughed, which was so unexpected that Iris smarted. 'Fair play's not an easy thing for a lot of kids to learn. I'd say that's quite a responsibility for Billy. You must be so proud.'

Iris had to wait a beat. Oh. No, she hadn't thought to be proud. Just — worried.

'It could be a great way for him to make new friends.'

Iris held back and thought, *Is she* lecturing *me?*

'Iris. It's an opportunity. You might find you lose his trust if you don't start trusting him, too.'

The smart deepened: a true hit. This morning she'd packed Billy's bag and was slipping in some extra snacks when he breezed past to refill Canary Woof's water trough. He looked at the birdseed bars she'd made, and the small container of nuts and pumpkin kernels. 'No, thanks, Mum. Not much into that now.' He saw her crestfallen face, and patted her on the arm. 'But points for trying. No big deal, right?'

To distract herself from the stupid prickling in her nose and eyes, she'd asked, did he know their phone number, and the number for the police and ambulance, if the bus — to which he groaned, '*Muu-uum!*' So she bit her tongue, and dropped him off at the meeting place, telling herself, as she looked in the rear-view mirror, *Don't look back, you don't need to look back . . .*

Tonight she and Liam would have their first night alone for — how long? What if they had nothing to say to each other now they finally had the chance to talk uninterrupted?

He would have had his first one-on-one session with Jenna. What if he reached a point in his session where it was clear he had to leave the marriage?

Thinking and over-thinking, the chain of what-ifs gathering more and more links, like the fairy tale where village folk get glued to the goose . . . Iris was sick of the stuck crowd of herself. At the Glad Rags counter, she swung her skirt back around the right way for the umpteenth time. She'd been losing weight since the Faye Prescott bombshell. (No, not that sort of bombshell. Iris thought Faye looked anaemic, actually. With a gourd-like face, and sharky teeth.)

All Iris's clothes hung from her shapelessly; skirts were rotating hula-hoops; trousers rode too low. Even though Billy seemed so much better, and Liam's first solo session, surely, would mean *some* kind of progress — today was the day that Brandy at Glad Rags commented, no word-mangling now: 'You're bad advertising, Iris love. Skinny as a rake. You need to make some adjustments.' Her gimlet stare meant more than to waistbands.

Abracadabra, alacazam — the whole story poured out of Iris: Jason, Billy, Liam; the precious, wrenching, bewildering lot of them. She half-expected the usual, 'What a bastard, how *could* he, I haven't met him, but what an *arse* . . . you deserve better . . .' But Brandy slipped off to make coffee, found some chocolates in the staff fridge, offered Iris the box, and said, 'You've been bottling all this up for *how* long? It's been eating at you, love. Look at yourself. You say you're getting counselling — well, have *they* noticed how thin you are?'

'The GP knows,' Iris said. 'She suggested anti-anxiety medication again, but I keep telling her the pills won't erase the fact Liam needed someone else, or . . .' Her voice hitched. Iris stared at the newspaper splayed on the bench. '. . . Or stop all the other terrible things that seem to be, I don't know, standing over Billy's future.' She gestured at the headlines. 'Climate change, war, shootings, recession, peak oil. God, when I think about that, I think, how will we even *make* anxiety pills when we reach peak oil? Better to tough it out now. Better get into training for the worse to come. Though sometimes — sometimes I think, I just want a holiday in someone else's head, you know? Just to get a break from my own *fucking* mind.' She blew her nose, took a sip of coffee. ''Scuse me.'

'Oh, no, darling, fuck away. I would. So to speak.'

They locked gazes briefly, then it was Brandy's turn to apologise. 'Sorry, love. I guess sexual in-under-endoes aren't that funny right now.'

Iris made a rueful face. 'They didn't actually have sex. Apparently.'

'Well, that's something, isn't it?'

'That's what the counsellors say. I'm so confused about it. It would be worse if they'd slept together. It would. It's just that part of me thinks, what hurts is the intimacy. And maybe sex is just, you know, rubbing body parts together once you're already so close that — oh, I don't know. I just don't know any more.'

Brandy turned pensive. 'Lots of people have affairs, Iris. Plenty of marriages survive them.'

'Yeah, but are they ever the same?'

Brandy sighed. 'Perhaps it's better they're not. Perhaps an affair comes along because things have to change.'

Iris unrumpled the colourful foil from her Turkish delight, stole a quick look at her. 'Speaking from experience?'

'I've been around a few more years than you, Ms Spring Chicken.'

Iris took in Brandy's gingery highlights, the dark roots of her hair, the fine silvery strands peering through, the two deep smile lines that she'd never thought to read as older than her. Brandy had seemed ageless in a plump, jolly way: her skin creamy, protected from the sun; her voice, with its Balclutha burr, often high, thin and breathless as a girl's.

'Tit for tat,' Iris said. 'I've told you mine, you tell me yours.'

'Tit for tat, I don't like that. Sounds like a strip joint.'

'For a real class act.'

They each unwrapped another sweet. Brandy turned hers over, examining the curlicued ridge on its finish. 'Oh, I really mustn't,' she said, then popped it straight into her mouth. Iris folded up her square of foil smaller and smaller, wishing she could tidy away the question that had pushed too hard on a private matter. Brandy *mmmed* at the melting milk chocolate, then said, 'Anything I say will sound as if I'm excusing your man by trying to excuse myself. But I had a flutter on someone once.'

Iris blinked at the horse-racing reference. Perhaps these verbal teeters had helped to make Brandy seem younger than she was.

'I was the bad girl in our marriage. Fell completely for an older man. He was my Seidō karate teacher. His name was *Aaron*.' As if that were part of the appeal. 'We started to have extra one-on-one classes when I was going for my grading. Then we started having a drink in the gym café after the sessions. Hubby and I were going through a bad patch. Kyle was hitting the piss hard after he'd lost his job. It wasn't even that so much, it was the way he just — didn't seem to *like* me any more. You know. No gazing in each other's eyes, no suggesting we go out, no coming over at parties, in that way that lets everyone know you're what's-it's-handle. Spoken for.' Brandy pressed her lips together.

'You don't have to tell me if you don't want, Brandy.'

'It's just a bit of a head-spinner, you know? Can't quite work out how it all happened.' She sipped at her coffee again, then set her cup down with a thump. 'No, I tell a lie. It's blindingly simple. Aaron, the karate teacher, he listened to me. He could look me in the eye; seemed to think I was interesting, you know? Thought that the fact I was starting up my own business, could work with my hands, all that, was *interesting*.' She shook her head as if at a mixed-up child. 'I *felt* interesting when I was with him. I even felt — worth looking at, to be honest. His eyes were like —' She fanned herself with one hand.

Iris's throat tightened. She could remember that look. *Narcissist*, she hissed in her head. *It wasn't ever really about you, was it, Iris? It was ordinary, mindless biology.*

She had to force herself to catch up with Brandy's narrative. 'He was a lecturer at the teacher's college, so I was pretty impressed with myself, you know?' Brandy scoffed. 'Anyway. He was married, too, but there was no sex any more, he told me. We went to Wellington with some others from the dojo for a tournament, stayed in the same motel, got drunk after the gradings, *really* sensible, *really* the Seidō way, and—'

Brandy patted the bun at the back of her head. 'It was stunning. Gorgeous, amazing, incredible sex. Things had gone all flat on that for so long with Kyle. It wasn't just *mechanics*, if you know what I mean. I really didn't fancy him when he was plastered. Anyway, afterwards — *bingo*,

I cried, and —' She stalled, looked up. Iris thought someone else must have walked into the room. Brandy said, 'He just couldn't handle that. He was like, "This is all wrong. It's not meant to be this heavy. I don't want someone I have to carry." As if I was crippled somehow. "I just wanted a good time," he said: "just a laugh." I'd sort of thought that was all I was in it for, too. Bit of flirting, bit of feeling good about yourself, then wham, all those tears. I think I was crying about . . .' She peered out to the street. 'About how I'd broken something. Or how something between me and Kyle was so stuffed that I'd go this far.'

Iris chipped at a crack in her mug with her fingernail, lost.

'And,' Brandy picked up again, pointing at Iris, as if this were what she must take note of, 'I realised, though I'd just wanted a good time myself, if the guy was going to act like that at the first drop, you know, he wasn't even the sort of bloke I wanted to have a laugh with. *And,*' — finger pointing again — 'when I heard him say those things aloud, about fun, and "carrying" someone, it was a slap in the face. I thought, that's not the real world, is it? It made me see how bloody depressed my Kyle was, you know?' Her full, pale face was now pink as a peony. 'So. Moral of the story.' She took a slug of coffee, then shuddered. 'Ugh, going cold.'

'Moral of the story?'

Brandy shrugged one shoulder. 'Come on, you're better with words. Something catching.'

'Catchy.' But Iris's own sense of injury was too intermingled with surprise at the rush of Brandy's monologue to come up with anything else.

Brandy stared at her cold coffee, turned the mug to and fro. 'Sometimes it takes a wrong to see what's right, that's what I think. Because I went back to Kyle, of course, and you know, tried to help him along.'

Iris raised an eyebrow. 'You carried him.'

'Yeah, for a while. Because that's what he needed. And that's the reality of a marriage, eh?'

Brandy released a smoker's cough: she had given up cigarettes, but her lungs were still in recovery. 'I'm not lecturing you, darling, you're all sixes and seven seas with it. You need to work it out between yourselves, but you know, for a while there I felt like — *fffff*.' She shook her head, so her silver hoop earrings swung to and fro. 'I was every shit you could think of under the sun. Wicked, slag, tart, horlet, nymphonoma . . .'

Iris couldn't help a short laugh. 'Harlot, Brandy. And nymphomaniac. But I get what you mean.'

Brandy gave a dismissive toss of her chin: words were irritations, any message should be clear despite them. 'I told Kyle, in the end, that I'd gone a bit doolally myself, had a crazy old lady crush. Which is worse than a schoolgirl crush, isn't it, because you should know better.'

The small brass bells tied to the shop door chimed as a pair of customers came in. Brandy called out welcome; the women drifted between clothing racks, fingering fabric, murmuring. Iris busied herself arranging brooches onto a small swivel display-stand for the counter. There was comfort in the simple physical action: slipping the brooches' backing cards over the tiny rails: hook, slide, turn; hook, slide, turn; trying different colour patterns. Copper, blue, copper, purple . . .

The women left without trying anything on, or buying anything. Brandy gave Iris an *oh-well* look. 'You know that jeweller round the corner? He says he hasn't noticed the effects of the recession on his sales. I think he's shitting me.' She ran her palm back and forth over the counter top. 'Still, it's early days for us here yet. And we've had that big cabaret job. Did I tell you lots of the cast said they'd be in to look around soon? Word will get out.' She sniffed. 'Or maybe that jeweller's sorts of clientele only comes from the upper inchalongs.'

Under Iris's breath, '*Echelons.*'

'Sorry?'

'Echelons.'

'Something like that.'

Iris spun the full stand, assessing her arrangement. 'So perhaps if you charged ten times as much for these, you'd sell more.'

Brandy made a face. 'Not that I don't love those, Iris, but that wouldn't be right, would it?'

Iris stared at the burnished copper surfaces; resting, resting the little pinball thoughts that wanted to go round and round, hitting walls, flipping back . . .

'You're thinking that's a cheek, Iris? Me wanting to do what's right.' Brandy said it without affront or edge.

'No, I was just — off in a daze.' She felt Brandy regard her, watchful and wry, warm and resigned. There was a sense of common ground in the room now, despite Iris's bruised feeling.

'Do you know what this whole bleat has made me think?' Brandy asked. 'One of the worst things about an affair, it's not the shame or the fear or any of the ways you beat yourself up for it. It's that you can't *talk* to anyone else about it.' She ran her hand up and down the counter, as if checking its finish. 'You'd think you'd get smarter as you get older, but you just don't.'

Iris felt a reluctant tug of sympathy. She'd wanted it to just be black and white, right and wrong, principles hard and fast as chess rules. She tried to push the conversation back that way again: bishop to her queen. 'Did Kyle ever find out?'

'Oh, yes, I told him.' She gave a quick sniff. 'I'm not a very good liar, for a start. And it felt like once I'd slept with the other guy, I was just about bringing him into the room with me everywhere, d'y'know what I mean? That's how constantly I was going over what I'd done. Because that's another thing. Even though I knew it was over, big mistake, memo to self, get a *life*, blah, blah, there was still this —' She pushed a fist to her own solar plexus, kept it pressed there. 'I tell you, I hadn't had it that bad since I was sixteen. And feeling such an *idiot*.'

Iris looked at her from under her fringe, wary, wanting to hide it.

'In the end I told Kyle, just to stop blurting it at a bad time. There's my Scots-Irish logic for you, as he calls it. Cheeky bugger.' She peered hard at her nails, found a nail file and started working at the cuticles, let the file clatter down, picked up a vintage halterneck dress and began unpicking the old, half-toothless zip.

Iris collected their coffee cups. 'How did he take it?' she asked, as she busied herself with rinsing them in the tiny corner kitchenette usually concealed from the shop by a curtain.

There was no answer. Iris kept her face turned down to the sink, waiting. 'Brandy?' she looked over her shoulder.

Brandy frowned as she worked the quick-unpick at the zip's edge. 'I was a wreck; he was a wreck. We were both weeping and wailing like band-sheets.'

Iris swallowed down another impulse to word-check.

'First, both of us wanted to take all the blame. Then, it turned around and it was both of us flinging mud. It was the worst. Kyle packed his bags and went to stay at a mate's. I thought I'd blown it for good, y'know? But after a couple of days, he phoned up, and said I was right.'

Brandy laid down the dress for a moment. 'He said he'd got to get his act together; he'd been pushing me away because he was ashamed of being out of work, even though he knew it was the times as much as anything. He didn't blame me for looking elsewhere. But he still wanted to make a go of things. And it has been different since then. It's like —' Brandy tilted her head, stared nowhere. 'Sometimes the things that knock you make you realise your luck, y'know?'

Iris held back from saying *It's different for you, you don't have kids* . . . because even saying that fell short of the hurt; and implied some twisted competition of suffering. Besides, Brandy's face showed how much she'd needed to confide; how bold it had been. The warmth in her voice also said the impulse came from wanting to help. So Iris just dried the cups, setting them back onto their hooks, where they gently rocked.

Brandy had the dress clutched in both hands now. 'Just give hubby a chance, eh, love? He's only human and he's had a helluva lot to deal with, too. We all crack differently under stresses and strains. What's that saying? The broken picture that goes to the wall, something-something-something. I know I'm glad Kyle took me back: it makes me sick to think where I'd be if he hadn't of.'

Pitcher. Well. Have. *Oh, God, I'm a grammar Nazi.*

'Mmmm.' Iris wiped the bench more times than was

necessary. Annoyance seemed to crackle through Brandy. She pushed the dress away, fossicked in one of the plastic crates she used for haberdashery. 'What d'you think *you* need to be happy, Iris?' Brandy sealed her lips around a number of pins that fanned out like lethal whiskers.

'God, that's a huge question. It's not — it's not a quick-unpick thing, is it? These things — they're complicated.'

'I mean before, what you said before. Something about wanting a holiday in someone else's life?'

'Their head. I think I said their head.'

'Well, that's not gonna happen, is it, sunshine? Not unless we're talking movies. But what about the next best thing to it?'

Iris quirked up the side of her mouth. 'What, *Wife Swap*?'

Brandy gave an exasperated *meep*. 'I mean, would you like to get away for a few days, on your own.' Telling, not asking: she seemed to be newly taking her 'older, more experienced woman' role seriously. 'Would it help you to clear your head? Because we've got a little crib, you know, a wee house in the Catlins. Kyle calls it Fisherman's Paradise. What with the weather there I say it should be more like The Rainway Station.'

Iris stared for a moment at Brandy's mischievous expression: the way she was trying to repress delight at her — for once deliberate — pun. 'I'm serious,' said Brandy. She clutched Iris's wrist briefly. 'You need a real break.'

Iris chewed her lip. She was thinking, *Is Billy all right at camp, will Liam talk to me about his session, does a break in the Catlins merit burning up more fossil fuels, what if there were some major national or family disaster while I was there, how do you do the right thing, how do you lead a moral life . . .*

Brandy's voice blissfully interrupted the fire-escape scramble in her skull. 'To be honest, when Kyle took some time away, even just those couple of nights, it scared me shitless, *'scuzay-vay mong frongsay.* I really had to front up to the fact he might be gone for good. It made the both of us see what was what. It might be what your Liam needs.' She stared hard at Iris. 'And you. Get out there, walk on the beach, maybe even go and swim with the Hector's dolphins — Kyle calls them the *what-the-heck, dolphins?* My Kyle, he's a riot really — take yourself some wine and crappy magazines, and let yourself off the leash for a bit. Eh?'

Iris studied the floor. 'Thanks, Brandy, for the offer. I'll definitely think about it.'

'You'd actually be doing me a favour. I need someone to mow the wee lawn. The bloke out there who usually does it has got a gamey leg right now, you could make sure the pipes are working, make sure the mice haven't got the run of the place — you're not afraid of mice are you?'

Iris gave a short, relieved laugh. (*Gamey!*) 'No. No, actually, mice, that's one thing I'm not afraid of.' How good to realise her neuroses didn't actually swallow the entire freaking planet. 'It's just, you know: Billy. After everything that's gone on.' She remembered him trying to fly in the middle of her argument with Liam. When the image of his face, white-green with pain and nausea, came back to her, the memory was almost worse than witnessing it at the time. *No,* she told her head. *Pack it away, far down deep, with the image of Jason too still, too quiet.*

Brandy sniffed again. 'Two or three nights, how's that going to hurt him, honestly? Be good for Liam, I reckon, to see what you usually do for everyone, eh? Be good for them, too. They can go all feral together if they want, can't they? Wear the same undies for three days, eat Cheezels for dinner, play computer games till midnight, or however kids these days rebel when their mums aren't around.'

Iris nibbled at her lip, then startled as Brandy slapped her hand. 'What are you doing to yourself, woman? Doesn't that hurt? Look at your arm!' She'd been twisting the skin again. 'Jesus, Iris. The poor blokes probably need a break from you, too. It'd do my head in having you worrying like that all the time, dog at a bone.'

Iris rubbed at the patch of skin. Brandy took Iris's chin in her fingers. 'Iris. Are you listening?'

'Yes?'

'Do you trust that doctor of yours?'

'She's good, yes.'

'Look. What you said about anxiety medicine. If you'd broken your leg, would you say, "I can't have a cask on it because one day there might not be any casks left?" If you, what, had an infected cut, would you say, "I can't have any anti-skeptic because that won't stop the death penalty in America?" It's all a matter of the wrong end of the micro-scope, isn't it?'

Cast. Antiseptic. Telescope. Iris felt tears and laughter cloud each other.

'I'm not saying those things you've been worried about aren't real. But it's the level that's not right. How can you do anything if you're all basket-case?'

Yes, Iris was exhausted by it.

She visualised the sea, lifting, rolling, tipping over, flattening out; long strips of sand, blank and calm. She imagined resting inside a small wooden house, *crib*, the comfort in that word, the cradling, listening to the timbers settle with the reassuring tick of an old grandfather clock, the susurrus of the wind, sun drying off the day. Like old childhood love murmuring through the walls.

'How soon could I take you up on it?' she asked Brandy. Brandy smiled, stood and went to a diary open on the counter: said she couldn't be bothered with that new-fangled iCal, and refused to buy an iPhone, 'I mean really, i-this, i-that, it's all i-'ll take your money, isn't it?'

She flipped back and forth through a few dates. 'Any weekend, if you just let me know.' Then she peeled a pair of keys out of the back of the diary where they'd been Sellotaped, separated them, and gave one to Iris. 'Here. It's yours for now. I should've stored one of these spares with someone, anyway, in case I lose this thing.' She waved the diary, and then ripped out a page, where she scribbled down an address and some directions, narrating them as she went. She sketched a little map, then sang. '*Ooo-ooo, ooo, yeaaah*. You know that one? That's our car song, whenever we go there. Right. I'm busting. 'Scuse me.'

Then she was off to the bathroom and Iris was left to feel the afterglow of her offer as she folded the map, and slipped it with the key into her handbag.

SO STUNG

THE GRATITUDE AND WARMTH from Brandy's new friendship, they should have made her calmer, shouldn't they, when she heard Liam's voice that night? Iris had done the groceries, buying luxuries to sweeten their first night alone; thinking he might need TLC, if he felt jarred by his session with Jenna. Replaying some of Brandy's reactions, she had also gone into a chemist to fill the GP's prescription for anti-anxiety tablets: though she did it with the same awkwardness she remembered from buying condoms as a university student. Embarrassed by her embarrassment, she shoved the box of pills down to the bottom of her handbag, almost tripping as she hurried from the pharmacy to the car park. *I don't have to take them*, she thought. *They're just an option . . .*

At home, she lugged groceries inside. Canary Woof and the answer machine were in a duet of urgent, high-pitched cheeps. What could the bird sense? Was it the school? Was there a problem at camp? She dumped the grocery bags and pressed the play-back button.

Liam's passionless monotone sounded from the machine. 'Hi. It's me. Look, I'm going to be late tonight. Something's come up. Oh, and I just wanted to check. Steve might need me to take a group out on the harbour this weekend. Wasn't sure of your plans. Anyway, don't know when I'll be in. See you.'

Fury cannoned through her. The chance to really talk: wrecked. Romantic, conciliatory dinner plans: wrecked. A weekend together for the first time since they'd moved south: bloody *wrecked*. The opportunity to put their relationship first: *ignored*. She was so stung she didn't even have time to think *too angry to drive safely*. She stalked to the bedroom, grabbed a suitcase, threw in a few clothes, her toiletries, some books, lugged it to the car, came back, grabbed the grocery bags again, shoved them into the boot, and slipped the South Island road map from the glove box. She sent Brandy a text: *Believe it or not off 2 Catlins now. U r life saver.* The mobile beeped back instantaneously: a line of happy emoticons, and the perfectly Brandyesque *strike while ironingz hot.* Iris flung the phone back into her handbag, snatched it back up again to turn it off, as if that itself were a message to Liam: *Unavailable. See how you #$@#$%ing like it.*

What would she have done if Brandy hadn't made her offer? Taken off to a motel, probably, the way her hot head had urged in the middle of that fight when little Billy decided he could fly. She drove with her knuckles as white as her press-lipped fury until she was near Waihola. There the sight of the lake and the tea rooms felt like instructions to collect her thoughts. She pulled up in the car park, and with the bitter aftertaste of *livid* at the back of her tongue, she phoned home. The answer machine clicked on. Bloody

Liam. She tried to keep her tone civil.

'It's Iris here. I've decided to have a couple of nights away. I'm borrowing a friend's place in the Catlins. Everything's fine; I just —' she shifted the phone in her hand, trying to think straight '— just need time alone. I'll have my cell-phone if anything really urgent comes up, but —' she stopped herself from saying, *but you clearly don't want to talk, so — slide it.* 'Okay. I'll be back in time for the end of school camp.' Then — partly in case Billy heard the message before it was wiped — she signed off with *loveyouguys.* And hung up fast, before Liam could run for the phone. She pulled out of the car park, belligerent, dismayed tears shunted away.

As it turned out, there was no cell-phone reception at Brandy's place. There was a landline, though, so no need to be spooked by isolation if there was an emergency. There she went again: catastrophising. Why should there be an emergency over the next few nights? The worst couldn't happen again so soon. It had already come.

The crystallisation of that thought sent Iris to the couch in the tiny living-room, where she cried herself to sleep, hugging a cushion like her own baby: the great swirling chaos of Jase, Liam, Faye, Pete, Steffie, Billy all carrying her off into oddly pleasant dreams: towers of pink and blue paper cupcake cases; a nameless man sitting in a black suit in a corner, to whom she brought food; the sculpture of another man whose face from one angle was only an empty bronze rim. She woke to the sound of a riroriro that she thought was Billy: Billy perfecting his descant.

The dissonance between her dreams and the night before, together with the Billy-toned sweetness, worked and worked through the sadness. Iris tried to sustain the note all day. She spent her time wandering the foreshore, collecting bird feathers, colourful shells, letting her mind empty. She'd assumed she'd come here to think. It turned out the opposite was more restorative. Eat, read, walk, sleep. Just letting the thoughts go, milkweed blown to the sky. No talk to anyone: even keeping her face down when she passed people on the beach.

On the first day, she thought she'd never want to leave; solitude was so much simpler than home. On the second day: ditto. Then as evening again turned down the lights, tears thrummed at the back of her skull. She dug around in her handbag, remembering the pills. She opened the box, scanned the leaflet about precautions, negative side-effects, musts and must-nots. Certain phrases raced up as if to slap her: collapse, self-harm, suicidal thoughts, *increased* suicidal thoughts . . . Panic swam. *Warning*, it should say. *Learning about this medication may induce the need for this medication.*

She shoved the leaflet back into the box, shoved the box back into the handbag, zipped the bag shut, threw a cushion on top of it, then sat on it, like Pandora in denial. It began to feel as if the room were being pulled into some dark, invisible plughole: reality draining through the floor. Had Pete, her brother-in-law, been on any medication? She'd never thought to ask. She couldn't start the course of pills without Liam there, in case . . .

Liam. His name brought warm turmoil. She stood up. He was still the one she turned to, when in any doubt, even in her interior monologue. It wasn't a monologue at all, then. It was a dialogue. Was that just habit? She wondered how she would feel if he pulled this trick on her — going

AWOL, being completely unreachable — not just dialled down. But the cone of silence, his flirtation with Faye . . . weren't they versions of this?

How would he like it if she found a lover? She tried to toy longer with that idea. Would it be flowers in the street from a stranger, a customer in the shop, a father at Billy's school asking her for coffee, then turning up with wine some time when Liam was out of town? Would the first move be holding her shoulders, clasping her at the waist, telling her he wanted her to tell him everything . . . Hang on. The man still had Liam's hands. His jawline.

There, underneath it all: there he was still. How she missed their old intimacy. When she really tried to think through a scenario where they were apart for good — splitting weekends with Billy — there was an intensified *Wait! No, wait! There is so much we still have to do; there are conversations we haven't had. Billy: how could we do that to Billy? This marriage is bigger than both of us.*

She shifted objects around aimlessly on the beach shack's two tiny bookshelves, then flicked, bored, through its pile of old *Reader's Digest*s and *New Idea*s. She tried to play a game of Scrabble against herself, losing interest within about three turns. She looked around the crib, which now felt stuffy, constrained, like a bodice two sizes too small. She paced the short distance between walls, then stood at the window and stared out at the gleaming moon-ribbon streaming along the sea's rumpled black. She visualised a dress borrowing its play of light on dark; imagined shaking it out for Brandy's astute eye. Liam would love it here; getting out on the water, well away from city views and the pressure of clients . . .

Stillness entered. She didn't want to punish Liam any

more — had just wanted space to breathe. She probably needed a longer respite, but a snake of nausea said, not this way. Not sneaking around as if stealing it, playing *he's the goose, I'm the gander, pass the same sauce.* It had to be upfront, frank, talked about.

THE MOST URGENT THING

LIAM CALLED HIMSELF A PRIZE IDIOT. He'd been playing for time with his white lie that something had come up; he'd still been decompressing after the session with Jenna. But after he'd driven out along the peninsula — never tiring of that molten blue harbour — trying to sort out his head, he swung back to town to find a florist and a bottle store. Then he went into Little India, so he could surprise Iris with takeaways. He'd been warming up to a big push. Not turning over a new leaf: more like doing a flip, a swimmer at the end of a lane, racing back to where he should be . . .

When he heard Iris's answer-machine message he felt vertigo, confusion. Friend, what friend? Who did Iris know who could lend her a holiday house? The way she said *friend*, all veiled — 'Don't cheat a cheater,' he said aloud, and then in self-disgust slammed a cutlery drawer shut.

Then, hell, bring on the disaster army, would you? He'd just decided to gorge on the takeaway feast as comfort when the phone rang. He dove for it, mouthful of naan balled up in one cheek.

'Mr Galbraith?'

'Uh-huh.'

'It's Elaine Hooper here, from Larnach Park School.'

He spat the food into a napkin. 'What's happened?'

'Nothing, nothing, Billy is actually fine, but we've had a bit of a double-whammy out here.' She sounded amped on crisis, actually. 'The camp's had a power outage. We were going to carry on anyway —' Liam was already thinking, lily-livered, namby-pamby, WTF call this wilderness camp, leadership training, don't they know how to light a fire? — 'but five of the children have come down with a tummy bug. It's not pretty. We've decided with no hot water, it's best to bring the children back to Dunedin. We're already on the bus now, and trying to contact all the parents. Can you meet us at the school in about an hour?'

Liam felt the giant forceps of a tension headache clamp his skull. What had Steve said the other day? Something about *this pukefest going round* . . . His sigh was close to a groan. 'Just as well one of us is home, isn't it?'

Miss Hooper's voice went high and tight. 'I'm sorry, Mr Galbraith, it can't be helped. As I say, we thought—'

'Yeah, yeah, of course.' He checked his watch. 'So I'll be at the school round eight.' As soon as the phone was down, he forked prawn malabari into his mouth. Canary Woof, whose cage had been left in the living-room for the day to catch some sunlight, scampered up and down his perch, for all the world as if glad Billy was coming home. Liam looked at him glumly. 'Missed him, did you, Woof?' The bird ran a few more fifteen-centimetre dashes. 'He might be bringing home a stomach bug, though, y'know.'

'*Rolfe. Rolfe*,' said the bird. Liam couldn't even laugh.

But Billy did seem the normal, well, box of birds when

Liam collected him from school. He claimed that it was only the boys in one cabin who were sick.

'Huh,' Liam said, 'early night tonight, just to be sure.'

'Where's Mum?'

'Oh, just — off on a bit of a break, I think. She wasn't expecting you home so soon.'

'I know!' Billy said, as if it were all part of the great excitement of being alive.

Liam coaxed him off to bed, letting him rattle on about what they'd managed to do on the truncated camp, agreeing to read more *New Zealand Birds* with him. His talk with Jenna still turned on high volume in his mind, Liam leaned down to rumple Billy's hair, then planted a kiss on his head. The boy's eyes sprung open in delight, which he instantly hid, as if camouflage would mean the kiss wasn't scared off. Sideswiped, Liam sat there, on his bed, till the boy was asleep.

Eventually Liam went to replay the answer-machine message. A Dear John, was it? He reined in the dismay; replayed it a third time, making himself concentrate on *everything's fine, back by Monday, loveyouguys*. He tried her cell-phone; texted her instead when voicemail came on. All he could think was *call me*.

Then he walked to the liquor cupboard, grabbed the one decent bottle in there — a single malt salvaged from the good old days — and poured himself a shot of sleep. Only thing being, before he felt groggy, he felt gutted and gregarious at the same time. He found his cell-phone and started a text to Faye. He got as far as *Hey, Faye what's up?*

'Fuckwit,' he whispered and deleted it. Then he called Steve.

'Oh, gidday, Liam.'

'How's it going?'

'Not too bad. You?'

'Shit, mate.'

'Billy still not too good? Or something come up down at the wharf?'

He took a moment to remember what reason he'd given for evading work that morning.

'No. It's just —' Liam took another mouthful of the Talisker, waited for the slow smoke of it to warm through his hesitation.

'Still there, Liam?'

'Yeah. Look, sorry to bother you on a Friday night —'

'Do you want to come round?'

'No, thanks Steve, that's the thing. I'm here on my own with Billy. Iris has taken off. She called and left a message. She hasn't rung you, has she?' Liam groped around for some other practical reason for phoning Steve. 'Or said anything to Hannah?'

Steve muffled the phone, then came back on. 'Nope. Hannah says she hasn't talked to Iris in ages. Says she keeps meaning to, but you know how it is —'

It was a polite porky; it had been a little odd for Liam to even ask. Now he had a vague recollection of some issue on Hannah's last visit to their place, but the whisky was melting anything except the most urgent thing . . .

'Okay. Thanks. That's all, really. Just wanted to pin down some facts.'

'Sorry, Liam, I haven't heard anything.'

'Okay.'

'So. She's got the pip with you.'

'Yeah. Not without cause.'

'How do you mean?'

'It's not too late, is it, Steve?'

'What, to call? Or are you talking about Iris?'

'Huh.'

'It's not too late to call, no. We were just Darby-and-Joaning in front of TV.'

'Hey, look. I won't go into it all now if you're settled in there together.' He swirled the single malt in its glass. 'Make the most of it, eh, Steve?'

There was some whooshing static, as if Steve were moving around the house. 'You don't know where she's gone?'

'Her message said she's in the Catlins, at a friend's.'

The silence gaped, but Liam had to stop the wrong penny from dropping. 'Nothing I don't deserve, Steve.' He swallowed. 'I'm no saint.'

There was another long, static-y passage where Liam thought Steve might have lost reception on the portable.

'Well,' said Steve, finally, 'me neither. All I can say, all I've ever come up with on this subject, and that's after a few hard home truths, too, I've been there — is love's a bitch, hormones are a bastard, and together they have little bleeders called misery and maudlin. Especially if you try to wean them onto the booze.'

Liam set down his glass in surprise. He must sound slurred, or else he'd swallowed too loudly down the receiver. 'Thanks, Steve. I —'

'Glad you called. You'll let me know if there's anything we can do, yeah? Like take Billy for the afternoon, or something.'

Although he couldn't hear exactly what she said, Hannah's tone in the background left Liam sure Steve should have cleared that with her first. He jumped in: 'I'll be fine, thanks for the offer. It's just a weekend. Good to talk to you. See you Monday.'

He hung up, slugged back the rest of his drink, heard in his mind's ear a song Iris used to play relentlessly; something about not being able to drown your sorrows because sorrow floats . . . But his hand was pouring another glass. His legs walked him around the house, back and forth. He put some Neil Young on low on the stereo; went to his mug collection and rearranged it again around the two new insanely cheap Toby jugs he'd received on mail order a couple of weeks ago.

When he stood back and looked at the reconfiguration his hoard still seemed unbalanced but, groggy, he couldn't work out what was wrong. He sat down with a hiss, fired up his laptop and started searching for more mugs online. Usually he found it satisfying: all the grinning faces; the bright glaze; the mindlessness of browsing websites. There were only a couple of foul green Crown Lynn replicas on Trade Me; not his thing. On eBay there was a mix of vintage Royal Doulton and Kevin Francis Face Pots. Too slick. Not as good as the lived-in character faces of the Royal Doulton. To his watchlist Liam added a Long John Silver mug with a parrot on its shoulder doubling as the handle, to show Billy in the morning.

There was something about staring at the battered old faces that calmed him down. He liked to imagine sitting in a pub with their type; listening to the hard-luck, shaggy-dog tales they'd be likely to tell. Iris thought his fondness for them was bizarre. But it was a harmless addiction, right? After all, he could be playing online war games. Or encouraging Billy to take up hunting, base-jumping or any one of the so-called adrenaline-junkie pursuits that sent her into paroxysms. She said, 'Weren't kayaking, tramping and caving enough?' He said, '*You* don't have to do them,' and she said, 'But what if something happens to the boys?'

She said. She had said.

Push it away. When am I not confronting it? I don't want to circle back to this tonight. I sorted some of my shit out today, I did. It's all about who's left. Billy and Iris. I hope, Iris.

Swig. Click, click, click, drink, browse, drink, browse.

Neil Young finished on the CD player; Liam tried some of his old Cure albums, not listened to for a decade or more, but found that at forty he couldn't stomach Robert Smith and his clenched ululating. The whisky needed older pain behind it: jazz, or the blues. He chose Coltrane, Byrd, Armstrong, Fitzgerald. He drank himself into the music then tried to drink himself out. Round midnight his head began to throb the warning that he'd better quit now or he'd be dog-sick in the morning. He fell into bed as if cut off at the knees.

Blank.

'Dad! Dad! You've got to hurry! Quick!'

Iris, car crash, roof off, there'd been a fire while he'd been whisky-coma'd, what the fuck, God my head! 'Yummp?' he managed. As he lifted his head it swilled with nausea and regret. Another yell came like a smack to the skull and the ordinary sunshine filtering through the curtains knifed his eyes. It ignited a painful, vibrant pink mandala right in the centre of his vision.

Billy came into the bedroom in a strange, jerky speed-walk. He was still in his BMXing-astronaut pyjamas, Canary Woof clutched in both hands like water in a desert.

His cheeks were streaked with tears, his face pale blue with disbelief: the network of veins showing through his skin.

Liam's stomach heaved as he swung his legs to the side of the bed, but he fought it back. 'Wassup?'

'Canary Woof is bleeding. I let him out of the cage and he flew around so amazing, Dad, I couldn't believe it, he knew where to go and how to show me, and I shut the door while I went to the loo and when I came back the neighbour's cat was at my window, it couldn't get in. The landlord's one's given up on Woof, but this one, it was sitting on the ledge outside, Canary Woof couldn't stand it, he was so scared, it was like, it was like, a *sniper*. Its green eyes were aimed right on him. And when I opened the door he tried to fly out and I tried to shut the door before he could and it's all my fault because he was aiming at the gap but then the gap wasn't there and—'

'It's okay, Billy, slow down. Just slow down. Easy, kiddo. Let me see.'

He held his hands out so Billy could pass the bird. Canary Woof's body quaked and he squawked in alarm when Billy opened his palms. Billy kiss-talked to it: 'Dad's just trying to help. It's okay.'

'Hell. Yeah. He's bleeding. We'd better take him to the vet.' Liam fumbled for his alarm clock. Seven o'clock. Christ. The time seemed to nail his headache in harder. 'Um, fire up the laptop for me, will you, Billy? I've gotta . . .'

Liam belted to the bathroom, vomited, waited for the fireworks behind his eyes to die, rinsed his mouth, brushed his teeth, called himself a wit-fuck for some variation on the theme, and gingerly made his way back to Billy, intoning in his head, *keep it together, keep it together*. Billy was still standing there, little bird clutched in both hands.

He hadn't turned on the laptop. He seemed to think force of concentration would keep Canary Woof alive.

Liam got the computer running; checked out the vet's open times. 'We can't go in until nine, Billy. We'll head in after your breakfast, okay?'

'That's not soon enough. He could bleed to death.'

'Right. I'll call them and see who does after-hours work.' Liam shuffled off to find the landline, making the call in the living-room. No answer on the emergency number either; the recorded voice said, 'If you reach this message I am attending another emergency. Your call will be redirected.' It was: back to the vet surgery answer machine.

Billy padded into the room then stood there, eerily frozen.

'Shit,' Liam said again, all inhibitions undone post-whisky: no tempering language in front of the boy. 'Can't rouse anyone, Bill-bo.' The hangover was turning into a white wall. He couldn't get past it.

'Google what to do,' said Billy.

'Eh?' He'd heard, but the intelligence of it hadn't sunk in past the only things he could think: Nurofen, water, bed.

'Google budgie and bleeding, or budgie and injury.'

Liam followed his instructions but something else made its way through the grip around his skull. 'If something's bleeding you staunch it, Billy. Can you find a paper towel or something? Will he let you?'

Colour came back into Billy's face, and Liam could see his concentration whirring. 'There's something about blood-feathers. I should know it about blood-feathers, but it's run out of my head all of a sudden, what order and how. Can you just Google it, Dad?'

'Okay.' Liam's screen-reading frown squeezed the whisky vice a notch tighter. 'Budgie blood feathers.' A website came up. His stomach pitched at the words 'Newly growing feathers need a fresh blood supply. Broken blood feathers that stay in a bird's skin essentially act as an open tube, letting blood run out.' He scrolled down a little; there was a slew of images of a stretched-out, bloodied wing, fingers carefully tweezing out the snapped shaft. He was up out of the chair, off to the bathroom, himself a broken pipe pouring out the very last of the drink. When he was emptied, it was as if the muscles in his stomach had learned what to do: sobs came now. His head churned with *Pete Jase come back Iris, poor bloody Billy, what a shit-crock of a dad, pull yourself together, isn't this what you were afraid of, if you fall apart . . .*

'Dad? Where are the tweezers? Or do we have something called needle-nose pliers?' Billy was outside the bathroom door, his voice now an excited-steady.

'Mum's dressing table. Tweezers.'

Billy knocked. 'I need a towel.'

'Just a minute.' Liam splashed water on his face.

'Forget it. I'll find something else.' Billy's impatience made Liam look up into the mirror. That was himself he'd heard. He dried his face, leaned on the wall for a moment as he assessed whether he was truly ready to leave the bathroom.

He unlocked the door and found Billy in the kitchen with the budgie wrapped in a tea towel, the laptop on the kitchen bench, perilously close to a water spill. Billy was murmuring something: it sounded like French on rewind; maybe his own bird-language. He pulled swiftly on a broken feather, and as he pulled on another, said, 'We need cornstarch and sterile gauze, that's what it says.'

Liam went to the pantry, found a box of cornflour.

Then back to the bathroom to the medicine cabinet. Found some gauze, shut the door, then opened it again. Panadol. Nurofen.

'Dad!'

'Coming.' He sped up a bit, his headache giving him a bollocking.

Billy needed Liam to open the cornflour. 'It says to put a pinch of cornstarch on the bleeding,' the boy said. The boy's worried frown was so like Iris it stalled Liam. Billy said, 'Quick please, Dad.'

Liam sprinkled a pinch of the powder on the spot where the feathers had been plucked out.

'Can I have the gauze now?'

'Yes, Doc.' Liam passed over the fine squares of material. The bird swivelled its head to and fro, with a thin but calm peeping sound. This boy really knew how to gentle birds. Billy pressed the material over the cornflour, and went to sit on the living-room couch with the bird cradled in his hands.

Liam poured himself a glass of water, knocked back two Nurofen. He closed his eyes: pain slid from the top of his skull and into his sinuses. He waited it out.

'Need breakfast, Billy?'

'Not yet.'

Course not. He wouldn't be letting go of that bird for a while.

'What's the time, Dad?'

'Ages yet before the vet opens.'

'I want to know what time I took out the blood-feathers. So we can say how long he carries on bleeding if this doesn't work.'

'Oh.' Liam felt so — junior. 'It's half seven.'

Billy made a clicking call. Liam gazed at his profile.

It seemed like Billy could see some part of the bird was wandering away, losing the will to stay in its body. He adjusted the gauze, the tea towel, his face in total concentration.

Liam went about a few chores: coffee-making, bench-wiping, chucking a load of laundry on — nothing too strenuous as he waited for the Nurofen to file off the edges of the headache. Eventually, with a mug of coffee, he went back out to sit alongside the boy. 'How's he doing?'

'Um, I think he's okay. There's no more blood coming through the gauze. See?'

'Hmm. Looks like a tiny island. Little blood map.'

'Canary Island,' said Billy.

'Ar, ar, humour,' said Liam.

'What?'

'Nothing. From *Mork and Mindy*. TV programme from when I was a kid.'

'Oh. Ancient history.'

'Watch it, kiddo,' warned Liam.

'Watch what, *Dork and Dimby*?'

'When'd you get such a smart mouth?'

'Came with the brain.' Billy started scratching at the miniature mohawk of pinfeathers on the top of Canary Woof's head. 'See these?' he said. 'He's moulting. We've got to help him get these out. He can't reach them himself. He looks punk.'

Liam set his coffee down and put an arm around Billy. He drew him close and planted a big kiss on the side of his head. 'You're a trooper, Billy. Some kind of bird whisperer, eh? Never seen anyone manage birds that well. Not even your granddad. I should've remembered about blood-feathers, but —'

'You've got an overhang.'

Liam looked down at his belly, thinking the boy meant he needed to get a larger size of jeans. 'What?'

'An overhang. Your breath smells like a fruity dog bum. Your eyes are red and you haven't shaved. You're Bleary McCleary.'

'Oh. You mean hangover. Sorry.'

Billy looked down at Canary Woof. 'That's okay. Toothpaste helps, you know.' He nestled against Liam's upper arm.

Liam watched the budgie's head tip as it trained one eye and then another onto the world.

Liam reached out a finger and took a turn carefully scratching and rolling the pinfeather shafts on the bird's head. 'This boy might be the smartest I've ever met,' he said to the budgie.

Billy kept his head resting against his dad. Then he lifted it, and Liam saw that he was looking at the trio of framed photos of Jason that sat on a bookshelf.

Liam tugged his own earlobe. 'Our Jase. A real people person. Energy to burn, eh?' He couldn't look at Billy again just yet. 'Always ready to try new things.' He took another fortifying sip of coffee. 'I always thought that'd be good for him along the way. He was no scholar, but I thought he'd make up for that in can-do and EQ.'

'You mean NCEA.'

Liam chuckled. 'No, EQ means emotional intelligence — knowing how people tick. He was like your Uncle Pete that way. But Pete was maybe too sensitive.' Billy looked up at his dad, and Liam pushed the boy's fringe out of his eyes. 'In some ways.'

'What ways?' said Billy.

Liam felt a sideways slip off the tracks. He took another

slug of coffee, waited until he could talk again. 'He didn't believe he'd be good enough for Jase on his own, after your Aunt Steffie died. But he didn't think through how it would affect all of us if he went, too.' Liam's free hand drummed on the air, as if it were trying to Morse something he couldn't say. He felt himself getting into it too deeply for the boy, the pit of grief that the whisky had washed him into. He pulled himself back. 'So, yeah. Jase was going to be a bit of a party boy. But you —' Liam set down his mug again. 'I think you could do anything you put your mind to. You could talk the birds down from the trees.' He gave Billy's nose a tweak. The boy was comfortably quiet, just watching the bird on his knee. 'Your mum thinks you could be good at languages. But I think you could just as easily be a scientist. Everything you know about birds; all that reading you do . . . either way, you've got the smarts, eh, Billy?' He gave him another cursory squeeze. Billy flashed a bright glance; his smile a curly bracket he tried to flatten out. 'You have to say that. You're my dad.'

'Not really. I've heard some dads call their kids all sorts of things.'

'Like what?'

'Numbnuts. Dillbrain. Lumpy. Lard-arse. The Accident.'

'Jeez. That's terrible.'

They gave each other a solemn look. Then they got the giggles. The very fact that they both got the giggles fuelled more. Pretty soon, though, Billy was saying, '*This* is terrible! I can't believe we're laughing! Canary Woof might be dying and we're laughing.'

Canary Woof tilted his head and barked. '*Rolfe. Rolfe.*'

The pair of them looked at each other, mouths in clown Os before they burst out laughing again. When they had recovered, Billy carefully re-checked the gauze. 'Definitely stopped,' he said. 'I still want to take him to the vet, though.'

'Yep.'

They sat there, pressed up against each other, primate to primate, as body warmth started its mending. Liam shut his eyes for a bit, and a memory coalesced out of the sleepy, hungover buzz in his head. Camping trips, as a kid: he and Pete side by side in the musty tent, being told to go to sleep while their parents sat outside, murmuring over a campfire. How almost every time they heard a ruru, morepork, little Pete would startle. *Wassat? Bush ghost?* And Liam would have to reassure him: sometimes giggling, sometimes annoyed that Pete was off again on one of his spooky fits. Pete always hutched himself closer, pressed his forehead against Liam's back. They'd drowse off together, warm and loose-limbed, Liam putting up with it even when it was too hot, because it was the best way to get his little brother to settle.

Liam opened his eyes and laid his palm on his son's head. He waited for all the jostling thoughts and remorse to quieten.

'We're gonna be okay, eh Billy?' he said, as if it were the conclusion to a subterranean conversation they'd been having for years.

The boy nuzzled his head further into Liam's hand. 'Yup,' he said.

Iris couldn't get reception on her cell-phone until she was so close to Dunedin it seemed pointless to call. She walked in the door, bracing herself for chilliness, hurt or disappointment. She found Liam and Billy both at the dining table, constructing an enormous kite out of bamboo struts and old sewing pattern paper she'd given Billy for crafts.

Canary Woof sat on Billy's shoulder. The bird was the one to look up first. It chirruped as if flustered, or perhaps in admonishment. Without a beat lost, barely looking up, Billy said, 'Hey, Mum, watch this.' He leaned closer to Liam so their upper arms touched. Liam made a high-pitched kissing noise. Canary Woof awkwardly hop-walked to his shoulder. Then Billy made his own high-pitched kissing noise. The bird hop-walked back. Then Liam picked up an old metal hoop that had once held a selection of cookie cutters. He held it up between their shoulders, gave the two-note pucker again. Canary Woof waddled through the hoop and onto Liam's shoulder. He seemed to bob in a series of tiny bows. Billy was grinning as if he'd done the trick himself.

'Canary Woof hurt his wing, Mum, that's why he's hopping, not flying. When he's better, we're going to see if he'll fly through the hoop, too.'

'Well.' Iris set down her bags. 'You two seem to have been busy.'

Liam finally stood, and met her eye. 'Billy's been a good kid.'

They stared at each other. Liam was pale, unshaven and his hair still sat in the little bristly clumps that showed he hadn't showered since sleep. 'You okay?' he said. From the look of him, she should be asking him that.

'It was good to have some time on my own.' She swallowed. 'I'm kind of pathetic, though. It didn't take me long to miss you lot.' She held out her hands as if to say, *no tricks*. 'This would all be so much easier if I didn't.'

Liam's mouth pouched: vulnerable, sheepish, tragic, sweetly boyish, maddening, familiar all at once. 'I'm so sorry, Iris,' he said. 'I've been an idiot.'

She let him stew in that for a bit. She picked up her bags again, moved them to the couch, sat next to them and started to go through the pockets. It was only after she'd unzipped and zipped them all that she realised she wasn't looking for anything: she was neatening her thoughts, reassuring herself that her mental resolutions were safely stored.

She looked up and there he was, expression as mixed as before. Her fussing hands fell into her lap, as she took a deep breath and offered in exchange, 'You haven't exactly had an easy run this year — I guess I should have cut you more slack.'

Now they couldn't meet eyes, and an interruption from Billy, for once, was a relief. The boy was whistle-kissing to the budgie.

Canary Woof hopped onto Billy's shoulder and trundled down along his sleeve until he sat in Billy's palm. With a cheery tinge of cheek, and a raised eyebrow that made Iris blink, Billy said, 'I guess things just might be quieter in my *room*, Canary Woof. I'm going to put you back in your cage now. Better not tire you out. The vet said you might be *subdued* today.'

As Billy left, Liam walked over to the couch. He gestured, asking Iris to stand. She watched him for a moment, then hauled herself up. Wrapping his arms around her, he whispered, 'Don't leave, Iris. We'll work it out. We will. I'll try harder.'

With her face buried in his neck, she said his name like a question. They pressed closer, and of course that was when Billy came lolloping back in. He hauled to a stop, then lolloped out again, singing in a giddy yet convincing falsetto *Gross! Gross!*

DELICIOUS SIZZLE

SO THEY TALKED, AND TALKED. Then they talked some more. Blocked grief, rushed grief, misread anger, back to the family sessions again, oh, blah, not *again*, Billy was kind of *over* it. That meant, Jenna said, it was probably time to wind things down, for him at least. Two more sessions booked: and then she thought the family could handle most of it by themselves.

'Handle the jandal,' said Billy.

'The way life flip-flops,' said Liam.

'Dad joke,' sassed Billy.

'Is there therapy for that?' said Iris, and Billy got more giggles, big time.

So it's not like Billy needs a sticker chart to tell him how he's doing. He knows that things are getting better. The hot sad tingles don't happen so much any more. He doesn't want to flap, jump, caw and scream. Some major amazing things have happened. Too many to list, really, but some he even writes down in his not-exactly-a-journal — the notebook he uses . . . okay, maybe four times a year.

The first one happened after his parents had one session with Jenna on their own. They were still going about their *marriage*. Sometimes they said *marriage* like the way Dad said *tax* or *warrant of fitness*. They both picked him up after school, Mum pale and Dad's eyes all puffy and red, like a chameleon who'd been in chlorine. His dad had said, 'Billy, can you come here a second?' Billy braced himself for more heavy talk, which was all so — *kwonk*. Dad said nothing: just rugged him up in a hug. Later, they sat on the couch; with Dad's arm slung round Billy's shoulder, they played Doodle Jump on the laptop. It might sound crazy. (Once they'd all started talking, just about everything they'd got jammed into their separate heads sounded crazy. Maybe crazy was the new not-crazy.) But right then, Billy felt like some part that had gone missing flew back into himself. Maybe not flew. Poured back. Like a dry pond refilling with water. Happy ducks could swim on it. Oh, it was pretty hard to get away from birds completely, but that was okay.

Trisha and Jenna said everyone had their interests and birds were one of his: it didn't mean he had *developmental issues*. Not like Cory Busby, a boy from school in Auckland, who screamed in malls, would eat only crispy food, had to be stopped from eating dirt and the silica packs that came with instant noodles, who was obsessed with red cars, and would sometimes just stand in the school grounds and flap his arms, getting himself hyper about something nobody else could see. Billy thought of him as a boy who'd been scratched, like a DVD, so he got stuck sometimes. You couldn't get him to skip forward, or even back, no matter what you said. But Billy liked Cory: he'd made life interesting. Jenna said, it sounds like he might have had autism spectrum disorder. Sometimes these terms are crucial; other times, they get in the way. And Billy said, maybe we all have our own syndrome. I have a Billy syndrome; Mum has an Iris syndrome. Jenna grinned, saying, w-e-e-l-l, it's much more complicated than that, but I enjoy your way of thinking. *Whatever*, Billy wasn't scratched in the Cory sense: he'd just needed birds in a special way, for a while.

Things had really turned pretty great. There had been the Orokonui Ecosanctuary visit for his own birthday, then he'd had two other birthday party invitations, so he'd been ten-pin bowling and to the butterfly house. He put those in his notebook. Mum and Dad had started a regular outing together to the movies on cheap nights and they'd found him a babysitter. Shayleen, the niece of Mum's boss, Brandy. She was actually kind of useless: sometimes Billy had to look after *her*. ('You forgot to turn off the stove. That smell is burnt rice.') But she was useless in a good way, because she didn't notice when Billy had a second ice-cream and stayed up reading till after nine o'clock.

Mum and Dad had started normal-talking again. Even about Jase and Uncle Pete. Billy wasn't too sure why exactly, but he didn't *want* the details. Couple stuff was weird and depressing when it wasn't going well. Then when it was, when parents got all huggy-wuggy and *oh, Liam, oh, Iris*, it made him want to lock himself in his room and draw pictures of Canary Woof until they'd stopped all the Freaky.

He supposed that seeing Jenna probably helped his mum and dad sort things. Either that or the fact that they were seeing all these movies meant that they had more to talk *about* now. So, anyway. Home was no longer 'so they all lived saddestly ever after'. And that meant he could enjoy the delicious sizzle of his secret. The school production. He put that in his notebook too. You should have *seen* the school production!

HIS OWN SWEET TIME

IRIS AND LIAM SAT down in the crowd. Around the hall people were unbundling themselves from down jackets, woollen coats, ear-flap hats, scarves, puffy gloves: outside, late spring had sent a storm. In front of Iris, a small Korean girl still had some hail clinging to her glossy black hair. The ice shone like seed pearls, as if with a fine sense of occasion. Iris scanned the large hall as familial pride glistened over the audience. Hairstyles were shinier, perkier; shoes along her row glinted with polish; couples brushed lint off each other's coats as if even the lint were delightful. Eyeliner seemed eyelinier, lipstick lipstickier, lava-lavas so bold on this shivery night. Everybody's postures were at their most meerkatish.

Wisps of chatter caught in Iris's ear. She fanned the photo-copied programme that small children dressed as monkeys had handed out at the main door. ''*citing*,' she said, quoting Billy, who'd been giddy with anticipation before heading backstage. Liam's public, impassive expression softened, and he kissed her temple. She felt the stirring of something. She deliberately let herself think: *Faye Prescott*. Did the sensation wane? A complex melancholy stood next to desire, like a trellis and vine so entwined it was hard to tell which was which. What was that all about? Knowing Liam more deeply than she had before? Gratitude for a second chance? Pride that she was so forgiving?

No. She was guiltier than that. When she'd come back from the Catlins and found Liam and Billy absorbed in their tinkering on the kite, Brandy's words had replayed: 'The poor blokes probably need a break from you, too. It'd do my head in having you worrying like that all the time, dog at a bone.' Iris had felt curiously redundant. As she sat there unzipping and rezipping her suitcase pockets, she wondered if she'd grown so lost in her own debates about right thing, wrong thing, what's best for Billy? that she hadn't seen how hard it was for Liam. Perhaps it reinforced for him that he was supposed to be the rock; left no room for him to listen to himself, in his own sweet time.

They still had a long slog ahead. Just last week, Liam had said to her, 'If you get that bad again, that thin and anxious, promise me you'll reconsider medication.'

'If you promise to keep up the counselling.'

He sulked, like a kid.

'Stalemate,' she said.

He sniffed under his armpit. 'Sorry, mate.'

Which, you know, was progress: bad wisecracks were better than iceman. What a labyrinth. But somehow, now that they were all talking again, the tangle seemed like the threads behind a gorgeously embroidered wall-hanging. The necessary mess.

'Penny for them?' said Liam.

She smiled, pressed closer. 'You know. The lifeyness of life.'

He raised his eyebrows. 'Guess that covers it.'

A man in a young gay couple to their left brought out a giant slab of a chemistry textbook. 'You can't *study* here, can you, Ivan?' said his partner. He wasn't really asking.

'I'll watch when Angelica's on. For her thirty seconds of fame.'

'You can't *read*!'

'Henry. I've been to school productions for all four nieces so far. I am a boredom connoisseur.'

A woman on the other side of Iris fidgeted, adjusting her waistband, tweaking her bra straps, readjusting her waistband again. 'Hmm?' said her husband, as if all the jiggles meant something.

'I just can't *think* in this outfit,' she said.

Thank God the lights went down then, so Iris could pretend she didn't see Liam's mirthful quivering. He was like a washing machine about to shake itself across the floor. She had to give his knee a sharp squeeze and hand him the programme as a distraction.

'What's Billy again?' he asked in an undertone.

'All I know is that it's a non-speaking part,' she said. 'That's all he'd tell me. He wouldn't even let me help with the *costumes*.'

Music struck up and Liam's voice burred in her ear. 'Maybe Chemistry Guy is right. Prepare to be bored.'

Jungle drums sounded. The curtains jerked back and the stage swarmed with dancing animals. On came a team of explorers in safari suits: out came a plot in a ubiquitous high-pitched drone and with so much tell-not-show that eventually Iris found herself craning to read the Chemistry textbook. Liam tugged at her elbow. 'There he is!'

She must have drifted off for longer than she'd realised. She wasn't quite sure why there was a blue spotlight, why all the animals had paws and hooves over their mouths, nor why all four explorers were agog, aghast and over-acting *marvellous, marvellous*!

But there was Billy, dressed in a tropical bird costume that for a moment seemed worthy of a metropolitan carnival. He lifted his wings and turned in the pond of blue light. Glossy beads trembled as he thrust out his chest and a giant crest of black feathers swayed behind his head like a peacock's fan. Where did they get it? The Santa Parade, a strip club, the Fortune Theatre? Iris realised she was braced for the sniggers, for the scrum of heads in the audience as people whispered and mocked. She was so sure someone would say it — 'That's Billy, the psycho bird kid, *hilarious*!' — that her attention lagged behind what Billy was actually doing on stage.

That sound: now there was *sound*. He'd said he didn't have a speaking part. But crisp and roof-hitting, in vigorous solo verses between the jungle-chorus, Billy sang. He was a skinny singing *Billy Elliot*! His thin chest looked as if it couldn't take the strain of the effort; he hit more than one bum note and at one point his voice seemed to hook in his throat so he had to cough, yet his expression pantomimed impish delight. During each run of the chorus, he gave a scurrying, scraping, spinning dance, swooping in and out of all the other animals in a way that didn't quite seem choreographed, because the other children were kept on their toes to scoop each other out of the way: a zebra and was it a gibbon clutched each other, cheerfully teetering, as they tried to keep up their end of the song. Yet as Billy passed each cluster of children forming a semi-circle, they caught his energy. Ripe and sunny with the juice of himself, he was like a light source; and they were a panel of sequins, glittering as he zoomed and carolled past them. His song ended with a cheerful, parodic, squeaky yodel and the whole stage gave an arm/wing/hoof-raised *hey*! as the finale.

A large part of the audience might have been clapping and stamping and whistling with relief that another school production that tried to give absolutely everyone their moment of glory was finally *over*. ('It's almost *ten o'clock*!' a woman in front of Iris impressed upon her girlfriend in a raised voice, close to dismay.) But Iris and Liam had sore hands, sore faces, from the pounding applause and broad, unselfconscious grins.

'I didn't even know he was brave enough to sing!' Liam shouted over the clapping and more bowing. She shook her head. 'Me neither!'

On the way home, underneath all of Billy's chatter, his, 'Did you like the bit when . . . ? Did you think the zebra was . . . ? Did you see that elephant try . . . ?' Iris was trying to compare tonight to something. She was looking for some lost object, or a thought that had been important, something she wanted to ask. It wasn't until she was drifting off to sleep that it came to her. The picture that Billy had drawn of all three of them: the grey, rainy picture the counsellor had shown them. How she had felt that she couldn't really translate it at the time. Now it seemed so obvious. All along, all the time she'd been digging through the past and dismantling things with her worry, there was Billy's bird-ery, storing up all the infectious energy of play.

It had seemed like a kind of obsessive-compulsive ritual; she'd worried herself sick that it had been a mutated quirk of sadness, that his bird act had been the spectre of loss. But maybe it had been a way of preserving joy. For there he was, in the costume he'd helped to make at school; not letting her intrude with her fussing and her what-iffing; as if to say, 'Look what *I* can do!'; belting out the songs the music teacher had coached him in; still fully capable of imagination, inventiveness, *fun*, despite what the family had been through.

Maybe every time he'd bird-mimed in those strange rituals, he'd been showing them how his vitality would still spill out, any route it could. They still had Billy, and Billy was going to be so very much himself.

A SHIFTING TESSELLATION

FRIDAY MORNING, BILLY WOKE warm and half-afloat from his dream. He ran his hand down his chest, where he'd felt the hard keel-bone hold the hull of him steady as he'd become airborne: skimming over fields, streets, buildings. It felt as if he was bathing in the dry, dark-blue air. It was twilight: he could see shapes and forms clearly but yellow, orange and white lights gleamed below, as if the whole city held candles in some vigil. In his half-awake mind he replayed the way he tilted, as the creatures he was with — for now he realised he was in a small flock — sped down a narrow canyon. He looked to the side and the boy beside him didn't meet his gaze, but still Billy knew the other one was aware of him. There was a smile somehow, in the soft dark of the feathers, the silver ring around the gem of the eye, the green along the wing-tips. Like a stone plummeting from a cliff, the cousin-bird dropped away, but Billy knew he had plunged only as a gull would, and that he rode the currents just out of sight. He felt his presence like the air racing over his own sleek head.

The dream of flight meant that all day there was content-ment behind his tiredness. He was in fact so exhausted after two performance nights that he didn't realise his bedroom door hadn't fully clicked shut when he trotted off to the bathroom during one of Canary Woof's free-flying sessions in his room.

After the bathroom, he trailed out to the kitchen to beg Iris for a popsicle. They argued about whether it was warm enough; the French doors were open to air the house in the sunshine; but there was late snow on the hills and a chill threaded along the corridor. Canary Woof must have seen his chance. From bedroom, to open door, to shotgun hallway in the old renovated villa; take a wrong turn, hive back and zip — straight out the front: that door also propped open to the huge cool blue tent of sky.

When he realised what had happened, Billy ran into the road and got an earful from a courier van. He went all sobby at the knees from the two shocks of bird-gone and horn-blast.

Over several days the whole family regularly stood on the doorstep and called and whistled. They lay a ring of birdseed all around the house. Canary Woof didn't come back. Billy was moony. Billy was blue.

Liam said, 'Canary Woof must have realised he missed his chance that time in the tree house. That time he was in shock; this time he was ready.' 'I thought he liked it here,' said Billy. 'Oh,' said Iris, 'maybe he just, maybe he did, but he just felt — he needed to see the world.'

Weeks, and some weepings later, Billy still wouldn't hear of visiting the pet store for another bird. Then one mild day, he saw his school-friend David just ahead, on the local playing field they cut through on the way to school. Billy jogged to catch him. His run disturbed a flock of sparrows on the grass; they lifted into the air in a shifting tessellation of brown against the clear blue sky. In the middle flickered a single bright shape. The whole panel of birds tilted, turned, swooped; it expanded like a tossed handful of dust, then condensed again, clotted as a cloud, before it fanned out. In the middle, glinting, was the gasp of one yellow parakeet.

Billy stopped in his tracks. He closed his eyes to clear them of the threads and bubbles of tiredness he sometimes got, in case . . . He opened them again, and the flock was swooping back down, settling again onto the field. The sunflower-coloured parakeet's head twitched up and down, peck then check, peck then check, constantly on the I-spy for trouble.

Billy hunkered down, puckered and whistled. The bird hopped a little nearer. 'Is that you?' Billy asked.

'^<!^<!^<!^<!^<!' answered the bird.

Billy tried to speak in kind. '^?^?^?'

The bird did a little strut. '*Rolfe. Rolfe.*'

'Hey!' said Billy. 'It *is* you!'

David had turned around and spotted Billy. Retracing his steps, he loped closer, calling out, 'Hey, Billy, watcha got?'

Billy gestured: *come here!* David joined him and crouched, too. The bird gave him a bold, one-sided stare.

Billy chirruped. Canary Woof *rolfed*. David unbalanced from his squat, he laughed so hard. Another boy, passing on the way to school with his mother, pulled up nearby, squinting at them. 'Wasso funny?'

David grinned. 'Billy's found a mini-dog in a bird suit.'

The mother gave a tolerant smile.

'You're barking up the wrong tree, David!' said Billy.

David rolled around on the grass, oblivious to the fact that his lunchbox had fallen out of his bag and spilt his sandwiches.

'You boys will be late,' said the mother, moving her own son along.

'You guys are weird,' said the little kid.

'Yeah?' said David jauntily.

'It's a good weird!' yelled Billy, at the kid's back. 'The interesting kind!'

Billy and David picked themselves up and started walking backwards to school, feeding out crust from David's sandwiches to the flock of birds as they went: two happy Hansels knowing exactly how to get back home when the time came. Billy la-la-lahed and skirled. Canary Woof, before cramming crust into his beak, sky-called '^<!^<!^<!^<!^<!' in return.

EPILOGUE

TRANSLATION II

The sun signs in heat on the stones;
the stones print their signs against the grass sheaves.
The grass whispers within the birds' ken;
the birds sing by ear the clear green syllables —
so on the bright lawn, beside the shadow-hedge,
beneath his sleepy skin
the child murmurs an idioglossia:
dreams himself native
to the first, universal language.

NOTES AND ACKNOWLEDGEMENTS

The first ten pages of this novel were published in *Landfall* (Dunedin: OUP, 2015). My thanks to the editor, David Eggleton.

Billy gleans his random facts about birds from various books and websites, some of which include:

Tim Birkhead, *Bird Sense* (London: Bloomsbury, 2012)

Andrew Crowe, *Which New Zealand Bird?* (Auckland: Penguin, 2001)

Dave Gunson, *Big Book of New Zealand Wildlife* (Auckland: New Holland, 2011)

Narena Olliver's website, www.nzbirds.com; specifically the article on the pouakai.

Te Ara — the Encyclopedia of New Zealand (www.teara.govt.nz)

Iris reads *The Dress Doctor: Prescriptions for Style, from A to Z* (1959) by Edith Head (New York: Harper Design, 2008). Liam quotes two Emily Dickinson poems: "Pain expands the time" J 967/F 833 - Line 1 and "If I can stop one heart from breaking" J 919/F 982. Reproduced with permission from Harvard University Press from *The Poems of Emily Dickinson*, edited by Thomas H. Johnson, Cambridge, Mass.: The Belknap Press of Harvard University Press, Copyright © 1951, 1955 by the President and Fellows of Harvard

College. Copyright © renewed 1979, 1983 by the President and Fellows of Harvard College. Copyright © 1914, 1918, 1919, 1924, 1929, 1930, 1932, 1935, 1937, 1942, by Martha Dickinson Bianchi. Copyright © 1952, 1957, 1958, 1963, 1965, by Mary L. Hampson. The epigraph for *Billy Bird* is a haiku from Tomas Tranströmer's 'The Great Enigma' in *New Collected Poems*, translated by Robin Fulton (Bloodaxe Books, 2011). Reproduced with permission of Bloodaxe Books.

Thanks to staff at Mirror Counselling, Musselburgh Medical Centre and the Southern District Health Board's Children and Adolescents' Mental Health Team, who all answered questions, showed me around their premises and loaned me reading material, as did poet and psychotherapist Michael Harlow. Thanks to Pete Swaab for returning me to Keats; to the University of Otago Robert Burns Fellowship for supporting the early writing stage of *Billy Bird;* and to the University of Otago Wallace Residency at the Pah Homestead, where the first draft was finished, and where the parakeet appeared in a sparrow flock.

Further drafts were made possible by the generosity of the Caselberg Trust, who granted me a short 'Down the Bay' residency, and Dame Gillian Whitehead, who let me use 'Harwood House'. Thanks to Total Fiction Services (Chris and Barbara Else) for their super-league stamina, critical acuity and keeping me in the family. Thanks to Majella Cullinane. Thanks to Harriet Allan and Sarah Ell for their alert and warm editing.

Thanks tenfold to Danny Baillie, who has understood the strange compulsions of the writing life ever since we sat outside the Schönbrunn Palace in Vienna, 1992, where we watched squirrels and ignored the palace's 'numerous attractions', having found our own.

Also by Emma Neale

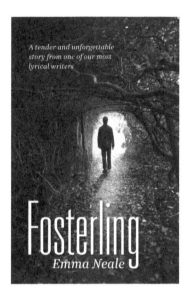

A moving, compelling story about society and our reactions to difference, convincingly evoked, beautifully written.

A young man is found unconscious in a remote forest. He is over seven feet tall, his skin covered in thick hair which reminds onlookers of an animal's pelt. When he wakes in a city hospital, he is eerily uncommunicative.

Speculation begins.

Medics want to run tests on him, the media want to get his story, and the public want to gawp and prod. When a young woman befriends him and he starts to talk, his identity seems to grow more complex. On his release from hospital, events drive him into hiding. Yet how can a young man of such uncommon appearance find true refuge?

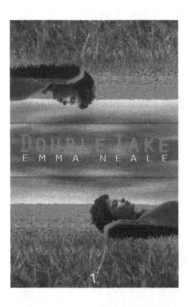

A rich, absorbing novel that explores the drive for creativity and the dynamics of family.

'Peas in a pod. Cherries on a stem. A pair, a set, a perfect match, people seemed to so quickly think . . . as if twins were a tribe of two with a secret understanding, existing in a self-contained, mysterious world . . .'

Growing up, the Marshall twins seemed to be ideal siblings. Yet when you're so akin to someone else, who are you, really?

Candy discovers a gift for music, yet in nearly every aspect of her life Jeff is there — pre-empting, mirroring. To work out who she genuinely is, Candy begins to believe she must separate from her brother for good. But at what cost?

Taking us into the world of grotty student flats, fiery politicos, eating disorders, and the convolutions of sexuality and first love, this is a beautifully written novel.

A stunning coming-of-age novel about running away.

'I think I saw Jenny today. A hemisphere away and fifteen years later . . .'

But could it be the same person that Marie now sees, the friend with whom she shared so much? The friend with whom she thought she would face all the uncertainties of adulthood. The friend who disappeared. This chance sighting in a railway carriage takes Marie back through the years to try to understand what happened to her best friend and why. In facing the past she is forced to confront her own fears and admit that running away is not always the answer — although for some it might be impossible to run far enough.

Intriguing, moving, vividly portrayed and beautifully written, this is a stunning first novel dealing sensitively and assuredly with the complex issue of coming of age.

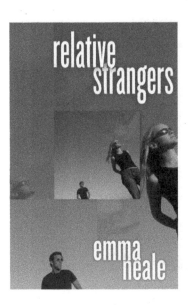

Moving, acutely observed and psychologically deep, this fine novel captures and illuminates past and contemporary relationships.

Colin should have the house to himself this Christmas. His flatmates are away and so is his girlfriend, who has gone on holiday without admitting the chill in their relationship. So who is the distraught woman in his lounge, along with a pushchair and screaming baby?

Like it or not, Colin must play host to this intriguing, uninvited guest, whose revelations begin to work loose his own tightly guarded secrets.

A moving and lyrical novel about enduring love.

'I was the girl who killed her brother.'

Julie loves her brother, calling him Little Moon and turning to him in times of difficulty. But the terrible accident, when she is only five years old, stains her life and the relationship between Julie's mother and her second husband, Ryan.

The intensity and dependency of this relationship is matched only by that between Julie and her mother, each shielding the other. But who is really being protected? A beautifully written novel, intriguing and insightful.

For more information about our titles go to
www.penguin.co.nz